*Also by Steven Key Meyers*

### Fiction

*That's My Story: Two Tales*

*Save the Max Man!*

*My Mad Russian: Three Tales*

*The Wedding on Big Bone Hill*

*Queer's Progress*

*Springtime in Siena*

*All That Money*

*Good People*

### Non-Fiction

*The Man in the Balloon:*
*Harvey Joiner's Wondrous 1877*

### Plays

*A Journal of the Plague Year,*
*and Other Plays and Adaptations*

# A FAMILY ROMANCE

## A Novel

Steven Key Meyers

*A Family Romance*

2021 Revised Edition

**SMASH
& GRAB**press

# A Family Romance

*For my parents, and for theirs*

What you really want to know is never in a book, and no one can tell you.

—Richard Jefferies
*Bevis*

Never excuse; for when the players are all dead, there need none to be blamed.

—Shakespeare
*A Midsummer Night's Dream*

# I.

# *Washington, D.C.*

# 1.

THEY HAD TO TAKE an elevator not reserved for Senators, a slow upwards haul. Nat Handler told himself he wasn't nervous—he'd been meeting famous lawmakers all day—but found his hand checking the knot of his tie as the attendant cranked open the door.

Hardy Owens, grinning from embarrassment at having to show a cub around his hallowed Capitol, and at the shiny provincial innocence of this particular cub, led the way. As for Nat, he was reminded of first days at boarding school and college. The day's one gleam thus far was a flash of fellow feeling offered by the skinny junior Senator from Massachusetts, Jack Kennedy, who bounded up into the facing seat on the Capitol subway—back then a contraption resembling the open carriages of horse-and-buggy days—and, putting out his hand with a ready smile, introduced himself.

Nat was surprised at how gaudy the Capitol was, even these inner recesses; every inch faux-marbled or stenciled, covered with fresco or mosaic, lest—he supposed—King George should crawl back in through some patch of wall left bare. If the aim was grandeur, to awe with the majesty inherent to the people of a Republic, the effect was just—

gaudy. It owed something to Rome's baroque churches, perhaps also to its bordellos.

Owens, speaking into an office, held open one of its double doors.

"*Hell*, yeah," came the drawl from within. "Bring him on in, want to meet *him*."

Squeezing past Owens, Nat located the speaker behind an enormous desk, virtually an aircraft carrier of mahogany: Senate Majority Leader Lyndon Johnson.

Standing up, Johnson came around and put out both hands. A shapely secretary sat beside the desk, her notebook resting on a borrowed patch of flight deck beside a stack of papers. She looked glad of the reprieve.

"H'wra *you*? Telling Hardy, glad to meet *you*. He taking care of you?"

The grip was bone-crushing, but Nat withstood it, and had to look up only an inch or two. "Glad to meet you, Senator."

"Well, that's fine. Sit down, gentlemen, get to know Randy's newest fair-haired boy."

Randy Orpen, founder and Editor-in-Chief of *Orbs* magazine, was Nat's boss, and Owens'.

"Don't want to take your time, Senator," said Owens, still hanging at the door.

"Sit yourselves on down, done here in a minute. Where were we, darlin'?" he asked, falling backwards into his giant leather chair.

Nat took one of the chairs indicated and so, reluctantly, did Owens. Boxes cluttered the room; Johnson was in the process of moving his headquarters downstairs.

The young woman held up the top sheet of paper.

"This came from the Dallas Chamber." She handed it over and, without looking at it, Johnson sailed it into the air.

"No time for that shit," he barked. "Write 'em a letter."

The secretary scrambled to retrieve the sheet. She was young and blooming, and in stretching to the floor revealed the roundness of her bottom. Johnson smirked at Nat.

"Next?" he said.

"Mayor Planter of Blanco sent —"

Johnson grabbed the letter and tossed it.

"Remind Mayor *Patootie* I'm a busy man!" he thundered as she went to the floor to retrieve it. Nat half-thought that the Leader was appraising his response to his performance — not catching but following his eye. He also detected in Johnson's, watching the secretary's lithe, lunging form, a wet avidity. Her breasts knocked against each other as she came up from the floor. Owens glanced at his watch and, bored but resigned, planted his feet flat and rubbed his crew cut as he looked out the arched window behind the antic Texan, where lay the heart-stopping prospect of the National Mall, straight down to the austere fact of the Washington Monument, beige-brown in wan January sunlight.

"Midland's after you again about —"

"Let 'em know — but *nice* — that soon as the 'publicans give me a breather, I'll look into their little matter." Toss and scramble.

"The Wilbarger County Commissioners want —"

"You tell 'em — really *tell* 'em — that the way Wilbarger County voted last time, be a cold day in *hell* they see *me* again." Paper went flying and the red-faced secretary scrambled, haunches working. "Remind 'em even their fucking pipeline's puny next to what's on *my* plate."

Finally Johnson had dealt with his correspondence. After his secretary crawled, red-faced and panting, over the floor picking up every last scrap, he dismissed her with an appreciative look at her departing backside.

"Well now, sir: Welcome to Washington," he said to Nat,

and Nat suddenly was aware of undergoing the most penetrating, all-embracing survey and investigation of his person he had experienced in the 21 years since his mother's death. "They tell me you're Texas?"

"My parents, sir. I'm from New Mexico and Arizona, but Dad was raised in Commerce and my mother in Vernon — Wilbarger County."

"Don't say?" said Johnson with a half smile.

"Yes, sir. Her brother was sheriff for years, his son still is."

"That right? Look, anything I can do for you, you tell me, all'ight?"

"Yes, sir."

"Wanted to see who Randy was sending us. Welcome to Washington."

A few minutes later the orange dome of the Capitol was receding behind their cab. The cast iron, freshly daubed with Rust-Oleum, was exposed for the first time since being swung high into the heavens by steam engines during the Battle of Gettysburg.

Owens, student and worshiper of power, told Nat he'd been accorded a glimpse behind the curtain, and Nat almost said, yes, just like *The Wizard of Oz*. But he didn't; kept to himself his sense of the great man's insecurities. His colleague wouldn't understand, but only look at him with dismay. Owens did add that his western background might work out after all.

Nat could read his mind: He, Hardy Owens, was cut in the Ivy League pattern of *Orbsites*, whereas Nat was — what, exactly? University of *Colorado?* Master's work at the University of *Kansas? Really?* Well, maybe New York knew best. New York usually did. Or maybe Randy was slipping? That was another possibility.

On Connecticut Avenue near Dupont Circle Owens

nodded Nat out the door at the Bender Building, the District's newest, most glamorous office building. Its ground floor was occupied by Paul Young's Restaurant, office adjunct and expense-account haven whose red-walled, red-carpeted décor would be characterized at an Inaugural party two years in the future by Joseph P. Kennedy, the new President's father, as looking "like a high-class whorehouse!" Upstairs, reached by elevators whose new-fangled buttons lighted at the warmth of a hovering fingertip, was the *Orbs* bureau.

Nat passed the pretty young receptionist and found his desk in the bullpen. He greeted some colleagues, arranged a drawer, got in on a laugh about Senator Dirksen, used the men's room and descended again, to stroll to his stop and wait for a bus going out 16th Street to the District Line. Dreary green and yellow streetcars also passed, rooftop cables sparking and snapping.

A D.C. Transit bus eased to a stop. Nat boarded and found a seat. Unfolding his *Evening Star*, he read the front and editorial pages, then rested it in his lap and looked out the window. At one stop a bus headed the other way, filled with weary black women, paused across the street—maids and housecleaners going home. Nat looked around his bus: almost entirely white, almost entirely male, if also weary.

Finally it pulled up to the curb at the strip shopping center on the Maryland border. Getting out, Nat saw Viv at the wheel of their Plymouth station wagon, a 1956 model in beaten green. Jack, aged seven, slipped over the front seat to join Jimmy, five, in the backseat. Pausing at Viv's window to kiss her—*smack!*—he went around and got in. On the seat between them was a grocery sack of gin and bourbon, Tom Collins mix, tonic water and two cartons of Kent cigarettes. As they drove out, Jack was punching his brother's arm and Jimmy was howling.

Ignoring them, Nat asked, "Any luck?"

"Nothing I liked," said Viv. She was house-hunting every day, but between the postwar boxes off Viers Mill Road and too-palatial colonials, it looked like being a long search.

A few minutes later she turned off Georgia Avenue towards the Park Silver Motel, but drove past its cantilevered entrance and parked around the corner.

"Come see," she said. Nat looked at her with perplexity but, collecting the kids, she walked into a tiny park surrounding a gazebo roofed by a giant acorn.

Unfolding himself with a groan, Nat stood by the car gathering his trench coat. Realizing he wasn't with them, Viv turned, and Nat walked over. He was looking more at the neighborhood than at the park—downtown Silver Spring's blocky big-city outline of the Woodward & Lothrop and Hecht Co. department stores, a White Castle guarded by sparkly cement bears, the inviting neon sign of the Anchor Inn. Dinner there sounded good.

"This is *the* silver spring," Viv told him. "What they named the town named for? Look: It says Abraham and Mary Todd Lincoln used to come out in their carriage for picnics. Isn't it sweet?"

"Huh," said Nat, utterly uninterested.

## 2.

THAT SATURDAY, HARDY OWENS gave a party. He told Nat everybody was looking forward to meeting Viv.

Nat put on his best blue suit, Viv a new dress more formal than her others. Its linen set off her Indian jewelry — weighty Navajo squash-blossom necklace, bracelets, rings and earrings inlaid with turquoise, coral and shellac broken off a phonograph record. In addition, she wore the latest model contact lenses, tiny curvatures of glass that nonetheless hurt her eyes — *scalded* them — causing perpetual tearfulness.

As Nat tied a tie skinnier than any he'd worn before and Viv sprayed Chanel No. 5, they nervously took stock of themselves in the motel room mirror. They saw that though both were yet young, and Viv retained youth's freshness, Nat was imposing on face and body rigid male assertion and control; practicing expressionlessness, too, the art of giving nothing away. In his job, it was best so, and it accorded with his idea of manhood.

"Where did you say his wife's from?" Viv asked.

"Don't know that I did."

"Hawaii, did you say?"

"Did I?"

Viv was unnerved by Nat's protestations that he didn't remember, how his eyes and mouth and the set of his head were abandoning her; how he was capable of scrutinizing her as though he'd never laid eyes on her before. Sometimes he put a thumb to his teeth and *studied* her. Stepping up to a higher-powered plane of his career, Nat had room in his mind, it seemed, only for the essentials; not for her. So she armored her warmth and shyness in similar expressionlessness. And yet for a moment they found each other's eyes in the silvered glass, surprising each other like swimmers underwater.

Enjoining Tommy not to let the three younger boys stay up late, they went downstairs from the two connecting rooms and drove out.

They found the address in Georgetown easily enough, on a street of doll houses. Viv gasped at their cuteness, but cars longer than the houses were wide were prowling for parking spaces, so they ended up leaving the Plymouth two blocks away. She was not happy about walking so far in heels, but declined Nat's suggestion that he drop her off; if she had to meet his colleagues and their spouses, she wanted him at her side.

They rang at a red door flanked by brass carriage lamps and attended by black iron jockeys in red iron silks. A moment later their host filled the doorway, and they ducked inside.

The absurdly tiny scale of the house disarmed them — miniscule spaces stacked on top of one another, a patch of garden off the dining room. Getting drinks, they revolved through the rooms. It was charming — another aspect of frontier, Viv realized, but an unexpected urban one. Surely it had been part of a mews, some servant establishment long ago, or not so long ago, before being so expensively redone? Twelve feet wide; even given the three stories, miniature, unreal, toy-like.

And crowded with bodies, young, attractive bodies with a rapacious edge of desserts and desires that confused her. Finding he'd misjudged the evening's formality, Nat took off his tie and undid his top button; Viv felt overdressed.

She liked Hardy's wife, Leilani, the Hawaiian beauty queen — the beauty taken on faith, her appearance was so exotic. Listening to husbands exchange war stories, Viv sampled canapés — cheeses doused in pepper sauces on imported crackers, toast rounds garnished with cream cheese and capers — and ate shish-kebabs. A sprinkling too young for the War had served in Korea instead, which was of no interest to anybody, but most were Europe or the Pacific, and they joshed one another; the really harrowing stuff, the stories that glazed eyes open to bottomless wells of grief, tonight (as most nights) went untold. Owens loudly lamented the poker-playing prosperity he'd enjoyed in the South Pacific, and otherwise the most serious conversation concerned likely candidates for President the following year.

Viv met *Orbs* staffers, plus some from sister publications housed in the same bureau. There were even a few non-*Orbs*ites, Washington *Post, Evening Star* and *Newsweek* men. Gradually she relaxed. For some ten years she'd attended parties as wife of the boss or coming man; after being editor of the paper in Grand Junction, Nat was the Chicago *Orbs* bureau's hotshot. If Washington in a way felt like starting over, so be it.

The wives — homemakers and housewives, though most were better educated than their husbands — while they chatted up Viv were trying to make up their minds about Nat. Charming and attractive, they agreed, but also with something elusive and not so easily categorized about him. A tall, good-looking man, a little awkward, intelligence beamed behind his glasses as he deployed the gregariousness of the shy person able to shove shyness aside for a given span. His Indian-chief profile made them nervous, but of course he was sanctified by New York. They had to be nice to him, and his wife, too.

Dancing to a hi-fi's rock-and-roll started in the biggest cleared space of the house — not the living room, furnished with slender Hepplewhite pieces and china figurines, but the top-floor bedroom. The dancers improvised handholding lines and figures, where bumping into each other was part of the fun. Soon those catching their breath on the staircase made it impassable.

Nat didn't dance — preferring to talk politics downstairs — but Viv accepted her host's invitation. Grinning, unseen by anyone, Owens touched her intimately, and she immediately backed off, but said nothing. Liquor blurred the proceedings, broke down barriers, made everyone silly. Viv found herself laughing with other wives in her highest register.

Later they were seated in the garden — ten feet square, with a space heater and hanging colored lights — where, one hand claiming Viv's shoulder, Nat told his set-piece about shipping out to war from Providence, Rhode Island.

"Viv found a factory job —"

" — tying lures to fishing lines," she volunteered.

"Pregnant with our first, not showing yet, and I had to find her a place to live, safe, comfortable and affordable, and — Well, it was wartime, wasn't easy. But we finally did it, honey, didn't we?"

Viv's wan smile was no match for Nat's bursting grin.

"Spare bedroom in a house belonging to the most *motherly* old gal you ever met. Oh, the sweet old thing took one look at Viv and adopted her right off! Felt so good, darling, knowing that Mrs. Coffman would be looking after you."

"Did it work out?" Leilani asked Viv.

Patting Viv's shoulder, Nat stepped on his own punch line.

"Let's just say— You know, Rhode Island has some funny laws about brothels? Turns out, it was that kind of house!"

Cries of hilarity greeted this.

Indoors, women and men merged, went out of focus, until one of the younger men—no one knew whether accidentally or not—managed to pull a strap or undo a snap that left a woman standing in her bra, arms crossed, dress puddled at her feet. More cries of hilarity, and then, if lingeringly, it was over, and Nat was getting the car, at the door rescuing Viv from Owens' embrace and driving her home.

"Went well, I thought," he said.

"It was fun," she answered.

He was thinking of that girl standing there in not even a slip, and of some of the other women, too. Oh, the young women of Washington! Viv's fall of golden hair had long since darkened and been cut. They'd been married, what, almost 16 years? Four kids ago? And she was still the only woman he'd ever been with, War and all?

He drove them to the Park Silver sure and straight, one eye squinched shut. Walking upstairs, Viv remembered their occupancy of so many apartments, so many houses, always impermanent. Now a motel.

Bone tired as she was, in bed Nat reached over, opened her supine and at first reluctant body and went to work; went to work with a roughness new since their arrival in Washington.

Finished, he rolled off, placed a beanbag-bottomed ashtray on his chest and lit a cigarette.

## 3.

THOUGH HOUSE-HUNTING MADE Viv anxious, she did enjoy stepping into every possibility pretending to be someone without history; all was future, all potential. Who did she wish to be?

For weeks nothing satisfied her. Then in Wheaton she found Hunter Mill Estates, a half-built new development that took its name from a vanished but well-sounding colonial gristmill, more recently scrubby pine forest along a polluted stream. There were four models, "contemporary" rather than "modern" in design, strewn in pastels on quarter-acre lots over a landscape graded into mild rises and gentle declivities.

She explored each model home. One featured columns and great double doors with lantern and chain above them; too fancy, trying too hard. Another sprawled over multiple levels, with sunrooms and porches; too California, Viv thought. One model was just too small.

Then there was the *Vanguard,* named for the newest space rocket: Of brick and siding, with a cathedral ceiling hoisting a wall of windows over the living room, half-staircase going up to four bedrooms and two bathrooms, stairs down to a walkout basement with family room and half-bath, plus a carport. Several Vanguards—priced at $20,000—happened to be nearing completion on Jeckyll Road, on Hunter Mill's outer edge, paralleling sheared-off woods a hundred yards behind.

They moved in, early settlers, one February day of utter stillness. An inch of snow had fallen, and their moving van was almost the sole vehicle on the roads. After a few hours' thaw came the Hecht Co. truck with their new bed, headboard divided into compartments.

By sunset the house was littered with half-empty boxes, though the beds were set up and made. Viv didn't like to sit without curtains, but briefly savored the living room's austere lines.

Nat was satisfied with the house because Viv seemed to be. She would enjoy furnishing it—buying attenuated Danish Modern pieces and banishing everything old or Indian downstairs. For too many years she'd had to pretend to like his dusty brown baskets and brown pottery—the dirt itself treasured—dun-colored Hopi lamp bases spangled with primitive devices, earth-toned Navajo rugs. Now the brilliant wash of light made her feel modern at last. She'd had the rooms painted off-white, deviating from white-white by a good two shades; it felt daring.

That evening, to celebrate, Nat whisked his family off to the Hot Shoppe in the parking lot of Wheaton Plaza, the region's first shopping mall. The orange-roofed Washington chain, founded by a local, one J.W. Marriott, was the kernel of the later hotel empire. In a booth, Nat read the menu's involved mythology of a pie-maker's rapscallion apprentice—which at least explained the towering neon sign of a kid hectoring an old man—but found his attention drawn outdoors, to the endless procession of cars circling the restaurant like Indians a wagon train.

Teenaged boys drove them, engines revving and rumbling.

Here came a '58 Thunderbird, there a '57 Corvette; a '50 Ford, '47 Buick, '55 Chevy, '48 Chrysler, '56 Oldsmobile, '55 Ford, '38 Pontiac — even a brand-new 1959 pink Cadillac *Coupe de Ville* nonchalantly steered by a duck-tailed youth peering past baby fat, each perky tailfin delicately presenting twin erections. Exhaust-pipes erupted in burbles, but the drivers' expressions never changed as around and around they went.

From the start Nat thrived in Washington. He had an attentive, attractive way with sources, a bird dog's persistence in following any trail once sniffed out and an easy touch in writing. Mornings, he wandered offices and hideaways, usually lunched with some source or official and, afternoons, sitting in the bullpen beneath the Herblock cartoons tacked over his desk, worked his resonant baritone on the phone, circling closer to his prey while a hunched shoulder kept the handset in place and he ran fingers through his hair. Nat liked the bullpen layout; it enabled him to keep up with everybody at the negligible cost of their keeping up with him.

Smoothing his notes into memoranda with the gifts of the novelist he knew himself to be, he telexed them to New York, and responded to editors' queries. Whole front-of-the-book stories came to rely on information he supplied, or even used chunks of his own paragraphs; very gratifying.

Washington — in those days called "D.C." only by its majority black population — was a company town ranked according to more minute degrees of status and power than even the military. It was challenging for a newcomer to tease out the precise relation of person to power; sometimes it wasn't the Cabinet Secretary but an undersecretary who wielded it, often not a dinner party's guest of honor but his wife or its hostess. Through these fascinating entanglements moved Nat, whose interest in getting to know *who* was *who* and *what* was *what* proved flattering to the players, and who, however new in town, as an *Orbs* correspondent carried a magnetic X-factor of his own; everybody wanted to be his friend.

His first assignments were the sort that always go to the new guy, but he enjoyed them nonetheless. For instance, *Orbs* secretly commissioned Andrew Wyeth to paint President Eisenhower's portrait for use in a future cover story. Nat was handed the hush-hush project, which meant scrambling down Gettysburg's landing strip after dark setting out candelarias for Wyeth's charter Cessna, driving him to sittings at Eisenhower's nearby farm — the General kibitzing with Nat as he dropped off or picked up the painter — debriefing Wyeth on the President's conversation and, in the dining room of the pre–Civil War Gettysburg Hotel, tactfully shushing him up. (Not Nat's fault that, to New York's consternation, Wyeth responded to his sitter's admiration of the finished picture by giving it to him.)

It was all bearable — save for the weekend visit by Randy Orpen's wife, Letitia Harrogate Orpen, the glamorous reactionary who served two terms in Congress and one in prison (for failing to pay duty on an emerald necklace). Though clearly a personage — that kind of American striver who, rising from nothing, savagely kicks out the rungs of the ladder she climbs — the way she treated Nat as a gofer grated. The low point came when she wanted to go riding in Rock Creek Park: Would Nat be a dear and find her a pair of jodhpurs? He did it, locating a dusty tack store off the C&O Canal tow path, but not for *this* had he entered journalism.

His colleagues were smart, ambitious, aggressive and competitive men who might as easily have been enemies as friends, except that antagonism towards New York — base of the writers and editors who chopped and mangled their memos into stories — knit the bureau into camaraderie.

17

It was a man's world, too, all right, a glaze of Southern gentility papering over the accepted fact that womenfolk were there to serve. But there were lots eager to do so. Nat found himself flung into an environment where even colleagues who proclaimed themselves happily married had girlfriends on the side or had resumed the endless college pursuit of getting laid. Happily married himself, Nat began to keep his eyes open; no harm in *looking*, even if the women were as *available* (presumably) as they were *sexy*.

To some, Nat seemed wanting in respect. At Paul Young's sandwich bar he'd been heard to remark that the men he met on the Hill, each in his own eyes larger than life, would not have particularly stood out at the Tuesday Rotary in Grand Junction, Colorado. Scandalized, everyone laughed; but did not the personages they daily dodged among reflect back on them a glow of greatness? Inside, they frowned.

And kept working their extravagant hours. When Nat got to the office at nine, it was to find them at their phones or clattering at their typewriters with the air of having been at it since dawn, and if he stayed until seven—which required hourly calls of propitiation to Viv—as he went out the door some were still jotting notes, telephones wedged to their ears.

His fellow *Orb*sites shared a social smoothness buffed in the Ivy League (or, in the case of their few female colleagues, at the Seven Sisters), and tended to radiate prosperity. His aggressively congenial new friend Hardy Owens, for example, came from north of Boston, a Dartmouth hockey star who made removing his upper plate a boast; scuttlebutt had it that he never bothered depositing paychecks until nagged to do so by the beancounters in New York. Owens was a quick reader of character and a good, fast writer, though in becoming his friend Nat had to overlook hints that he was limited, narrow and mean.

A single truncated Cornell semester apparently had not buffed Nat to the same perfection, though he was sure it was what got him into the Seabees after he was drafted, and being a Seabee helped the shorthand outline of his War pass muster. "Seabees," he'd mutter. "Western Pacific." It raised the specter of hopping occupied islands towards Japan, bulldozing landing strips under fire. Pressed, he might grunt, "Guam."

Seldom did he volunteer that his Navy rank was Laundryman Second Class; that he fought his war with washers and wringers, assigned to light duty following the boot-camp incident that almost got his foot amputated (though it was gratifying that the incompetence of Camp Peary's doctor had been so promptly rewarded with a posting to Guadalcanal). But someone had to do the laundry.

Nat knew that he stood somewhat apart, classed as an outsider, a rube; but the outsider's viewpoint can be advantageous to a journalist, and he was resolved to make it so.

## 4.

WHEN ASSIGNMENTS TO FOLLOW the 1960 Presidential candidates were handed out, newcomer Nat—to the dismay of some—got the prize of covering the Democratic front-runner, Minnesota's ebullient Senator Hubert Humphrey. Hardy Owens got the longshot Kennedy, others Symington, Kefauver and Lyndon Johnson; eschewing the primaries, Johnson was running from behind the scenes. (As sitting Vice President, Richard Nixon had the Republican nod sewn up.)

Nat enjoyed campaigning's frenetic pace, and liked his candidate, too. Late in April, rejoining him on the campaign trail, he brought Viv and the kids to National Airport to meet him. The working man's eloquent advocate introduced his wife and sons, and Muriel Humphrey gave each Handler a wallet-sized card, her family posed on one side, a cookie recipe on the other.

Candidate and reporter then flew to Clarksburg, West Virginia on an Allegheny Airlines DC-3. Virginia's vegetation was lush beneath them, almost every rise topped by a fine old house. As they climbed to cross the same line of improbably blue mountains Nat's pioneer ancestors faced, a thundersquall abruptly tossed the plane about. It pitched and dropped, while

Humphrey's big round head rolled against the cloth snapped to the seatback and he never stopped talking.

He was a cinch to win West Virginia's May 10 primary, which would be a big step towards the nomination — a necessity, too, after Kennedy's unexpected Wisconsin primary victory next door to Humphrey's home state. But everyone said his West Virginia lead was insuperable, and he was confident the United Mine Workers would endorse him; that would be the ballgame. (In the event, the UMW endorsed no candidate).

When Nat asked whether he wasn't afraid of Kennedy inroads, Humphrey reached up to adjust the air spraying over his face. Scorn and disdain competed before his expression settled into something more compassionate.

"Know Jack?" he said. "Looks so young, you'd card him before you sold him a beer. (*Wine,* more like.) No, miners prefer a working man like me. Can relate to someone who worked his way through night school." He didn't have to voice it: *Rich kid.* Everyone hates a spoiled rich kid.

He was freer in talking about the rich kid's father, Joseph P. Kennedy, himself famous for 40 years and at one time politically ambitious. Humphrey noted that Kennedy *père* was said to have made his first fortune bootlegging. "A crock," he said. "Like to have us *think* so. Never had the balls, just a big customer. Only got into liquor when it was legal again. Killer, all right — but strictly on paper."

Nat ceased breathing as the plane angled down at a mountaintop forest primeval that at the last moment opened up to a runway. He put away his pen and the little brown flip-cover notebook he took notes in, and Humphrey shook his hand.

Offered him a ride, too, in the car that met him, but Nat wanted to rent his own. He'd just been handed the keys to a

Mercury when a twin-engine Convair with a turquoise stripe along the side sailed down to a landing. Brush script on the nose spelled *Caroline*. Recognizing the Kennedy family plane, Nat went over to see who might get off. Wasn't JFK already in the state? And in Clarksburg, too, if he wasn't mistaken?

The Convair — bigger than a DC-3 — taxied up to the terminal, its door opened, steps unfolded, and from an Oldsmobile parked at the fence the youngest Kennedy, Teddy, the fleshy, good-looking kid brother, bounded past Nat and halfway up the plane's stairs. He reached to take the Gladstone bag a fetching brunette was lugging down them but, laughing, she drew back and said something Nat didn't catch, clearly in a playful tone. Teddy reached again, she yielded one of the bag's straps, and together they carried it past Nat to the Olds, before Teddy returned to get cases that matched her pink suit.

Meanwhile it was as though she'd reached out and grabbed Nat by the crotch: *Sexy;* maybe the sexiest woman he'd ever seen. Mid-20s, thereabouts? Petite — Teddy towered over her — but with a voluptuous figure beneath a beautiful face.

They ducked into the Olds and drove off.

Nat was left wondering who she was, and to ponder the happy family man's response.

As he drove out, the setting sun broke through to light up the scrim of trees an other-worldly gold. The sky churned through garish configurations as he negotiated Clarksburg's sooty stone and brick downtown. After checking into his hotel, he strolled the streets, cobblestones wet from the storm. Nothing appeared to date to later than about 1915. A more hardcore town he'd never seen.

Later he met up for steak in the hotel's dim restaurant with Hardy Owens and, though normally wary of associating with such — they always wanted help carrying equipment — an *Orbs* photographer.

Nat remarked that since Humphrey had scheduled a closed-door businessmen's breakfast the next morning, he meant—if Owens didn't mind—to follow Kennedy to early shift change at a coal mine.

"Knock yourself out," Owens snorted. "Don't know what Kennedy's thinking. They don't like him here. Catholic rich kid?"

"Speak of the devil," said the photographer. Jack Kennedy loomed at the doorway with his brother and the woman who got off the *Caroline*. They quietly took a table at the wall.

Nat's companions gave low wolf whistles. "Nice piece," the photographer remarked. "Got taste, give him that."

When Nat looked surprised, Owens said, "He's a dog, didn't you know? This one, who can blame him? Do her myself."

Judging from the backs of their heads, constantly nodding forward, both Kennedys were engrossed in her. Hair drawn back, she rested her chin on her palm, her other hand holding a glass of wine, the *Mona Lisa*'s smile playing about her lips.

Upstairs, Nat took out his Olympia portable typewriter and wrote up his conversation with Humphrey and impressions of Clarksburg, and through the hotel switchboard put in calls to New York—dictating a page and a half—and to Viv. Then he went to bed.

Early the next morning, almost before he knew he was awake, hair wet and stomach growling, Nat was guiding the Mercury out of town through hollow after foggy hollow, Hardy Owens and his photographer riding along. To Nat's surprise, the road soon dwindled to a single lane, though fortunately it widened at the many blind curves. Whenever a car met his, it pulled halfway off the pavement and kept coming. Nat did the same.

They caught up with the Kennedy cars cautiously nosing up and down the abrupt hills. The hollows reminded Nat of his father's father packing up and leaving the Appalachians behind when coal came in where he was tenant-farming on east Tennessee's Walden Ridge. A railroad spur was laid uphill and the first mine opened. At first convicts worked it, but then they began hiring men off the fields. Nat's grandfather wanted nothing to do with coal. Cashing in as best he could, he moved his family to Texas, where he began farming cotton — again as a tenant and, Nat thought wryly, with no greater success than with corn in Tennessee; but that was another story. He was grateful for his grandfather's gumption in getting out of the hills.

The mine lay in a hollow, its face beneath a hillside tipple past a truck yard and gravel parking lot. Miners arrived in their overalls three and four to car or pickup and clambered across to wait on stumps and fallen logs, lunch pails in hand or at their feet — waited grimly for their overnight brethren to come out. The sky was bright but the hollow misty and dim, aside from a lone, low-angled shaft of sunlight that picked out one particular log and made columns of fog swirl upwards around the miners sitting on it.

The doors of Kennedy's car opened and the candidate got out wiping his face. He'd probably been napping, probably wasn't particularly a morning person. Nat found Jack Kennedy interesting. True, an off-putting Harvard shine adhered to the man, part and parcel of that upper-crust *assumingness*, but Nat couldn't really hold it against him, finding his humor and easy irony engaging, if not, at their basis, especially warm.

But he also caught another strain, the strain of the *Mick* — of the despised and dispossessed — and found himself wondering how assured that Harvard gleam really could be, how deep it went, and whether the gap between Harvard and Mick might not be the matrix of something promising.

Kennedy shambled over to where miners waited in the sun. His suit was gray, cut slender—quite beautiful—and set off by a narrow tie fixed by a *PT-109* tie pin. The pin seemed to center the man, who was in motion around it, eyes moving, hand going up to muss his longish hair. He greeted the miners in a Boston accent. From twenty feet off, Nat could see no response beyond pale faces turning upwards for a moment, nothing readable in them, and dipping down again. Primordially immovable; no one intended to stir until the whistle blew.

Then Kennedy surprised Nat. Smiling broadly, talking animatedly, he plumped himself down in the middle of the log, made miners scooch over for him. Dropping into the sunshine transformed him into a prince from another planet, resplendent, warm, easy. He stretched out his hand and held it until the miner next to him shook it, got to his feet again and shook hands down both ends of the log. Nat couldn't follow the conversation, but clearly he was introducing himself and affably asking questions.

And within a minute a miracle occurred: These bone-weary miners were engaged and committed as they talked with this shiny, grinning Yankee who brushed back his unruly hair as he followed up with more questions, and then, striking fingers against palm, forcefully made a point. When the whistle finally blew and a gate opened and an army of men caked with coal dust began to stagger out, the day shift ignored it, eagerly crowding around Kennedy instead. As at last they trotted off to work carrying their lunch pails, he waved after them, thanking them for their calls of "Good luck!" and turned to grin at his handlers. But stayed on to shake the hands of those coming out.

"Maybe there's something to him after all," thought Nat, as Owens failed to suppress a yawn.

For the rest of the day Nat followed Humphrey. The Happy Warrior made stops at a barbershop, a bingo game, a VFW lunch and an Odd Fellows coffee. Nat had to admit he'd never known a more cheerful soul, which in itself was refreshing.

When, in late afternoon, Humphrey disappeared into a fund-raising cocktail party at a hilltop mansion of soot-streaked yellow brick, Nat returned to the gloomy hotel where he had a room and the candidates had suites.

As he was getting his key at the desk he saw the young woman from the *Caroline* turning a rack of postcards. She had the aura of one of the movie stars Nat had met from time to time, from Ann Sheridan on her unlikely visit to Grand Junction to Shirley MacLaine when he'd followed Khrushchev to L.A. the year before. Poised and self-possessed, she looked demure, hair in a bun (a *bun!*), bosom well covered *(bosom;* he laughed at himself using his mother's word).

He buttonholed a passing Kennedy aide to ask who she was, and the aide introduced them.

"Pam, meet Nat Handler from *Orbs* magazine. Nat, Pam Manchester, one of our best volunteers." Duty done, the aide wandered off.

"Saw you at the airport yesterday," Nat told her, "getting off the *Caroline.*"

"Did you?" she said in a low, tuneful voice, smiling.

"With a Gladstone bag. What was in it?"

Looking amused, she replaced a postcard.

"Cash."

"*Really?*"

"Just kidding. Extra clothes for Jack, that's all. Shaving cream."

Nat believed her first answer.

Her momentary focus on him was bewitching. He found himself contemplating asking her to have a drink, even dinner, just as research into the campaign. His madness passed — though turmoil lingered at his groin — and with a nod more curt than he intended he went upstairs to type up his day's memo, in which she did not figure.

Nat was pleased that paragraphs from his memos made it almost intact into the following week's *Orbs* cover story, a portrait of Kennedy as interloper that conveyed something of the playful and determined spirit behind the handsome features.

And to the political establishment's surprise, Kennedy handily won the West Virginia primary, taking 61% of the vote to Humphrey's 39%. That knocked Humphrey out of the race, and made Johnson's strategy of winning by acclamation at the convention look shaky.

Nat felt bad for Humphrey. Nicer guy you couldn't want to meet, his sunniness at 5:00 a.m. coming into a diner filled with cranky reporters memorable.

## 5.

WHEN THE DEMOCRATS nominated Kennedy for President in Los Angeles that summer, Nat was there, haunting the Biltmore Hotel and doing his best to penetrate the machinations that saw Johnson get the Vice-Presidential nod. In the end he never learned why, with his splendid Senate career in full flight, LBJ would accept No. 2 and the obscurity it promised even in victory; no one seemed to know. He was dismayed by the Kennedy campaign's scorn for Johnson — *Uncle Cornpone* they called him. Amused, but a little offended, too, Nat detected Mick defensiveness in the nickname's rudeness.

The conventions not only sorted the candidates, but *Orbs'* general-election assignments: Hardy Owens got Kennedy, and Nat the Republican candidate (and odds-on favorite), Richard Nixon.

Though conceding Kennedy was probably more fun to cover, Nat found his man fascinating — a cold fish, standoffish, buttoned-up, not in the least likable, an introvert doing that most extrovert thing, running for President. Nat's clashes with Nixon's press man, Herb Klein, who did his best to insulate the candidate, became a daily feature of the campaign.

Only once did he see Nixon's façade crack. The Vice President cancelled a day's campaigning to fly north and ask a Detroit mogul for money behind the gates of a Grosse Pointe estate. The index to his anxiety was that after returning to the campaign plane, massive donation in hand, he started drinking before it took off. A quick bourbon, another, and the cursing began. The usual Nixon whose smile bristled with teeth relaxed into something possibly more true to himself, sour, profane, paranoid and angry as he held forth on "*Commie son of a bitch*" this and "*rat's ass*" that.

Finally the candidate's wife came up, sat on her husband's armrest and reached for his glass.

"That's enough for *you*, Buster," Pat Nixon said.

Nat's campaign highlight came when he and Hardy Owens traded assignments and for two weeks he followed Kennedy through the Midwest and to his family's compound of beach houses at Hyannis Port, Massachusetts. He flew Viv up for a weekend. She enjoyed seeing the town and walking the beach and sitting behind the Kennedys at Sunday Mass. Jacqueline Kennedy, beautiful and poised, was completely at ease with the ritual. Her husband, however, seemed impatient and distracted—to have perfected a Catholic pose while thinking his own thoughts. Nat meanwhile stood or sat but, in best Protestant pride, never kneeled.

Both Owens and Nat felt the benefit of the fortnight's fresh perspective, but the picture that graced the magazine's *Editor's Desk* the following week showed Nat interviewing Kennedy—JFK serious, Nat skeptical, notebook in hand. The caption read *Handler & Kennedy*. Viv cut it out and slid it into the edge of her dresser mirror.

Six weeks after Kennedy's thin surprise victory, Viv's redoubtable mother arrived for a long Christmas visit, intending to stay through the Inauguration and even watch its parade from *Orbs'* bleacher seats.

LaCinda Halderman was in her 60s now, but handsome as ever in her woolen suits and pearline earrings. The family room, with pull-out couch and half-bath, was given over to her. She doted on her grandsons, and they adored their grandmother. Viv noted the contrast between her mother's austere treatment of her, growing up, and the overflow indulgence washing over the boys, but was glad of it. LaCinda took the kids to Gifford's for sundaes and banana splits and the whole family to dinner at the Olney Inn and the Water Gate Inn, and swept Viv up to New York for shows and shopping, after which purchases arrived for days.

Christmas morning was a blowout of boys opening presents: books, records, Cape Canaveral rocket sets, machine guns that shot noisy bursts from glowing red muzzles. Jimmy thereafter could wear official mouse ears while watching *The Mickey Mouse Club*, a Popeye cap watching *Popeye*, Hopalong Cassidy hat and chaps for that hero's reruns.

Nat spent an evening photographing everyone in front of the dining room drapes. Setting up lights and reflectors left over from his newspaper days, when he sometimes doubled as photographer, he posed them individually and in groups. Bathed in light, they blinked, uncomfortable, caught out — except for LaCinda, whose open-eyed regard for the lens was regal.

Then, a few days before the Inauguration, something happened. LaCinda couldn't catch her breath. Viv took her to the family doctor, who diagnosed congestive heart failure — LaCinda knew all about it — and forbade her to smoke or drink — she knew all about that, too — but descried no immediate danger.

However, she decided to forgo the Inaugural Parade, even before a foot of snow fell the night of January 19 and disrupted all plans. The plan had been for Tommy, a high-school senior too cool for parades, to drive them to the bus stop. Instead, undaunted — it never occurring to her to stay home — Viv broke a trail through the snow for her two youngest, trekking a mile to University Boulevard. It had been plowed and buses were running, so they got downtown and found their places among frozen, happy crowds at Pennsylvania Avenue and 14th Street.

From their perch they saw the new and old Presidents pass on their way to the Capitol, trapped like specimens beneath the bubbletop of the spectacular Truman-era Lincoln limousine, the aged General swaddled in top coat and muffler, the youngster beside him not even wearing a coat.

After the swearing in and the Inaugural Address, there came the traditional stage wait — lunch — before the new President led his parade back to the White House. Viv realized she'd never been so cold, not even in their year-long North Dakota sojourn: Cold invaded her bones; fingers and toes throbbed before dying altogether, and Jack and Jimmy mewed with misery. She hustled them across to a Peoples Drug Store, where they bought hot drinks and schmaltzy souvenirs. Jack proudly pinned to his coat a big JFK button dangling blue ribbons. Braving the outdoors again, they climbed back to their seats.

And were rewarded with the sight of the limousine, now open to the skies, sliding past with the new President and First Lady smiling and waving, she vivacious in a pink pillbox, both coatless (that evening Nat assured Viv that Jackie had been swaddled in unseen blankets). Fusty old Eisenhower was nowhere to be seen; the world had gone from black-and-white to full color.

In fact, Nat at that moment was driving through a half-tone landscape of snowy fields and dark skies, following Ike as he was driven home to Pennsylvania. Keeping a respectful distance, at first he felt impatient to have been assigned to escort the ex-President, but soon enough was relishing being part of the formal turning of history's page. When the gates to the farm had closed, he turned around and hurried back to Washington.

Meanwhile the cold, and the floats without number, and the marching bands thrown out of step by echoes off buildings numbed those in the bleachers. Long before Fred's Boy Scout troop could march past, Viv shepherded the kids to the bus for home. The roads clear, Tommy piloted the new Plymouth to meet them. It was a 1960 three-seater station wagon in blue and white, sheet metal peeled back over the headlights like suggestive eyebrows and sweeping back to tailfins even taller than the old one's. Its expressed eagerness to eat up the road was insincere, however, for it was as sadly underpowered as its predecessor.

A few days later they crowded into LaCinda's train compartment at the Silver Spring station. Jack was amazed to discover that lifting the seat cushion disclosed a toilet. They set her marble suitcases on the ledge, kissed and hugged her, and retired to the platform. She waved tirelessly through the big window, smiling from her blue wool and powder, her large eyes carrying the knowledge of what was to come, until the train rolled her from sight.

A week later she was in the hospital with a heart attack. Viv flew out to be with her. Two mornings after that Nat picked up Jack and Jimmy at St. Andrew's School. Sister Madonna helped them get their coats and lunchboxes, but no one would tell them what was going on. As they left Jack said to a classmate, "Look silly carrying my lunchbox at recess, don't I?"

At home Nat broke the news of LaCinda's death, and drove them and their brothers to Baltimore's Friendship

Airport for the flight to Denver.

The boys found compensation in the plane. The plush DC-7 was attended by kind stewardesses; only the thrum of propellers was tiresome. At the rear was a lounge with a curving banquette where they took turns. Also they visited the cockpit, blinking at revelations of light bursting through onrushing clouds over fanciful silver meadows, and the co-pilot pinned to their shirts pilot wings enameled in United Airlines colors.

# 6.

WITH KENNEDY'S VICTORY, *Orbs* named Hardy Owens its chief White House correspondent. Fair enough; in trailing after him for months, he'd grown close to the new President; had Nixon won, Nat likely would have gotten the same push for *his* wagon (he explained to colleagues with even less Latin the derivation of *career* from *carrus*).

Early in the new Administration, Nat began cultivating the Attorney General—and vice versa. Robert Kennedy, the President's intense younger brother, became his best source on civil rights, which the Kennedys gingerly began to promote. RFK even permitted Nat to listen in on an extension—off the record—as he spoke with the Rev. Martin Luther King, Jr.; the best Nat could do was write New York a confidential memo.

The Kennedy Administration seemed firmly in command of its destiny, despite early hiccups. In April, Cuban exiles "invaded" Cuba's Bay of Pigs under supposed American military sponsorship, except that no help was forthcoming. The ludicrous plan was devised when Eisenhower was President, and emphatically rejected by him; but the military got it past the new President, and accordingly a troop of exiles landed and was slaughtered.

It was a fiasco but, crucially, Kennedy appeared to learn from the experience, and the setback didn't poison Washington's glamorous new atmosphere. The young, handsome, rich First Family delighted the city.

Such a time for parties! Hardy Owens regaled Nat with accounts of state dinners—the *hors d'oeuvres*, food and wines, the First Lady's charm, the pleasure of rubbing shoulders with the great. Viv herself gave more dinner parties than at any time before or after, every few weeks putting the leaf in the table and asking five or six of Nat's colleagues or competitors and their wives out to Hunter Mill for an evening of cocktails, shrimp scampi or beef stroganoff, hand-cranked ice cream, more cocktails.

The most notable occurred one May evening. The living room was resounding with behind-the-scenes tidbits when an Allied Van Lines tractor-trailer turned into Jeckyll Road and with a *whoosh!* of air brakes pulled up beside guests' cars. It carried LaCinda's furniture.

Viv coped with aplomb. The movers carried everything down the grassy slope beside the house—only weeks earlier black crews had unrolled turf like rugs over the bare dirt—and inside through the sliding-glass doors. Viv circulated through the living room, refreshing drinks and passing canapés, checked the oven, stirred pans on the stove, dashed downstairs to supervise placement of her mother's things. Upstairs, voices discussed sit-ins across the South, Goldwater's intentions and their hostess's grace under pressure.

Though not asked to state dinners, Nat and Viv attended parties at Hickory Hill, the beautiful Virginia estate where Robert Kennedy lived with his fairytale family of (as it was then) seven children.

The best occurred one hot June night in 1962. Humidity blanketed them and gnats helmeted their faces as Nat and Viv walked up to the house from Chain Bridge Road, where a young man had taken charge of LaCinda's snazzy red-and-white 1955 Pontiac "hardtop convertible."

Inside the front door chaos reigned. Ethel Kennedy, cleaning up a mess at the bottom of the stairs, yanked Viv's hand and gave Nat a boisterous welcome as her husband chased his sons down the hall and pulled on a dinner jacket. The eldest boy showed Nat and Viv his treehouse in a mighty hickory, two rooms level with the top of the hill on one side, towering over the lawn on the other.

Amused, Nat and Viv walked across the lawn towards the pool and its flagstone terrace. The sun was slowly descending. It made for a handsome setting—Japanese lanterns swaying from tree boughs, to one side men in toques preparing to barbecue beef and pork, on the other bartenders manning banquet tables.

They found drinks and friends. Viv met powerful men and their wives, but was thrilled most of all to place her hand in Judy Garland's as the star happily held court. She lingered there.

Nat wandered on. It was delightful. With every drink voices were pitched higher and louder. Among the hundred guests were Peter Lawford, the actor and Rat Pack member married to a Kennedy sister, and Teddy Kennedy, running for Senate in the upcoming midterm elections, along with the Secretaries of State and Defense, the heads of the National Gallery and National Symphony, Senators, Congressmen, White House and Justice Department aides. It had the charm of a place and time off the clock. As the only *Orb*site there, Nat was received with gratifying interest as he chatted about Faulkner or civil rights. The cries of the children running in red pajamas among the guests, together with the cicadas and a jazz combo, made for a lively background.

With everybody else, Nat turned to watch when their host prevailed upon Judy Garland to sing. Or kind of: She insisted that he join in, and there issued a weird duet of *The Trolley Song*, RFK off key and tuneless, ever a lyric behind. *"Zing, zing, zing,"* sang Garland, and Kennedy brought up the rear: *" – zing, – zing, – zing."* Garland kissed him, to cheers.

As guests began eating, a new black Lincoln Continental, sleek and perfectly proportioned, came rolling down around the house and across the grass towards the pool. The car's slab sides waveringly reflected the lanterns as it turned, chrome-ribbed taillights glowing. It was trailed by a station wagon filled with men in hats.

The President stepped out from behind the Lincoln's wheel, and a thrill passed over the terrace. Unaccountably wearing sunglasses, he smiled, teeth gleaming. A dark-haired young woman got out the other side, while men unfolded themselves from the station wagon; they kept their hats on. The President, laughing and surrounded, strolled with his passenger, brothers, several sisters and brothers-in-law towards a table on the pool's verge. Nat caught fragments of his excuses for Jackie — *"just too tired"* — as he got an acknowledgment — *"Nat"* — and a touch of the fingers.

The President's arrival jazzed the party even more. He and his companion traded barbs with neighboring tables as they caught up with the liquor and started eating ribs; infectious Presidential laughter rang out. The Secret Service men sat down near by and accepted Cokes and barbecue. Nat and Viv, her eyes watering from her contacts, grabbed plates and chairs, as it happened next to the Defense Secretary, who was holding forth on how useful Viet Nam would be as a laboratory for updating Army equipment; already a handful of military advisers was in the country.

"Our new boot, for instance?" he said, eyes fluttering

behind tortoiseshell rims like Nat's, a thumb squashing the facets of his crystal glass of Scotch. "Remember the boots in the War? The *blisters?* These new ones, every step pumps out water! March through any jungle, any swamp, feet will stay dry! No more trench foot!

"And the *rifles?* This new M-16: One press of the trigger, 20 rounds! *Twenty!* Makes our guys invincible!"

But Nat was watching the President's table, especially his gorgeous companion and her complexity of curves. And recognized Pam Manchester.

Soon a band member put down his horn and began singing Chubby Checker's hits *The Twist* and *Let's Twist Again,* and the cleared part of the terrace filled with women doing the twist in long dresses, men twisting in suits and dinner jackets. Nat thought *jungle abandon* as Viv pulled him into their laughing midst.

A yell and the first splash came. Nat broke away in time to see, amidst screams and shouts of glee, Teddy Kennedy bobbing up in the swimming pool in jacket and tie, shaking water from his head and grinning, and to see Ethel Kennedy push Arthur Schlesinger into the deep end.

Mayhem; within seconds a dozen were splashing in the water or climbing out. Waves of laughter came from the President and everybody else.

Nat apprehended the caste system in operation: Those in the pool were Kennedys or close aides or friends like Pam Manchester (laughing, her dress a second skin, she clambered out into a towel someone held open for her). No one else, no civilians, as it were—certainly no one who couldn't afford a new suit and shoes—got wet, and not a drop reached the President. At the height of the melee, Nat instinctively shunned the water's edge, but realized he needn't have; no one would have touched him.

Towels were passed, an ironic ovation given—too self-conscious for Nat—and more drinks. Pam Manchester walked over to the President's table and plopped herself down, tidily wrapping one towel into a turban and using another to chafe her legs and arms. Playfully pretending she was dripping on him, Kennedy shooed her towards the house and was joshing the soaked but happy Teddy as Peter Lawford wandered off.

Hugging herself like a Venus de Milo with arms, Pam passed Nat at the terrace's edge.

"Looked like fun, Pam," he said.

She laughed without looking. "It really was."

"Haven't seen you since West Virginia."

She craned round, and he saw recognition click into place. "*Nat*, right?"

"Good memory." She smiled. "See you came with the President. What's your role in the Administration?"

"Oh, I'm the girlfriend," she answered on a note of raillery, and trailed towards the house. She stopped and turned around. "Not really, Nat," she said, and spelled it out: "I'm kidding. Just old friends."

Sighing, Nat watched her walk into the house, then turned to see Lawford tugging two lissome blonde things towards the President, who pulled them into chairs.

A few minutes later, when she emerged in a dress obviously not her own, Pam paused to size up the scene at the President's table. For a moment Nat thought she looked angry. Altering her direction, she fetched up, smiling, at a table of Justice aides.

Nat was chatting—not with the clearest of heads—with friends from *USA*1* and *Newsweek* when he saw the President stand up and wave over one of the men in hats. Making his goodbyes, JFK helped both blondes into the Lincoln's backseat, climbed in after them and was driven away. The Secret Service wagon followed, its turn signal winking as it went up the hill.

The party began to wind down. Viv yawned; she'd latterly been making conversation with a three-star general's wife. Ethel Kennedy and her husband said jovial goodbyes and young men trotted for cars.

Someone tapped Nat on the shoulder.

"Nat, can I possibly hitch a ride? Seem to have lost mine."

"Sure thing, Pam."

He introduced her to Viv—"Pam works on The Hill," he hazarded; "Actually, the World Bank," she said—and they walked out front to the waiting Pontiac. Presumably the TWA bag on her shoulder held her wet clothes. Nat tilted the seat forward and, shoving aside a Frisbee, she got in the backseat.

"Great party, wasn't it?" he said as they crossed the Potomac. "Best I've ever been to, I think."

"Had its moments, certainly," Pam allowed. "Unless the mosquitoes got you?"

"Don't think so," Viv said promptly.

"Only hope no one got poison ivy," Pam said. It sounded considered and weighty.

She directed them to a house on R Street, hardly out of their way in those days when the Capital Beltway was an unfinished monument to itself, concrete columns rising from red clay at future overpasses. She shared the house with six other women, she said, and they called it the Gruberian Embassy in honor of their absentee landlord, one Col. Gruber. There she thanked them, and they waited as she walked up the steps, opened the door and turned to wave good night.

"She seems nice," Viv said.

"Nice," Nat answered, "and I get the feeling very smart."

"Certainly striking."

"I think the secret to her beauty is that it's so sculptural and rounded."

"She works at the World Bank?" Viv asked, Nat's lyricism setting off alarm bells.

"I guess, but actually she's the President's mistress, or one of them."

"*What?*"

"Didn't you see them arrive together? I met her back in West Virginia." Sophisticatedly crossing hands on the steering wheel, he turned into 16th Street.

"Nat, I don't like that. He's got that beautiful wife. . . . And *we* had to drive her home?"

# 7.

A FEW DAYS LATER Nat had lunch with Hardy Owens. He enjoyed filling him in on Hickory Hill; Hardy had never been. But he wanted to consult with him, too.

"So, Hardy," he remarked, "the President brought a young lady with him."

"I'll bet he did," said Owens.

They were eating steak by the red-shaded lights of Paul Young's. High-class whorehouse? Nat liked it.

"Met her in West Virginia during the campaign. Remember the sexy one who had dinner with him and Teddy? Looked like the Mona Lisa?"

"She a wop?"

"Don't think so. Rents a house on R Street with some other girls. They call it the Gruberian Embassy, after the guy who owns it."

"*Cute,*" snorted Owens.

"Says she's the President's girlfriend."

Owens' face went rigid, his jaws bulged, he buttered a roll in a distracted manner.

"But maybe not any more, is my impression. Arrived in his personal car, but he left with two other girls. Pretty brazen all around. Everybody saw. Viv and I had to give her a ride home."

Owens bit fastidiously at his roll. Fastidiously sipped water. Cut a morsel of steak and speared it with his fork. Caught a waiter's eye and pointed to his Scotch. The waiter brought a new one and carried the empty glass away.

The push Kennedy's election gave Owens' career was a big one: He'd started writing a weekly column for the magazine called *The Pinnacle*, and begun appearing on the Sunday TV news panel shows *Meet the Press, Face the Nation* and *Issues and Answers*, where, incongruously for a man not 40, he cultivated a late manner, harrumphing twice before he asked a question, as though to indicate that in a better-ordered world the questions would go to *him*.

"*Well*," he finally said, and harrumphed twice. "Quite a few women in this town will tell you they're the President's girlfriend, or used to be, and they're not all lying, either."

"I was struck by what Viv said. She was offended, said if she'd known she might have voted for *Nixon*."

Owens snorted.

Nat continued, "*Orbs* should —"

"Nuh-uh, *no*." With a clatter, Owens let drop his knife and fork, and had to wave off a waiter who thought he was signaling the end to his meal. "Nothing we can do with it, not *us*. Look, the guy's a horndog. Lots of guys are, and what's it matter? He's President, why not get some fun out of it? *Needs* fun. And *Mrs*. Kennedy's perfectly happy, that's all that matters."

"But —"

"*No*."

"Besides being the biggest scoop I can imagine" — Nat was talking fast — "look at the chance of his getting involved with the *wrong* woman, someone from the Soviets, or the Teamsters, or the Mob? Or getting one pregnant — can you *imagine?*"

Owens harrumphed urgently. "Nat, Nat: Granted, the history books might be interested. If George Washington played around? Pretty racy reading! But there's nothing *we* can do. Want to make Uncle Cornpone President?"

"If he's *that* vulnerable —" Nat shook his head. "This one seems a little pissed off. Woman scorned?"

"But why would she make a fuss? They never do. Think she wants a scarlet letter on her jacket? *'G'* for *Girlfriend?* Just nobody's business. *Orbs* would never run her story. Too racy even for *Spiral,*" he said, naming *Orbs'* sister picture magazine. "No, he's safe. There's this, too, not to be melodramatic: To do a story like that might be as much as her life's worth — or yours."

Nat scoffed.

"Come on, Nat, power at that level? Jack's not naïve, *trust me.* Not the first, either. Grover Cleveland married practically a teenager in office, and Warren Harding? *Notorious* — begat a child two steps off the Oval Office! And you've heard about FDR and his secretaries? Not to mention the masseur who used to jerk off his *enormous* cock? (Got that from Junior's ex-wife, believe it or not.)

"Now, Nat, this isn't a story *anyone* can publish. Pursue it and you won't get *anywhere.*" Owens smiled wide, pulling in his lips with unconscious menace.

Nat glowered. "The fix is in?"

"I wouldn't put it like that, not at all. But you're doing so well, and Viv likes Washington, right?" Smiling, he harrumphed twice. "Now, how about some nice lemon pie?"

Nat was still brooding about his scoop in August when he and Viv rented a cottage with friends on North Carolina's Outer Banks.

The eight-hour drive wended through a Virginia landscape

that effortlessly harkened back a century, or even two, U.S. 1 winding through colonial hamlets where old houses and inns crowded up to the pavement's edge.

At lunchtime, they came upon one of the few eating places in Virginia *not* bedecked with NO COLORED and WHITES ONLY signs; Nat refused to patronize any establishment so emblazoned, especially after his six months in Little Rock covering Central High School's desegregation. He shepherded his family to the threshold, where they experienced the never-to-be-forgotten sensation of being whites entering a black establishment; a *frisson* dissolved by the proprietor's graciousness.

Interstate 95's first open stretch zipped them past Richmond's enormous, aromatic cigarette factories. Near the North Carolina border, they crossed the Great Dismal Swamp, where dead trees rose chalk-white out of mirror-still waters, then skimmed past peanut fields that stretched to the horizon. A chain gang was scything roadside weeds, 20 black men in striped uniforms and striped hats laboring in the brutal sun under shotgun-toting white guards. After a stop at Anna Gallup's fruit stand to load up on peaches, tomatoes and figs, they crossed the shaky wooden bridge across Pamlico Sound and found the cottage in Nag's Head. The Cottles — Doug and Deanna, he of the New York *Times* — had just arrived with their kids. All the kids got along, and Deanna Cottle was one of Viv's best friends.

A spit of barrier islands, low and scrubby except for a few big dunes, the Outer Banks are under nonstop assault by a baroque curl of waves. Some few fishermen have always eked out a living, operating out of sound-side harbors and preserving an Elizabethan *patois* that has them saying they'd *lief* do this, *lief* do that.

Since the War, vacationers from Washington made up the

bulk of visitors. Amenities were so few that they selected themselves as those content to swim, sun, read and rest. The slow beach road passed clapboard cottages on stilts and newer, earth-bound ones of stucco. Along its twenty miles were two mom-and-pop groceries, a handful of restaurants and motels, two fishing piers, an ice cream parlor and a used-book store—a raftered space filled with dusty volumes, including a treasure trove of turn-of-the-century juvenile fiction, *The Rover Boys* and every spinoff known: *The Submarine Boys, The Motor Boys, The Aviator Boys.*

Their cottage's two sun-bleached stories peered from stilts over the sand berm bulldozed into place after Hurricane Donna eroded the beach in 1960. Motley pieces of rattan and oak furnished the place. There was no TV reception, and radio was chancy. Nat was immediately, gratefully "off."

A few days in, he was on the back porch drinking beer at sunset while Doug, a barbecue expert, kept an eye on his coals at the bottom of the stairs. The wives were in the kitchen, the kids on the beach stamping the sand to phosphorescence, the surf pounding out questions never answered, when Nat brought up the President's girlfriends.

Doug was amused. Pam Manchester he hadn't met, but he did know two or three women who claimed to have slept with Kennedy. It was something one heard at dinner parties, usually as a boast. He'd told his editors about them, too.

"But my shop won't touch it," he said. "Not with a ten-foot pole. *Dynamite.*"

"I don't get it. Don't people have a right to know?"

Doug sipped thoughtfully. "How's this: Do we have the right to tell them? What did Jesus say, 'Let him who is without sin—'?"

"Come on, Doug, what's *Jesus* got to do with the President of the United States? I really don't get it. In a democracy, to keep *this* from the people? Not *our* role to protect *anyone* from his own behavior."

Doug said, "Look, if you think there's a book in it, and you're serious about wrecking your career, I know the guy can help you do it: Luther Pike."

"You know Luther *Pike?*"

"Friend of Deanna's father. I'll give him a call, you want."

Pike was a New York publisher with a niche of his own: Any book carrying his imprint promised salacious thrills, was automatically notorious. He was always in court fighting—and winning—obscenity lawsuits; consequently his readers' thrills were righteous ones. His latest crusade concerned a Beat writer's magnum opus, *The Tome of Aversions*; it took four court victories to get the dirty book into the stores and onto the bestseller lists.

The sudden possibility of publishing his scoop—and as a *book*—jolted Nat. The surf's hammering brought the unexpected thought that the idea was *cheap*. If he pursued it, what *he'd* be doing was about as cheap as what JFK was up to.

"Thanks," he said. "Maybe I'll give my shop time to change its mind. Let you know, Doug. Thanks."

"Sure, Nat. Just be careful what you wish for."

They watched lights steaming along the horizon as a ship rounded Cape Hatteras.

## 8.

NAT WAS NOT SO OBSESSED with his scoop that he missed the first September hints of crisis, the whispers about missiles being trucked through Cuban villages at night and frantic U.S. preparations to launch a surveillance satellite.

When he was on Guam awaiting his part in the invasion of Japan, which the Pentagon expected to produce *one million* American casualties, the U.S. dropped the atomic bomb on Hiroshima. Nat remembered the moment he heard about it as one of the happiest of his life, if dampened immediately by the query of a Guamian woman who worked in his laundry, "What about the children and women?" That bomb didn't end the war, so the U.S. exploded another, this time over Nagasaki, killing thousands more civilians. Japan surrendered and the invasion was called off.

The postwar peace was kept by ever larger arsenals of ever bigger bombs, America's counter-balanced by the USSR's. But in the fall of 1962 American reconnaissance confirmed that the Soviets were placing nuclear-tipped missiles in Cuba. The possibility — *probability,* some well-informed types had it — that the superpowers might soon blow each other up pushed the President's sex life clean out of Nat's head.

What worried him was that he couldn't shake loose any more information than that. His usual sources clammed up. One day he cornered Robert Kennedy getting out of his car in the Justice Department courtyard, and even then got no answers. But that in itself was a kind of answer. And there was no ignoring Washington's thickening tension, which seemed projected onto the leaden skies, a string of offshore hurricanes banishing autumn's usual blue buoyancy. Nat afterwards remembered a charged overcast as being the weather of the Cuban Missile Crisis.

Getting home one evening querulous and unsettled, he took his martini out to the screened porch. Viv was strolling the back yard in company with two youngsters in dark suits whom he might have taken for Mormon missionaries save that they were pointing beneath him.

"Right there's best, ma'am," he heard. "*Earth* between you and the radiation."

"Viv?" Nat called through the screening. "Viv?"

He heard her ask, "If we give the go-ahead, how long before it's ready?"

"You understand, we're busy."

"*Very* busy," echoed the other.

"*Viv?*" called Nat.

"Nat, these gentlemen are here to give an estimate for a fallout shelter."

He went outdoors, and they shook his hand and gave him a brochure, and as he went back inside were going two doors down to give another estimate.

"Eighteen hundred dollars," Viv reported.

"And finished when?"

"End of the year."

"Too late," said Nat, though he knew no more about what was coming than that. As seemed called for, he poured another martini.

But the tension had days left to build. News came of more Russian ships approaching the island. Nat heard that at Cabinet meetings the Vice President was urging that the Air Force be given the permission it wanted to bomb the missile sites, but that President Kennedy was resisting.

Meanwhile, schoolchildren drilled. Jack reported that Debbie Marsh, who sat in the window row of his fifth grade classroom at St. Andrew's, had been assigned to leap up at the atomic flash (which everybody knew would come over the White House, twelve miles to the southwest) and close the blinds while her classmates ducked under their desks to await the blast wave some seconds later (surely closed blinds would prevent flying glass?). But Debbie Marsh cracked under the pressure and changed places with Anne O'Connor.

After the blast wave passed, the children were to go single file into the hallway and take their places against the walls, heads between their knees, to await the descent of fallout. Twenty minutes later, when things were as good as they were going to get, Sister Madonna would release them to walk home.

Those who lived farther out were assigned to go home with classmates who walked to school. Thus Jack informed his mother that after the Bomb dropped George MacDuffie would be coming home with him. On the designated drill day, they walked home together, then morosely watched *Robin Hood* and *Rocky and Bullwinkle* until George's mother picked him up.

Though impressed by the school's planning, Nat doubted things would go so smoothly, and doubted the nuns thought so, either. He could only imagine the screaming, radiation-scorched, eyeless hulks of children who might live to crawl down Jekyll Road picking their way between particles of Strontium-90 and Caesium-137.

On October 22, the President addressed the nation. Grave and handsome in black and white, the lens flaring as though to underscore his words when he lifted his face from his paper, he described the blockade—"quarantine"—the Navy at his order was setting up around Cuba to prevent more missiles being landed, and demanded the withdrawal of those already there.

The quarantine worked, Russian missiles duly made the voyage home, and the crisis passed. Dangerous as it seemed at the time, details that emerged later made clear how very close World War III had come. That peace endured seemed due to President Kennedy's imagination and courage, with his brother's help, and even without knowing the whole harrowing story, people had an instinct about it. The President won an upsurge in popularity, and Democrats gained Senate seats in the November elections, brother Teddy being among those elected.

In his gut, Nat had not expected normal life to resume; had thought, *This is it!*

Saved the world? Maybe Kennedy was entitled to his girls, after all?

One morning in December, a rumbling was heard at Nat's breakfast table, whose customary sounds were those of newspaper pages being turned, chinks of spoon against bowl, cigarette coughs. Outdoors, diesel urgings were building up and coming closer.

From the dining room sliders, Jimmy yelled, *"Daddy! Mommy!* They're tearing up the woods!" A fleet of earthmovers, attended by graders and dump trucks, was working behind the trees; they saw the tops of trees falling and fugitive glimpses of yellow. Birds flew up; squirrels, rabbits, groundhogs, possums and raccoons fled towards the houses. It was an awesome spectacle.

Nat left for work, but Viv, upset, all day watched earthmovers go back and forth while enormous tangles of wood burned. By dusk they had pushed the forest wall back another hundred yards and sheared off one entire hill, leaving a cliff 20 feet high.

But all was quiet and only a few fires still glowed by the time Nat got home and, with a chink of rocks, lifted his martini. Viv was already planning an impenetrable hedge of bamboo.

Within days, surveyors were staking out new streets and homesites, and Viv daily watering her hedge.

## 9.

AT THE END OF the year France sent the *Mona Lisa* to America—plucked the world's most famous painting off the walls of the Louvre, placed her on board the liner *France* and sailed her to New York. Under police escort she was driven to Washington and hung in the National Gallery of Art, to remain for four weeks.

On Tuesday, January 8, 1963, the President and First Lady hosted a diplomatic reception for *La Giaconda*. Nat and Viv attended, he in black tie, Viv in a formal from Woodies; Hardy Owens had wangled the invitation.

The masterpiece presided from within red velvet draperies over an oblong chamber thronged with guests. Navy guards in white flanked the picture, the French flag to one side, the American at the other.

The President and First Lady entered to *Hail to the Chief,* Jackie Kennedy's strapless pink Empire gown flowing from her admirable shoulders, with white gloves pulled past the elbow and diamond earrings dangling. They greeted the French Ambassador, who presented France's Minister for Cultural Affairs, André Malraux, the personification of the Gallic intellectual. Nat thought the First Lady's hairdo resembled a tricorn Napoleonic hat, but never had he seen anyone so deliriously happy; she posed in front of the picture as though showing off a family portrait, while Malraux stuffed his hands in his tuxedo pockets.

Speaking from a rostrum at the side, the President pledged the U.S. would develop "an independent artistic force and power of our own" to rival France's. It went over; everybody laughed. Clearly he was delighted to have the Leonardo at hand to help dispel Washington's lingering rusticity.

Nat couldn't take his eyes off the *Mona Lisa*, however hard to see through her bulletproof glass; from most angles glare wiped her from view, nor was the height at which she hung helpful. Of those assembled, LBJ came closest to looking her in the eye; Nat thought Uncle Cornpone looked awed.

Viv and he joined the reception line, where he was startled to hear *"Nat"* and, turning, to find behind them Pam Manchester in blue silk. Like a debutante, she was holding the arm of a uniformed youngster. Air Force, Nat guessed.

Nat reminded Viv they'd met, and Pam thanked them for the ride home all over again, and somewhere in there he had the impression the military man clapped his heels.

When they were still two couples off, Nat saw the President's head bob like a predator's at the scent of prey. Immediately ahead of them was the region's biggest Chevrolet dealer, who was reserved, even haughty, until Jacqueline Kennedy smiled at him, when he melted — gave the First Lady both hands, would have sawed the President's arm off, save that Kennedy adroitly slipped his hand into the French Ambassador's, and turned to greet Viv and Nat.

A few moments later Nat looked back to see the President's fingers lingering in Pam's, as something animated Mrs. Kennedy to paddle her shoulders gleefully.

Champagne flowing, no one wanted to go home until,

finally, the Presidential party showed signs of leaving. Nat went to retrieve his and Viv's coats.

As he returned, he heard a Harvard accent call *"Pamela!"* across the room. Mrs. Kennedy, the Ambassador and Malraux were departing, the First Lady beaming into Malraux's craggy face. Moments later, her husband was going the other way with a Secret Service contingent and Pam Manchester.

Stuffing both coats in Viv's arms, Nat lunged across the room, past the jilted cadet in dress blues, and followed them through the great rotunda, beneath golden Mercury balanced in flight above hissing waters. Outdoors in the half-circle drive he saw Kennedy help Pam into a black Lincoln, get behind the wheel and, a car following, drive down Constitution Avenue.

Nat ran outdoors, sprinted through the frigid air to his Pontiac parked on C Street and gave chase.

The Lincoln continued to Pennsylvania Avenue. The taillights disappeared, but Nat knew where they were going. He'd followed by instinct — the instinct, he told himself, of a reporter after a story (reporter *obsessed* by a story, maybe, but so be it, he thought: *Obsession does a lot of good work).* Turning up K Street, at this hour a shorter way, he found a parking space next door to the Gruberian Embassy and was sitting there, lights out, when the President wheeled up with his escort, double-parked and, laughing, took Pam indoors.

A third-floor light went on. Nat waited, freezing. Finally he realized it was pointless to try to outwait anybody or to imagine what might be taking place upstairs; he knew what was taking place. Pictured it, and couldn't stand it: That body uncovered, those legs opened.... Gnashing his teeth, he started his car and pulled out. Startled, a man with a hand to his pocket stepped out from behind a tree.

The National Gallery was dark; no one was waiting outside, and no one answered Nat's pounding on the bronze doors. Finding a phone booth, he called Hardy Owens, and was jovially informed that Viv was having a nightcap with him and Leilani.

He drove to Georgetown and picked her up.

Viv had his coat, but was very angry.

"Left at a reception with no way *home?* Don't know when I've been so *humiliated,* Nat."

"You knew Hardy and Leilani were there."

"Was it that woman? The one the President's involved with?"

He admitted that it was.

"And *you? Are you* involved with her?"

"*No!*"

But her fury lasted all the way home—the straight shot out 16th Street, the Georgia Avenue-University Boulevard loop-and-roll through suburbia and into their carport.

Everyone was asleep except for Tommy, home between college semesters and sprawled in the family room watching Johnny Carson, the new host, interview an author in the *Tonight Show*'s third half hour.

Nat watched, too—discovering that underneath his easy, funny banter, Carson was a good interviewer—then went upstairs and eased into bed, apparently not waking up Viv despite the mattress's judgmental creaking.

There he masturbated to images of Pam Manchester—stroked himself extravagantly, with the full powers of one in command of his fantasy, able to direct her to do whatever he wanted, rolling her this way and that, producing a cavalcade of sensation and—turning over and crushing a pillow with his face—a handful of semen.

"*Jesus,*" he thought, rolling onto his back, "it's not just the story, it's *her.*"

And saw Viv sitting up and looking at him in horror.

# 10.

GETTING HOME FROM WORK the next evening, Nat found the kids packed off to a neighbor's for dinner and Viv furious.

Not that they had a fight about it. They never fought; *never*. But when in the course of their discussion Pam Manchester's name came up, Viv said it might be best if Nat were to stay elsewhere for the time being.

He was just as adult about it. Taking some clothes and the Olympia, he drove back downtown (in the Pontiac, leaving Viv the station wagon she needed for the boys) and took a room at the International Inn, the new high-rise on Thomas Circle designed by Morris Lapidus of Miami Beach fame that featured a glass dome over the swimming pool.

Later that evening he began a new routine. Had to—was compelled to. Picking up a sack of sliders at White Castle, he drove to R Street and parked. Then sat; sat hating the obsessiveness and longing that had him sitting there, especially when nothing happened.

The next evening he did the same thing, and was rewarded by the sight of a two-car motorcade arriving at the Gruberian Embassy and seeing Pam come outdoors and get in the President's Lincoln.

Two nights later, it happened again. This time Nat followed them to a carriage house behind the Foxhall Road mansion of a Senate pal of the President's.

Another night, he trailed them straight to a White House gate. Nat drove on by, thinking he shouldn't be surprised the President thought he could get away with it. If Marilyn Monroe shimmying in a skintight dress and singing *Happy Birthday, Mr. President* at Madison Square Garden hadn't let the cat out of the bag, what could?

Other nights Nat saw the President enter the Gruberian Embassy, emerge after an hour or so and return to the White House. After seeing him safely through the gates, Nat would go back to his hotel and have his way with Kennedy's mistress.

But then it apparently was over. In a week of frozen R Street vigils, Nat didn't see the Lincoln again. He called off his surveillance—sped to his room and didn't come back—one bitter night when he was stamping the floorboards to keep warm and Pam stole up and, thumping his window, yelled, *"Who the hell do you think you are?"*

That shattered his fantasy of offering himself in the President's place. But he told himself it was a useful wake-up call. What he had to remember was that Pam Manchester was just one of *many* Kennedy women—a part of Nat's scoop, but only a small part. He needed to find as many of the women and the facts as he could to develop the story. Come right down to it, Pam he didn't need at all. And surely if he compiled enough evidence, persuaded enough of the women that he could help tell their stories, *Orbs* would have to publish his scoop?

As for the supposed cheapness of writing about President Kennedy's affairs? On consideration, Nat rejected the notion. What the *President* was doing was cheap, but a journalist investigating that behavior? Performing a public service.

Also he needed to move back home.

He telephoned Viv, and met her for dinner at Villa Rosa. On his promise that there had never been anything between himself and Pam—*technically correct!*—and he would have nothing to do with her going forward—*no need!*—and that he loved only her—*true!*—Viv took him back. The kids were reserved for a time, but said nothing.

As winter ended and spring began, Nat worked on the story on his own time, lunch hours, evenings, weekends. Finding Kennedy's women was the easy part. Colleagues gave him names; everybody seemed to know some of them, though no one could figure out what to do with the knowledge. Even a female colleague from *Spiral* intimated over lunch at Paul Young's that she'd had a Presidential fling herself. At a dinner party, an *Orbs* correspondent's wife declared to the table that so had she.

Thus Nat found himself proposing to a number of women that he interview them about their affairs with JFK.

Some refused. Some wanted a fee; Nat demurred, payment violating journalistic ethics.

But others spoke to him. They were of two general types. The first were poised and educated daughters of a monied or professional class easily seen, had Kennedy not been married, as appropriate companions for him. Winning and attractive, each had a spark of humor, fun and sexiness, and every one of them was protective of her Jack Kennedy. Adopting an avuncular manner, peering kindly over his spectacles, Nat found several of them, within those limits of protectiveness, surprisingly forthcoming.

The other kind were professionals—call girls living genteelly with no visible means of support, or streetwalkers on the decline from the profession's loftier levels. These last tended to be more overt and provocative, trying to get a rise out of Nat, bawdy in speculating what he was *really* up to.

One of the first type met him for lunch at Harvey's, the Dupont Circle steakhouse unchanged since Lincoln's patronage. The red-papered rooms gleamed with gaslight chandeliers and a staff entirely African-American. Andrea was 28, a married Bryn Mawr graduate considering law school, and not ashamed of having had a fling with the President — to the contrary. And she wanted to talk about it, so, even while delivering injunctions as to her anonymity, told Nat everything he wanted to know.

A lady of the second sort met him in a booth at the bar of the Hotel Washington, in the Treasury's shadow. It was a tired old place — chandeliers yellow with dust, carpets threadbare — for all that the Speaker of the House lived upstairs. This lady, while keeping, as it seemed to Nat, an eye out for trade, declared the President to be a perfect gentleman, generous and appreciative, and imparted nothing more, though she intimated they could get a room if Nat so desired. He declined, and the interview ended abruptly when she somehow managed to seal a deal with a man winking from the bar whom Nat recognized as a goody-two-shoes Congressman from Oklahoma.

On days when his research lasted into the evening, he would find a phone booth from which to tell Viv that the House — or Senate — was still in session *(true enough!)* and he'd be an hour or two more. Instinct told him to keep his inquiries to himself.

A consequence of pursuing JFK's love life was that Nat tingled with desire 24 hours a day like a teenager. Finding these women, sitting down with them, deploying such seductive charms as he possessed in trying to win their cooperation left him in a maddening state of arousal, just when Viv was not so interested.

By May, Nat's dossier was fat with notes outlining the President's extra-marital sex life. But to turn them into a coherent story required that he focus on a single foreground figure, on some one particular woman.

Who better than the most dimensional, and the one whose affair spanned the longest time?

He needed Pam Manchester after all.

# 11.

NAT RANG THE BELL at 5:30 on a sunny afternoon.

The Gruberian Embassy was a town house of yellow-painted brick with a fanlight over double front doors. A pretty house on a pretty block, Nat noted. The houses dated to the nineteenth century, their stone and brick fronts now mostly cream or white. And a storied block in Washington history: In 1919 an anarchist exploded his bomb a few doors down at Attorney General Palmer's, and though the bomber was the only casualty (except for the shattered windows of FDR's house across the street), the resulting uproar led to expanded powers for the FBI and an apparently lifetime sinecure for its chief, J. Edgar Hoover.

A young woman answered the door. "Yes?"

"Hello, my name's Nat Handler. Is Pam Manchester in?"

She flashed a smile. "Come in and I'll see."

"Thank you."

Nat waited in the entry hall, hearing women upstairs call to one another, before Pam, a hand to her hair, started down the staircase.

"Oh, it's you," she said, stopping.

"Pam, I wanted to apologize for parking outside that

night," Nat said. "No excuse, except I was on a story — "

"Oh, it's OK, Nat. Come on in." Her face softening, she came down the rest of the way and led him into the parlor, which had a handsome Federal mantel and substantial old furniture. Voices wafted in from elsewhere. Indicating the couch, Pam perched at its far end.

"Believe the bastard dropped me all over again?"

"Did he?"

Looking at her, Nat realized that his high-minded reason for seeing her was merely an excuse: *He wanted to see her because he wanted her.* Another thing for the family man — entertaining a not unpleasant gathering at his crotch — to ponder. But he was sure he had everything under control.

"Can I offer you coffee, or a cocktail?"

"No, thank you. Just glad to find you in."

She smiled. Her resemblance to the *Mona Lisa* included the smile — vulnerable, he thought, but knowing, too; possibly not without cruelty.

"Pam, I've a request to make. As you know, I'm a correspondent for *Orbs* magazine. I do journalism but, like they say, journalism's the first rough draft of history."

She nodded solemnly, though he detected amusement. Sitting slightly forward as though she were the petitioner, she looked fresh and delicious. The room smelled wonderful, and part of it was her.

"I follow, Nat, I think, but exactly what is it you want of me?"

"When we met in West Virginia, you were keeping company with Jack Kennedy. In the long run, that relationship's *history*, but right now, today, it's *news* and, with your help, I want to report it as such. Voters deserve to know."

She laughed out loud and, murmuring an apology, lit a Pall Mall, inhaling until it sizzled. "And what do I get? '*Floozy of the Year'?"*

"Same as I do, Pam: The satisfaction of speaking truth."
Accidentally, he licked his lips.

"A seat on the truth train, I can dig it," she said, smiling. "I
heard you were talking to girls. Nat, you'll laugh—"

"No, I won't."

" —but I had feelings for him. Stupid, I know."

"No, no."

"No, *stupid*. Never the deal with Jack. So you want to know
all about it? From start to sad, sudden finish? *Finishes?*" She
tapped ash into an ashtray.

"Yes, please."

"How I fell in love? A little bit? And now can't reach him?"
She exhaled with a sigh. "But you don't ever fall in love just a
little bit, really, do you, Nat? I think you understand. Look,
keep my name out of it and I'll talk to you. But you do know
you'll never print it?"

"So they keep telling me."

"I think someone will visit you first. But hell, sign me up."
Folding her hands on her lap, she said, "Take off your
glasses."

"Not sure that's a good idea."

"Just for a minute."

He lifted them off his face, and her blur looked deep inside
him.

"Do you have Indian blood in you?"

"Won't deny it."

"OK, let's talk," she said. She wrinkled her nose. "But not
here."

"My office?"

She just laughed.

"Restaurant?"

"A hotel suite would be more conducive to conversation,

don't you think?"

"Don't know about *that*," he said, though in fact he was *thrilled*.

She leaned back and sighed. "Then I don't know."

He swallowed. "Well, how about the International Inn? It's nice."

"Fine."

She agreed to meet the next afternoon.

THE ORANGE AND TURQUOISE suite he took on the fifth floor looked onto trees in fresh full leaf. It was still May; summertime's mugginess hadn't yet descended. As he set the Olympia on the sitting-room table, Nat assured himself that all he was after was the story. Not *his* idea to sequester himself in a hotel suite with the sexiest woman he'd ever seen. He would simply, professionally, elicit what she had to tell him. That was all, just *words*, and where can the harm be in *words?* No danger in shutting himself up with her, because he had no intention of inserting himself into the story *(so to speak!)*.

Or if there *was* danger—came the stray thought—Viv need never know.

But he was excited—*very*; felt his body trembling expectantly, found himself swallowing, changing his saliva, altogether as jumpy as when he was 18 years old and stalking Viv and her boyfriend.

He called downstairs for room service coffee, iced tea, sandwiches and cookies.

Pam was late. Waiting, he watched TV from the small bedroom's bed, one foot jiggling nonstop. Between cartoons Cap'n Tugg took his boat down the Potomac to escape the gang chasing him, was just telling his parrot *they were in for it now!*, when a knock came at the door.

Startled, swallowing hard, Nat answered.

Pam strode into the sitting room in sunglasses and silk scarf. Her dress was of apricot-colored flowers on white. The scarf reminded him of Viv armed for Mass.

"Hello, Nat," she said, unwrapping the silk, a glance through the bedroom door taking in his body's imprint on the bed. "Well, where are we?"

"Over there, I thought?" he said, indicating the table while he went into the bedroom to turn off the TV's blather: *Lord, is she sexy!* "Hungry? There's this, but we can order anything you want."

"I'm fine, thanks," she said, taking the chair he held out.

"Well, *great.*" He sat down opposite, wishing he'd thought to close the bedroom door. They could see the bed from where they sat. But getting up now was somehow not possible. "You look wonderful."

She shot him a look. He regrouped as he picked up a pencil, self-consciously flipped open a fresh legal pad and said, "Well, why don't you tell me how you first met Jack Kennedy?"

She lit a cigarette. So did he.

"Oh, let's see. . . . Came to town after college — Wellesley, class of '56 — and took a course at Katharine Gibbs. As luck would have it, I got a job at his Senate office, and must have caught his eye.

"Well, I remember, actually. I was typing a letter to a constituent and he came over and dictated a change, I finished it, he looked it over, looked *me* over." She sighed. "Such an attractive man.

"Totally secret. Knew from the start it wasn't *real*, that we could never even go to the movies, but that didn't matter — when he's there, boy, is he *there*. Randy guy, too, Nat, if you want to know.

"Accidentally slept over at the Embassy once. He woke up

in the middle of half a dozen career girls fighting over the bathroom. Was he a sensation at the breakfast table! Did my reputation no end of good. Usually I'm a fuddy-duddy."

"I don't believe *that,*" Nat said.

She smiled. "Maybe it's because I knew he was married with a child and ambitions and it was so totally hopeless that I fell in love. Gave it that element of sadness, you know, that makes things more *real,* more—what's the word?"

"Poignant?"

"*Poignant,*" she agreed, stabbing out her cigarette. "He *is* adorable. Saw less and less of him, though, then nothing at all. Well, he's busy for sure. Then I took that money to West Virginia. Told you about that. His Dad's security guy showed me what 200,000 bucks looks like—which *(paugh!)* is like a rotten salad that belongs in the garbage—and put it and me on the plane. And Jack and I were together again. Even met his mother. Have you met his mother?"

"No."

"Everyone talks about his father, but take it from me, it's the *mother.* And then that damn party at Hickory Hill. But then the *Mona Lisa.* But now, again, haven't seen him in months.

"Oh, well, I'm a big girl, but can't help it if it makes me a little bit sad and a little bit mad. Nice to talk about it with someone sympathetic."

For two hours, Nat coaxed her to tell about their assignations, fill in the *wheres* and *whens.* Taking his notes, he tried to ignore the sexual funk that seemed to arise in the air around them. But sex was what they were talking about, after all.

At last she ran out of words, which brought him back to the fact of sitting with her, close to her, sounds of traffic picking up outdoors, his once pristine legal pad a blackened mass of notes. Was he being *too* professional, feeding his obsession with just-the-facts? Was it time to change modes for one more personal, more, as it were, *frontal?*

Excusing herself, Pam got up and went into the bathroom. Nat noticed she ran the tap while using the toilet, like Viv's mother and aunts. When she came out, she called from the bedroom to ask if it would be all right if she stretched out for a minute while she tried to think of more to say.

He shot to his feet, saying, "Yes, do, but first. . . if I may. . . . Excuse me," and discreetly went past her into the bathroom himself. *Time to make my move.*

*Move?* What move would that be? *Kennedy* would go out there and fuck that woman. Could he live with himself if he *didn't?* Nat stepped out of his shoes, slipped off tie, shirt, undershirt, pulled down his pants, kneed out of socks and shorts with the thought, *Now we're getting somewhere.* He looked at himself nude in the mirror. *Not bad for 38.*

But apparently guilt, even as it enhanced his excitement and made him tremble, prevented his erection. *Am I really going to do this?* he asked himself, knowing the answer to be, *No, not really.* But he bought himself a last moment's fantasy — *Well, but maybe* — by pairing his shoes and setting them against the wall, before he stood up and ejaculated, gushing with a sensation as abstract and enjoyable (except in the circumstances) as a wet dream's. Guilt and desire had short-circuited his body. He'd never heard of such a thing.

"*Goddamn* it!" he whispered. "*Fuck!*"

And *yuck!* Appalled, he washed himself and got dressed, the issue now not *would* or *wouldn't*: He *couldn't.*

He tied his shoes and opened the door. From the bed, Pam called archly, "Fall in?"

Going past her through the bedroom, he sat down at the Olympia and rolled a sheet of paper into it.

"Pam, really have to thank you," he called without looking

at her. "You've made a real contribution."

She swung up and put on her shoes, stood up, came into the sitting room tying her scarf. "Happy to oblige," she said. "Just remember, no names." And left.

Nat waited five minutes, checked out, and walked back to the office to type up his notes on his bigger typewriter there.

Washington's a tough town to walk in. The streets radiate out from the center, so walking goes against the grain, requires tacking back and forth.

But Nat's thoughts went back and forth, too. First he berated himself for not being a seducer, then for even *thinking* of betraying Viv. His ghastly orgasm was wrenched from him, he knew, by excitement for Pam hitting—head on—guilt about Viv.

But he couldn't feel such potent guilt without a reason for it, and that reason was plain to see: He loved his wife. He came all over himself because he loved Viv and, push come to shove, his body wouldn't let him to do anything with another woman.

At Connecticut Avenue, a motorcade of older Cadillac limousines passed. It resembled a parade of elephants, each with a hump and the twin chromium tusks called *Dagmars* after the famously busty model. Nat guessed it was the Vice President returning from some busy-work task.

And told himself, *You're no Kennedy. Better get used to it.*

And sighed.

*Alone with the sexiest woman in the world, and she was giving me signals, and I couldn't get it up.*

And, ruefully, *But I'm so lucky to have Viv.*

## 12.

NAT DECIDED TO WRITE UP a précis in memo form of what he had and show it to his Bureau Chief, Will Grady. That would give his editors every opportunity to assign him to break the story wide open.

He took care writing his memo, coming into the office over Memorial Day weekend for peace and quiet. On the *Re:* line he typed *The President's New Clothes*. Beneath, he stated that President Kennedy was pursuing multiple affairs, had been doing so throughout his marriage and Presidency, and told in brief from start to finish the story of the affair with Pam Manchester—without naming her—including her trip to West Virginia, its pool-party end, its renewal beneath the *Mona Lisa's* gaze. Mentioning, but not naming, some dozen other women who had or had had relationships with Kennedy, and discussing how these affairs threatened his re-election and legacy, he emphasized *Orbs'* responsibility to portray the man accurately, warts and all.

Tuesday morning, Nat telephoned Grady's secretary from the bullpen to ask for an appointment—not necessary in an office with an open-door policy, but he wanted to signal his seriousness.

At the hour named, he walked in with the original of his memo (the carbon copy safe at home; the office still awaited its first Xerox machine). Sitting down opposite Grady, he told him what he'd been working on. Grady looked interested, intimated he'd heard as much and reached for the memo.

He read the first page with concentration, and buzzed his secretary to hold his calls. Gratified, Nat lit a cigarette and looked out over Dupont Circle's rooftops. What made Washington's trees so prominent, he realized, was how low the buildings were; from any angle of approach the city still offered a 19th-century aspect. His boss turned pages, from the last one paged slowly backwards and lifted his face.

"Hot stuff, Nat. Well done."

"Thanks, Will."

Grady leaned back. "Look, you meet these girls around, they all have the same story. I don't imagine it's anything we care to pursue."

Nat's heart sank. "But think of the security risk: How does he meet them? Who knows there's not a ring targeting him? With maybe the Russians behind it? Supposedly one of these women is a Mob mistress. How's that square with the war on organized crime? And I hear rumors of births and abortions. Kennedy could be in a real mess here."

"Nat—"

"Can't tell me others aren't working on this. Phil Graham spilled the beans to some out-of-town reporters last *February*. Want *Newsweek* to beat us? Will, all I ask is that you show the memo to New York. If they call me off, fine."

"All right, Nat, but you sure as hell can't telex this. Take it up yourself, hand it to Helmut. I'm sure Randy'll want to see it, too. And they'll tell you what to do."

"Thanks, I'll go up in the morning." Nat got to his feet.

"But tell me," said Grady, also rising, "why do you want to

crucify Kennedy, anyway?"

"Don't *want* to, Will. Just doing my job: Following the truth wherever it leads."

Sighing unhappily, Grady told his secretary to put his calls through.

Next morning, Nat took the 9:00 a.m. Eastern Air Lines shuttle from National Airport to New York. They ran a second section to meet that morning's rush, so with some strategic loitering he found himself sharing a Super Constellation with just 20 other passengers.

From LaGuardia he took a taxi to *Orbs*. His briefcase held a change of underwear and a shirt, though he didn't know if he'd be staying overnight. That was up to the powers that be.

The new, 50-story Orbs Tower was part of Rockefeller Center's leap across Sixth Avenue, the first of the gigantic bookends that came to line The Avenue of the Americas. As usual, Moondog, the blind musician in a Viking helmet, stood sentry outside. At the risk of betraying that he was from out of town, Nat threw back his head to take in the whole handsome building of stone-clad piers framing panels of enamel and glass.

Upstairs at *Orbs* magazine's 12th-floor nerve center he handed his memo to Helmut's secretary and asked her to give it to him.

She carried it in and he sat down in the waiting area to read *Spiral* and *Ducats*. A few minutes later Helmut came out of his office, passing Nat with a wink and wave as he went to the elevators and punched *Up*. Randy Orpen's office was on the 34th floor. Twenty minutes later, Helmut emerged smiling from the elevators and came up to Nat.

"Nat, nice piece of work. Randy thinks so, too."

"Thanks," said Nat.

"Now look, as you can imagine, this takes consideration—

special handling."

"Of course."

"So go on home for now, all right? We'll let you know."

"Yes, sir."

Helmut shook his hand, Nat taxied to LaGuardia and was back at the office in time for a late sandwich at Paul Young's. He couldn't help feeling disappointed, but it was natural that before breaking a story that would shake Washington to its foundations they should want to think it through.

Meanwhile he resumed calling his sources, trying to learn when Congress would recess for the summer. Grady wanted to know.

## 13.

THINGS HUNG FIRE FOR three excruciating weeks, until one afternoon Grady summoned Nat to tell him New York wanted him first thing in the morning and he had a room reserved at the Warwick Hotel.

Tamping down his excitement, Nat called Viv and drove to National with his change of underwear.

As he flew over the green countryside of Maryland, Pennsylvania and New Jersey, he was thinking how *Orbs* should proceed: Cover story, of course, perhaps with sidebars about various pseudonymous women, maybe leaving it to *Spiral* to publish photo essays on any who might wish to cooperate.

He thought, too, about consequences. A year hence, the 1964 campaign would be under way; Kennedy had a year to recover from the public's learning about his womanizing before he ran for re-election. As for Nat, his career might be launched into a higher sphere. Alternatively, he might never be heard from again, not if the public chose to be offended with the messenger. The stakes weren't negligible, and the outcome not in his own hands. But it was exciting, and he was sure he was doing the right thing.

After checking into a tired-looking room on the 15th floor, he descended to the Warwick's bar, and later strolled into the dining room, where he remembered a few years back seeing the hotel's penthouse resident, Marion Davies, movie star and formerly Hearst's mistress. A most presentable old lady, she was dining opposite a younger man—her lawyer, he divined—who matched her drink for drink in the most impressive parade of drinks Nat ever witnessed until, unfortunately, the man passed out, his face landing in the mashed potatoes. Looking unsurprised, Davies had ordered another Mimosa.

That night Nat slept fitfully—he blamed traffic noise—and after breakfast walked to the Orbs Tower and went upstairs. He entered Helmut's office to find him and two colleagues laughing at a painting on an easel. Helmut turned to greet him.

"Hey, Nat, take a look, isn't this *great?*"

Nat had to laugh, too. Boris Artzybasheff's picture showed the Statue of Liberty on water skis, picking up her skirts and screaming with glee as she sent waves rolling at Wall Street.

"Nice," he said.

"*America on Vacation.* That's the cover you guys are doing." At the word *cover* Nat started like an old fire horse at a bell. "Taking your families on the road soon as you can—tomorrow, *today*—and getting the story. It's June 26? Deadline *July* 26. Come on, let's sit down, get specific."

They sat at a table spread with maps, and to his horror Nat realized nothing was being said about his memo. Instead, Helmut divvied up the country in terms of road trips. One colleague got New England and the coast down to Key West, another the West Coast and Pacific Northwest. Nat was to load up Viv and the kids, head up to the Pennsylvania Turnpike, work over through Ohio and Indiana, taking such fragments of I-70 as were finished, and from Chicago follow the entire fabled course of Route 66 to the Pacific Ocean at Santa Monica, California.

"*Route 66,*" Helmut repeated, smacking his lips as though Nat had lucked into the plum assignment of his career. "And don't stint, guys: We want the tourist traps, the alligator farms, the miniature golf, house museums, cavalry forts, motels, food. Snapshot of the country at play. Randy's thinking in Cold War terms—you know, Route 66 *versus* whatever Russia has. What is it, The Road of *Bones?*"

Nat lingered as the meeting broke up.

"But Helmut," he asked, "what about—?"

"What's that, Nat?"

"My memo? The President's girls?"

"Don't think we're interested, frankly. Anyway, this comes first."

"But—"

"That's what Randy wants."

And though he persisted, Helmut did not relent.

Downstairs, Nat called his friend Doug Cottle from a lobby phone booth: Did his offer to introduce him to Luther Pike still hold?

Doug asked Nat to call back in a quarter hour.

He did so from the hotel, and Doug told him Luther Pike wished him to call. Nat dialed the Luther Pike Press, and readily reached Pike himself, who in Long Island lockjaw urged Nat to come see him as soon as possible. He was in town? How about right now?

Nat got the address—16th Street, off Union Square—checked out of the Warwick and walked downtown amidst memories of being a teen-aged runaway in New York. A cab might have saved time, but he needed to work off some frustration.

Finding the limestone-clad building, originally a town house, and taking a rickety ride upstairs, he knocked on the door bearing Pike's brass plate. He waited. He knocked again. After waiting some more, he opened it to find four rows of desks whose occupants were engaged in covertly talking to one another. Through a glass wall at the front he saw a man at a desk with a young woman leaning over him. As she straightened up and came out to greet Nat, chatter ceased and hands reached to telephones and typewriters.

Nat shook hands with a slender man with a white mane and Mandarin manner. Bookcases displayed Luther Pike books, the covers' chaste typefaces and muted colors belying their lurid contents. Pike's voice, pumped from deep within, made mere whiffs at articulation.

"Nat, so pleased to meet you. Doug says your book's just what we're looking for. Jack Kennedy's a great man, but guess he has his weaknesses. Talk to me."

Nat talked. Pike was keenly interested, interrupting to urge him to put it down *in just that way*, to use *those exact words*, and insisted on taking him to lunch. "Brownies Restaurant, on the corner. Eggplant steak sound yummy? Soybean cutlet?"

By the time Nat returned to the airport digesting a soyaburger, he had a deal for *The President's Mistresses* — or *White House Adulterer?* — and in his wallet a check representing an advance of $15,000. He was going to write a book.

## 14.

"OH, NAT, SAY IT AIN'T SO," his Bureau Chief lamented from behind his desk.

"Signed the contract and banked the check, Will."

"You can't do that. I mean, it's a free country, but you can't work for *Orbs* — represent *us* — and at the same time write a book like *that*."

Nat stood up, unsurprised. "In that case, I'm afraid I resign, effective immediately."

They shook hands, and Nat shook hands also with his alarmed colleagues, and adjourned with some of them to an impromptu, alcohol-soaked sendoff at Paul Young's before driving home, one eye squinched shut, jobless husband and father of four. But planning on getting rich.

The one thing he rued was how quickly he had to write his book. Pike insisted it be in stores for Christmas. If Nat delivered his manuscript October 15, Pike's quick development process — "No one's faster! *No one!*" — could have the book on sale by December 1, giving Nat just three and a half months to write it. But Pike assured him it would be worth it — bestseller *guaranteed!*

"Press conference, stacks of copies behind us," Pike had

said. "You'll be famous, Nat, and *rich?* Probably print a hundred thousand copies to start. What am I saying? *200,000!* No, quarter *million!* Till then, top secret. Mum's the word!"

Nat belatedly realized he couldn't take the road trip he and his brothers had planned to visit their retired, aging father and his sweet second wife in Yarnell, Arizona. That reunion would have dovetailed with the Route 66 trip, but wasn't going to happen now.

He called to cancel, and told his father why — told him about the President's girlfriends and the big check he'd put in the bank.

"Isn't poking into that kind of thing beneath a Senior Correspondent's dignity?" his father asked. A few years earlier, when Nat informed him he'd been named *Senior Correspondent,* his Dad had laughed and laughed. "You'd be *The Man Who Took Down Kennedy?*"

Nat was stricken. "Goes to the kind of man he is, Dad."

"Sounds like he's the kind of man most men are, son," David Duncan Handler said gently. "And you *like* the guy. I do, too. Why tear him down?"

"It's not me, it's *him,* his *behavior.*" Nat heard the pitch of his voice rising, as it always did in dispute with his father. "President of the United *States,* and can't keep it in his *pants?*"

"I'm proud of you, you know that," his father said. "Wish your mother could have seen what you've made of yourself. She'd be so proud, too. We've had our problems over the years, but going after Kennedy? Not the way to solve them."

"Don't get you, Dad," said Nat. "Not about *us.*"

Next morning, without shaving — he was an author now — he set up shop on the dining room table. He fanned out his memo, his notes, fresh legal pads, sharpened his pencils, placed a stack of *Orbs'* grainy copy paper beside the massive Underwood from which he'd edited the Grand Junction *Daily*

*Item,* and began.

Began. Read some notes. Poured a cup of coffee. Read more notes. Looked out at the street. Nothing. But a minute later he could hear a car coming and watched it pass. Getting up, he looked out the sliders at the back yard, past sprouting bamboo to open ground furrowed by giant tires. Sat down again. Listened to Viv push the kids outdoors to play, "but no yelling."

That Nat's was no usual suburban pursuit became obvious the second hour. Their neighbor Carol, whose husband was CIA—they'd brought his-and-her Peugeots home from his Paris posting—dropped by unannounced for coffee and was fascinated when Viv barred her entry.

"Nat's *home?* On a *Thursday?* Viv, what's the *matter?*"

She would not be put off, but walked right in.

"Hi, Nat," she said. "Everything all *right?*"

He brusquely reassured her, even as she came up close and darted eyes over his papers. He stood up and she withdrew, treating Viv to a half-hour's goodbye, the women mirroring each other's postures—arms crossed, then hands on hips, then lounging against a wall, then hands supporting elbows—in a frieze that leisurely took them from living room to foyer, out the door and across the carport.

The kids discovered that they lived in a mausoleum, silent but for an incessant shushing meant to preserve Nat's concentration: He was on deadline, a word they had long learned to dread.

When Jack and Jimmy settled down to afternoon TV— reruns of *The Mickey Mouse Club* and *Make Room for Daddy*— Nat began appearing at the top of the stairs with appeals to lower the volume. The boys crept closer and closer to a more and more muffled television, before giving up and retreating to their room to play with a Kenner construction set, only to have their Dad hulk by, eyes glassy, avid for distraction.

"*Mom!*" they yelled. "*Dad's* here!" Viv helped them flee to a neighbor's.

A disciplined and determined writer, Nat slowly got words on paper. Scouring his cheeks with a sound that drove Viv up the wall, he would write a few words, then stalk around the house, sitting down with pad and pencil on the screened porch or in the bedroom, with quickened step return to go *rat-a-tat-tat* at his keyboard; until his fingers stopped again and he sat glaring outdoors.

When a paragraph proved especially recalcitrant he would rise up and, huffing a tuneless melody, go around watering plants, frowning out windows, checking the mailbox. In trying to unsnarl particularly knotty passages, he was even known to mow the lawn. Otherwise he sat staring into space; writing a book, he assured Viv, takes a lot of staring into space. And when torn to the surface—the telephone ringing, a kid laughing—he was apt to be snappish.

For the kids it was torture; for Viv, too. Nat followed her around the house, bobbing up to see what she was doing, ask whom she was calling, what she was cooking, where she was going.

Worst was when he set off down the street. Once Viv saw a neighbor lady dart outside and bring her children indoors away from the strange man.

As Nat's typist, hers was a major part in the undertaking. During most of the time he was off at war she supported herself and their firstborn by typing, putting off forever the completion of her own degree. Now her fingers' expert *tap tap tapping* delivered up batches of typescript that grew steadily towards the 60,000 words Pike said gravitas required.

But she liked no part of the project. "Nat, it's like pimping," she protested after typing a chapter that described accommodations his women made to the President's bad back. *"Disgusting."*

"Viv, it's a story so hot no one else dares touch it."

"Why do *you* want to?"

"Not a matter of *wanting,* Viv, it's part of *history* — "

"It's *gossip,* Nat. What if it elects Barry Goldwater? *Goldwater,* Nat? Want that on you?"

"Hey, Barry's a good man. Knew him back home, remember? Stayed with Dad at Keams first time he ran for office."

"Nat!"

One morning, a white, four-door Chevy Bel Air parked in front of the house. Viv noticed it as she poured orange juice, also that the man in a fedora behind the wheel kept the engine running, possibly for the sake of air conditioning. She couldn't see his face. He appeared to be waiting, but she didn't know what for.

"Nat, there's a car out front," she said when he tramped to the breakfast table. "With a man in it."

Their sons were at the table, each reading a section of the Washington *Post.* Nat asked for the front page; handing it to him, Tommy plucked *Metro* out of Fred's hands, Fred took *Business* out of Jack's, and Jack took *Sports* from Jimmy. Jimmy turned the Wheaties box around and read the back.

"How's Bill Gold?" Nat asked.

"Good," Jimmy piped up. Gold's congenial *District Line* column appeared next to comics on one of the *Post's* five glorious pages of them.

"Nat," Viv prompted.

"Public street," he answered.

But car and man didn't budge, and after breakfast Nat found he couldn't concentrate, so, to Viv's terror, went outdoors and approached the Chevy.

Its driver got out as Nat came up—a large, unsmiling man in his late fifties or so, good looking in a squarish kind of way. Disarmingly, he removed his fedora to bare a crew cut— incongruous in someone his age, but to Nat signifying law enforcement or military.

"Mr. Handler?"

"Yes. Who are you?"

"My name's Bob Argent. Like to speak with you. Take a turn down the block?"

Nat was curious, so set off down the sidewalk with him past the neighboring Vanguards.

"Mr. Handler, I work for Ambassador Kennedy," Argent said.

"Do you really?" Nat asked, startled.

"The Ambassador asked me to talk to you about your project."

"Indeed?" The President's father, crippled by a stroke soon after his son's inauguration, could no longer speak. Nat had seen him in his wheelchair being posed like a puppet amidst his family.

"He's concerned. He'd appreciate it if you didn't write about the President's private life."

Nat was charmed. Deep as he was in his book, energizing as he found it, it wanted the last bit of enticement for an agent of the subject's to try to call him off.

"That's as may be, Mr. Argent, but—"

"Call me Bob."

"Bob, I'm not sure you or the Ambassador—or the President, for that matter—understand what it is *I* do as a reporter: Seek out the truth and write it, in the conviction that—"

"Come on," said Argent. "You're a man, Mr. Handler. Man of the world."

"Sure, but—"

"The Ambassador's prepared to be generous. Happens to be an opening at USIA, high up. What do they publish, 50 magazines around the world? *And* produce The Voice of America? Salary's good, too, if you're not civil service."

Nat was speechless: United States *Information* Agency? Voice of *America?* Had he just been offered a *bribe?*

"Bob, I'm insulted," said Nat. "I'm—"

"All right, Mr. Handler. Here's something to consider, though. The Ambassador's protective of his family. Now, these nice ladies have been helping you out of the goodness of their hearts. Wouldn't want it to end badly for any of them, would you?"

Thinking *Time to head back,* Nat turned around, saying, "Well, in the first place, *Bob,* I don't respond to threats, and in the second place, *Bob,* my sources are confidential—"

"Come on," Argent repeated. "You know, I used to be a G-Man. Been worth my while to stay on terms with the Bureau, and I can tell you Director *Hoover's* taking an interest, too."

Never had Nat seen so world-weary a smile. The eyes within their crinkled skin were flat, and sorrow permeated a face that was not without sensitivity. He realized that *his* truth-seeking took place on an altogether more luxurious plane than any Argent had access to.

"OK," Nat said. Hearing himself, he was afraid of accidentally giving Argent hope, but the other's eyes didn't flicker. "I mean, I've heard you out, you've been clear. Whatever I do from here on in is my responsibility. I've been warned."

"Oh, not *warned.* Well, and Miss Manchester doesn't wish to see her name in print, nor to see mentioned any personal dealings between you, whether at her house or at the International Inn. Plus, she sees you on R Street again, she's calling someone. Old friend of the family's.

"And Mr. Handler, I'm no heavy. Sixty-one years old, for Chrissake. But heavies the Ambassador knows."

Nat announced, "The way of truth may not be the easiest, Bob, but it's the way I have to go." (To himself: *God! Even on the fly, how pompous can you get?*) "And please don't hang around my house. Makes my wife nervous."

"Wish you had more imagination, Mr. Handler, that's all," Argent said with a little nod, before getting in his car and driving away.

## 15.

JUST THEN A HAZARD of living near Washington showed itself: Relatives visited. In the hottest part of the year, Viv's Aunt Ida and her husband arrived to stay a week.

Al Henderson was 70 years old, but that didn't stop him from wearing exclusively his old Civil Air Patrol uniform, however raggedy it looked. Nat was fuzzy on what the Civil Air Patrol was until Al, gravely and at length, was pleased to fill him in, Ida sitting by rolling her eyes. She was thrilled to be seeing Washington at last — the Lincoln Memorial, the Capitol, the Smithsonian — but embarrassed by that uniform, rare plumage even in a town of flocking uniforms. Wherever they went it drew questions, as did the medals on Al's chest, which were for, respectively, five, ten, 15 and 20 years' volunteer part-time service. But Al happily snapped off salutes and explanations.

It was a trying week. Making the best of it — truth be told, Nat wasn't that unhappy to be torn away from his manuscript — he and Viv took guests and family on daily trips downtown, where Viv and her aunt disappeared. The younger boys particularly enjoyed the National Archives and its horseshoe tunnel behind the founding documents and —

visiting it at Al's insistence—the Army Medical Museum. Inside its red-brick precincts, untouched since the Hayes Administration, Nat was amazed at such exhibits as the pickled leg with elephantiasis, four dozen pickled pairs of testicles, a dissected and pickled penis, a vagina *ditto*, the pickled fetuses and the skeleton affably sitting in a corner, bequeathed by its original possessor. Al frowned over the newer exhibits featuring horrific photographs of air-crash victims; Nat steered the boys away from those.

And with them climbed the Washington Monument, the stairs being free (Al splurged on the elevator, which cost a dime), pausing for breath on landings where stones chiseled with names and dates had been donated by the various states. The view through the top's narrow apertures disclosed the entire sweltering city.

Down below, they visited the National Air Museum, housed temporarily in a block-long Quonset hut near the office shacks thrown up during the War that still covered much of the Mall. Outside, missiles and anti-missile missiles bristled; indoors the museum was stuffed with relics in the mode of an attic. The Wright brothers' dusty Flyer, its fabric half rotted, hung from the shadowy ceiling near *The Spirit of St. Louis* and the Bell X-1. On the floor lay the crumpled wreckage in which Wiley Post and Will Rogers died. Al Henderson ambled up one side and down the other at a determined and proprietary pace.

They also toured the White House, freshly refurbished by Jacqueline Kennedy. For the first time in years the rooms reflected their early Nineteenth Century heritage and showcased original pieces restored to it (the nation saw the results in the First Lady's charming TV special, hosted by Walter Cronkite with a cameo appearance by the President).

Riding home Al unexpectedly reminisced about shaking

President Warren G. Harding's hand in the Oval Office in 1921.

"Here with a Chamber of Commerce delegation," he said. "And when the others left, I stayed behind to tell him I came from the same town as his Postmaster General. 'Pueblo, Colorado?' he goes in his deep voice. 'That's it, Mr. President!' and shook his hand all over again. Fine-looking man. The ladies went for him."

"*Really?*" Nat asked.

"And how!" Al cackled. "And he for them! Real horndog, they say." Suddenly he looked nervously at the boys.

"Hear the same about any president since?"

"Kennedy, you mean?" Al asked with a wink. "Wouldn't surprise me one little bit."

"And would you want to know?"

"*Hell*, yes."

Nat felt encouraged, and so must Al, for he told the story of shaking President Harding's hand again.

Aunt Ida and Al went home, the kids returned to school and Nat spent several days at the Library of Congress doing research on previous Presidents' sex lives. When that turned up surprisingly little, he telephoned several historians to ask what they might know on the topic.

But they didn't have much light to shed, either. Harding, FDR—that was about it. One asked shrewdly, "What are you working on, a Kennedy exposé?"

Still, he made progress. But one September Saturday he broke away to take the boys car shopping. (Viv stayed home in silent protest.) At the local Lincoln-Mercury dealer, Nat first inspected several august used exemplars, but in the showroom the salesman demonstrated the added rear leg room of the just-received '64 Lincoln Continental and suggested a test drive. So while the boys luxuriated over leather and suicide doors, Nat considered whether black or white would better suit.

They drove home — by a supremely roundabout route — in a shiny black Lincoln Continental with white leather interior, leaving behind the Pontiac as a trade-in.

Nat couldn't get enough of it. The Lincoln's elegance was heartstopping. From the leather-wrapped wheel he looked past a glossy hood edged in chrome and led by an ornament resembling a telescopic rifle sight. The windshield swooped back, there were buttons and switches and gauges galore, power windows, power seats, AM/FM speakers front and back. The padded dashboard featured walnut framed in chrome. The up-to-date 1960s esthetic, controlled and understated, contrasted with the baroque confections of the '50s. And he needed merely put a toe to the accelerator to feel 320 horses surge.

The car's grandeur made the boys quiet and grave in considering their new estate, gave them a new way of looking kindly upon those in lesser vehicles.

Only Viv resented spending a pre-tax third of the book advance on a car, though when pressed she conceded, "It's very pretty."

After the publication hullaballoo was over and royalties started rolling in, Nat thought they might look for a new place, perhaps a horse farm farther out, or maybe a house in Cleveland Park or Georgetown. In any case the suburbs were wearing thin.

This idea Viv found agreeable, and took advantage of several open houses to get a sense of the market. She toured a horse-country manor with paddock, meadows and barn, plus garden terraces and tennis court, and strolled through a tall city Victorian of endless rooms, wonderful woodwork and multiple fireplaces, trying to envision the life she and Nat could lead in such spaces.

But, ever prudent, she thought it early to do anything definite.

## 16.

NAT'S DEADLINE LOOMED—and passed. He missed it, perfecting and polishing his prose.

Personally, he doubted it mattered if *Kennedy's Women* was out before Christmas: Not a book people would put under the tree, but one that would get due attention whenever it appeared. But Luther Pike started calling to demand the manuscript, first weekly, then, in November, daily. Nat couldn't penetrate his crust enough to gauge how upset he really was, but resisted, feeling he owed it to himself and to his subject to write as well as he knew how, and that took time.

But by the middle of the month, Viv typing up a flawless copy on heavy typing paper, Nat was feeling pleased. His manuscript was impeccably researched, if he said so himself, and gracefully written, too, so characterizing the President's harem as to meet the requirements of both anonymity and literature. Pam, for instance, so vivid in person, came across on the page, too, however blurred in detail. The result was a nuanced, readable account of JFK's womanizing—behavior made more human and more understandable, he hoped, by his treatment of it.

Finally, Nat packed the manuscript in his briefcase, along

with some overnight things, and on the sunny Friday of November 22 drove himself, after a quick lunch, to National Airport, where he caught the one o'clock shuttle for New York.

Watching the autumnal landscape pass beneath, he was excited, but delivering his book was surprisingly bittersweet. It wasn't the novel he'd longed to write since he was a boy; he doubted his mother would have been jumping up and down for joy. However clean his prose, the subject's salaciousness, and the possibility of its doing harm to a President he admired, dampened his satisfaction. But JFK wasn't his friend, not really, and how can writing truthfully ever be *betrayal*, anyway? When truth's the only thing?

So he was prey to a combination of unease and satisfaction—no, *joy*, really; yes, *joy*—as, briefcase in hand, he walked past the stewardesses smiling beside the plane's door and down the movable steps to LaGuardia's tarmac.

Enjoying how much cooler New York was than Washington, he crossed into the terminal, past those waiting behind velvet ropes to board the return flight. But stepping onto the shiny waxed floor washed him with so distressing an atmosphere that he had to stop to assess what he was perceiving. The man behind banged into him, swinging a Samsonite briefcase painfully into the back of his knee. All around them people were wiping their eyes or crying outright and hugging one another.

Perplexed—surely he hadn't walked unseeing past a plane crash on the runway?—Nat trudged towards the cabstand. But though he'd done it a dozen times before, this time he got lost, found himself in a corridor to nowhere. He backtracked, and as the terminal opened up around him saw a woman go up to four men and say something that made all five burst into tears. A ticket agent on the phone stared in horror at nothing, a hand balled to her lips. On a TV screen above a bar, Walter Cronkite glanced at the clock over his shoulder, took off his glasses and wiped his eyes.

When he finally found the cabstand and took a seat in the foremost Ford, he had to wait for the driver to break away from a group of his fellows. He got behind the wheel exclaiming, "Believe the goddam Texans *killed* him?"

Nat—angry at not knowing what apparently everybody else knew—shut him up by asking him to turn up the radio. When had he last felt so lost? WABC was mid-story about somebody being taken to Parkland Hospital. Nat's first, inane thought was that he belonged to Parkland *Pool*, near Hunter Mill, but then a voice confirmed President Kennedy's death. Horror and denial were fighting when they lost the radio to the Queens-Midtown Tunnel.

If he were still at *Orbs* Nat knew he would be busy and involved, possibly even be in Dallas, more likely rushing upstairs from lunch at Paul Young's to do something useful in bringing a fuller picture of events to people. Instead, he was sitting on grimy vinyl hearing tires hum in a tunnel, headed to deliver his book; a book obviously now dead in the water, made by Dallas unspeakable, obscene and shameful. He remembered seeing at a New Mexico shrine a caged eagle that cringed in shame; now he cringed, too.

Back on land the radio spoke up, Kennedy still dead. Off Union Square Nat took the wheezing elevator to the Luther Pike Press. The staff was crowded into Pike's office, where a radio was shouting, " —that they took for *backfires* — "

Nat joined them. Pike signaled the others to leave.

"Bad luck, Nat!" Pike told him. "Bad *luck,* I say? Sign from *God*. Can't go ahead with the book, obviously, but in a funny way — or no, not so funny, I realize — at least no one needs to *know*. God, what a near thing! If you'd met your deadline? Makes me *shiver!* Offer you a drink, but under the circumstances—

"Now, Nat, hate to get legal, but that advance I paid you? Conditioned—read your contract—on your delivering a publishable manuscript. Now, *'publishable'*—term of art, bit mushy, sometimes open to interpretation, but in this case it's clear: This book is *not* publishable, whatever the state of the manuscript—and I'm sure it's *very good*. So if you'll kindly repay your advance, we can shake hands and be quits, no lawyers."

"Of course," Nat said stiffly. "Don't have my checkbook with me."

"Oh, next week will be fine," Pike said.

Elizabethan horrors continued all weekend. Nat studied Oswald's mug shot on TV, the kindled, smirking eyes bespeaking a serene self-possession, the joy of the son who has killed his father. But was what Oswald accomplished so very different from what he'd been trying to do himself?

With the nation he watched the assassin paraded out that he might be shot in turn.

Only with the stateliness of the lying in state and the funeral could anyone hope that events were taking place within history and that life would go on. The arrangements, however improvised, had an awful dignity. The casket reposing in the East Room and beneath the Capitol dome, the daughter's gloved hand fumbling under the flag that wrapped it, the son three years old saluting it, Charles de Gaulle and Haile Selassie marching a mob of world leaders up Connecticut Avenue to St. Mathew's Cathedral. Every ceremonial was observed, down to the horse-drawn caisson and the riderless horse behind it, boots backwards in the stirrups. The horses plodded across Memorial Bridge to the columned house at Arlington, where the coffin was lowered into the ground.

As the widow lit the eternal flame, a flight of fighter jets—flying, Cronkite informed them, in the "missing man" formation—thundered over Arlington Cemetery escorting the Boeing 707 that had borne the President's body home. Nat watched the jets roar across the TV screen and out of sight, but seconds later the roar resumed and the house began to shake. He and his sons burst into the back yard to see the fighters at treetop level shooting their shadows over the ground, while just overhead Air Force One thundered with the wrath of the gods.

# 17.

NAT SUPPOSED IT PRESUMPTUOUS to think himself worse off than others when the whole world felt wrecked, but who except Kennedy himself was so extinguished by Oswald's bullets? (Well, aside from Vaughn Meader, the witty JFK impressionist.) He had no job; no horse farm was in prospect. It reminded him, but on a greater scale, of Pope John XXIII's death the previous June, when Viv's pastor, Monsignor Coyne, suddenly and with no good grace was sporting the surplice of an ordinary parish priest, answering merely to *Father* until the new Pope could confirm the old one's appointments.

After a painful conversation with Viv and a call to their broker to sell AT&T stock, Nat wrote Luther Pike that check. The rest of the month and all December he stayed indoors, depressed, wandering from room to room, until he thought to take out some short stories he wrote in college and try to breathe life into them. Viv gamely did the typing, until he pronounced them DOA. He kept his beard, by now of a length that attested to wisdom.

Thanks to Viv's inheritances from her grandfather and parents (her father's World War I gassing doubtless contributed to his fatal heart attack at 53, just before he and

Viv were to meet for the first time since she was a little girl)
the Handlers could withstand a spell of joblessness. Nat put an
ad in the paper offering to sell the Lincoln, but had no takers.

A few days after Christmas, the weather continuing warm,
Viv proposed a ride in the country, just the two of them. She
said she wanted to talk.

Leaving Fred to mind the younger ones, they set off, the
Lincoln magisterially nosing out of Hunter Mill. Within
minutes they were running past the white fences and brick
mansions of horse country. Every few miles they came upon a
crossroads of wooden stores and shanties that, except for the
still ubiquitous NO COLORED signs, seemed unaltered since
the Civil War. Nat knew the countryside was doomed. New
editions of Hunter Mill Estates would plant crops of split
levels in the pastures, shopping centers and drive-ins would
replace the crossroads. Because that's the way life goes, he
thought; more reliably a series of losses than of gains.

As they headed vaguely up the Potomac, they began
passing Civil War landmarks—sanctified stretches of earth
and woods, until at Antietam, where split-rail fences set off
batteries of cannon and dead oak leaves cartwheeled across
the battlefield, they got out and strolled hand in hand.

"You wanted to talk?"

"Nat, I've always been so proud of you. You're so good at
what you do. You've always made me feel a part of it, and I've
done my best to help. But remember Williston? Told you I'd
leave you if you didn't get me out of North Dakota?"

"Oh, yes, I remember."

"Twenty below, weeks on end? I was dead serious. Nat,
you can't moon around about your book forever. If you want
me with you, you've got to get a job.

"Oh, Nat, I love you. Remember how good Grand Junction
was?"

Grand Junction, Colorado, was her Arcadia, where she was happiest. Thinking of it, she saw herself, as in a movie flashback, in her long, flowing hair of ten years earlier.

The town stands on an arid plateau bordered by the purple shelves of the Book Cliffs. It was where Nat found another newspaper job after Viv commanded the move south.

At first it seemed no lovelier than North Dakota. They rented a house downtown—"downtown" in a town of 15,000, yet the largest city between Denver and Salt Lake. But soon Milt Pierson, owner and publisher of the *Daily Item*, drove Nat out to a farm on the dusty outskirts.

"Going on the market soon. Want to move to California, be nearer the grandkids. Not asking much, and if you need help with the down payment, just ask. Call it a farm, but it's only five acres—lease the hayfield to the fellow next door. Barn, few sheds, nice yard—and the house. Well, you'll see. Well, here it is."

And they turned off B½ Road into the cottonwood-shaded drive of a tall white farmhouse with porches all around.

"Oldest house in Mesa County, not mistaken. 1880, thereabouts?"

From Milt's Packard Nat riveted his gaze on it. "Well, Viv will have to see it. How much are they asking?"

"Eight-five, is it? I expect eight thousand will do it."

Nat drove Viv and baby Fred up the driveway the next morning, soon as Tommy was on the school bus.

"Oh, Nat, it's beautiful!"

"Milt said to knock."

They did so, and were admitted by a friendly, white-haired, miniature couple. In the manner of farmhouses, the ground floor was open and flowing but for a room called the library closed by French doors; Nat looked at its shelves with excitement. Upstairs were four bedrooms and another large bathroom. There was a shed used as a garage, a barn stocked with goats and chickens, and three cats plus two dogs—an English sheepdog and a setter—who followed them around with metronomic tails. The animals went with the house.

The lawn was green, courtesy of the irrigation ditch that edged the property. Asparagus grew on its bank.

They negotiated over coffee, and came away with a handshake agreement to buy house, farm, appurtenances, goats, chickens, cats and dogs for $8,000.

"Think it's a good deal," Nat said, pulling onto B½ Road.

He and Milt Pierson hit it off, at a time when Milt wished to back away from day-to-day responsibility for the newspaper he inherited. Hired as a reporter, Nat soon became city editor, then managing editor. Within weeks—days—he seemed to know everybody in town and everything that was going on, and showed himself able to get good work cheerfully done from his subordinates.

So far as Viv was concerned, Grand Junction was Eden. She loved the house, the lawn and the field lapping up to it; loved having her babies. Kids may not make for romance, but for her they were sufficient, even with Fate's twist that her four were all boys. Her yearning for a daughter caused her to play the odds with pregnancies two, three and four, coming up snake eyes every time, though so sure #3 *had* to be a girl that she painted the nursery pink and chose (oh, the *zeitgeist!*) the extravagant name of *Jacqueline*. Then gave birth to *Jack*.

The kids thrived. Tommy took care of the chickens, with whose eggs Viv began the family's great age of soufflés. Also she baked cakes and pies—always making a sugar pie from the leftover dough, so the kids didn't have to wait until dinner for a treat—and doughnuts, too, the holes a general favorite. Her grandmother had taught her how to cook by eye and palm; instead of recipes she had sequences rooted in muscle memory. Potato pancakes, shoo-fly pie, biscuits, popovers, waffles — everything tasted of the joy she found in making it.

She made friends with staffers' wives and neighbors, and on Wednesday afternoons was den mother to Tommy's Cub Scouts. In sunny weather she kept them running around outdoors, and on rainy, indoor days set them to folding newspapers into printers hats.

The old house took much care, her garden likewise, and she kept a busy farmyard; there was always something to be done. Viv hadn't a moment's rest, but was consciously happy every single day.

For six years life was busy and rewarding. Nat enjoyed running his own shop; his decisions ruled newsgathering in an enormous territory, he was one of the town's leading lights and, at a salary ultimately of $100 a week, one of the best paid.

Her mother's visits helped Viv see the enviableness of her life through another's eyes.

For the first one, LaCinda flew in on a Frontier Airways DC-3 that took a buffeting over the Rockies, and stayed a month. She quite liked the "farm" and, without saying so, was impressed by Nat's status. He gave her a plant tour, showing her around the double storefront with the newspaper's name across the windows in gold leaf. There was the pungent odor of hot type and a steady thrum from the presses running in back. Railings like a bank's divided the floor, with two separate offices at the side: Milt's with door closed, Nat's with door open. Meeting the staffers, including Nat's star reporter, the woman he promoted from the society columns to the police beat, LaCinda took in everything — the photographs and clippings taped to the walls, the swivel chairs, oaken desks, eyeshades, typewriters, the wire-service reports torn off the teletype and taped to the front window.

On the eve of her departure they gave a dinner party. Nat

barbequed steaks, while Viv made her mother's favorite angel-food cake with buttercreme frosting, topped by vanilla ice cream the boys cranked to perfection. LaCinda's enjoyment of her visit could be gauged by the gift she oversaw delivery of the next morning: a pretty donkey of sweet disposition named Clementine. The kids loved Clementine, despite her tendency to throw them.

Eden came to an end, however. The *Daily Item's* printers went out on strike for the right to join a union. Taking umbrage, Milt Pierson hired scabs to replace them. Sympathetic to the printers, Nat was deeply offended by the scab compositor who, eating a fried-chicken dinner brought in from the best restaurant in town, contemptuously dropped the bones into his hot pot of molten lead. The owner-publisher then held a meeting at which he required every employee to stand up and pledge fealty in a combination loyalty oath/no-strike pledge. When it came his turn, Nat rose trembling and heard himself say, "I quit."

Calamitous, save that it worked out. One of his reporters was the local stringer for *Orbs* magazine, and he let his editors there know about him. Nat was interviewed, hired, assigned to the Chicago bureau, and they sold house and donkey. But Viv feared it a portent when Clementine's buyer whipped her braying up the ramp into his trailer. The kids were crying, but Nat said a deal is a deal.

*Et in Arcadia ego,* was that the phrase? She got through Chicago—and then Washington! Where joy remained on hold as, doggedly—sometimes feeling abandoned—she tried to get the kids grown. The friendships with Leilani Owens and Deanna Cottle were lifesavers—teaching Leilani how to bake angel-food cake, eating lunches out. If life wasn't what she'd dreamed it would be, it was OK.

Viv and Nat strolled the Antietam battlefield without

trying to make sense of the historic charges and counter-charges, but respectful of ground so sodden in blood. As at their elopement, Viv told him she was in it all the way, disappointments and all; only he had to get a job.

As they returned to the car, a half dozen kids came running across the grass, calling as boys had done for a hundred years, *"Hey, Abe Lincoln, how do like your beard?"*

## 18.

NAT PHONED HIS FORMER Bureau Chief and asked to come in and see him. For all that Grady said he didn't see any point to it, he agreed to meet.

Clean-shaven, Nat asked for his job back.

Grady was gentle. "Brought a guy in from the Detroit bureau to replace you, Nat. Taking to it pretty well, too. Don't think we don't miss you, but that's the way it is."

"How about New York? Could it find me a bureau some place? Maybe Saigon?" It was his Hail Mary pass, naming what had to be the latest hardship post.

"Nat, speaking for myself, I felt hurt—a lack of for want of a better word *loyalty* on your part—when you left to write that book. Thought it beneath you, and not too nice to us, either. Just my personal feeling."

*So that was that.* "OK, Will. Thanks, I understand."

"How's Viv?"

"Oh, great, thanks."

On his way to the elevator, willing to avoid seeing any more of his old colleagues than he had to, one did come into view. The man who wrote the Duke of Windsor's memoirs had the office next to the Bureau Chief's; he was Washington man for *Orbs'* sister publication *Ducats*, the monthly business magazine. Now his door opened, and he said, "Hey, Nat, got a minute?"

For the first time, Nat found himself in Walt Hunt's office, paneled in teak and decorated along nautical lines. His desk held a model of the sloop he berthed in Annapolis.

"Coming back, Nat?"

"No, Walt, I wish, but apparently I blotted my copybook."

"Ever think of working for *Ducats*? Not that different. Well, not the same, either. Business instead of politics, but business is human, too. Mean a move to New York. Get your assignment, basically have a month to report it, another to write it—eight, ten thousand words usually. Not leisurely, exactly, but it's slower, no denying that. Pays better, too.

"More a long-form kind of shop, is what I'm trying to say. People think it's easier than it is, but it's satisfying, and we seem to have influence. Might agree with you—you're a good writer, don't think that's gone unnoticed."

"Yes, I'd be interested," Nat said.

Walt popped up and put his hand over the desk. "Good. Let's go up to New York tomorrow?"

Before going home, Nat drove out to Arlington. President Kennedy's grave lay within a picket fence that kept the floral wreaths and bouquets three feet deep within it from overflowing onto the lawns. A blue flame plumed up from the enclosure's middle. As yet there was no headstone. The raw plot surrounded by worn grass looked to Nat just about like what a democracy can offer—picket fence, mud, flowers, a flame. He was one of dozens looking on in grief and disbelief.

Then he took his happy news home. The next day, he flew to New York, got the job and, after a lightning house-hunting trip with Viv, closed—on the basis of a healthy new salary—on a $50,000 house in Katonah with a swimming pool and million-dollar view over the Croton Reservoir. The house sat on five wooded acres, its neighbors invisible, and was reached from the train station by making four right turns — perfect, Nat foresaw, for a man fresh from an hour in the bar car.

The morning of the move he drank his coffee standing up, skimming his last home-delivered Washington *Post* and, though reading with less attention than usual, he caught the item about Pamela Manchester's wedding at a Potomac estate. The accompanying photograph showed her lovely — *spectacular* — in white next to her groom, a Foreign Service up-and-comer.

# 19.

IRONICALLY, HIS FIRST assignment for *Ducats* brought Nat back to Washington to interview President Johnson. The story was about the new President's relations with the business community.

He'd done the reporting, interviewed his economists and industrialists, was ready to write, when he realized he needed a quote from the man himself. Calling the White House and explaining he wanted only a few minutes, he was given the chance to speak with the President while he got his hair cut in the basement barbershop the next morning. Nat took the shuttle and put up at the International Inn.

Interviewing the President on the fly reminded him, with a pang of pure pain, of an episode from his fortnight covering JFK in 1960. One day Kennedy had promised an interview but was running behind, so on a luscious September evening Nat asked his questions while Kennedy drove them from his Senate office to the Shoreham Hotel in a blue Pontiac convertible, fast, the top down. Eyes shining, a man on the verge of conquering the world, the candidate quipped and declaimed and — worryingly — gesticulated his answers. It was like being on a date — a good one.

The next morning Johnson was just being tucked beneath a striped sheet when Nat came in.

"Hey, there, Wilbarger County, h'wra *you?*"

"Just fine, Mr. President. How are you, sir?"

"Did some diggin': It's *your* uncle led the posse that put away that Oklahoma yeggman Frank Holloway!"

"That's right, Mr. President. What was it, 1916? The last great posse."

"And your grandma was friends with Quanah Parker!"

"Ran cattle off the same creek."

"Man, Comanches come round *our* place, warn't no *social* call. *My* grandma crawled under the house with both hands clapped over my daddy's mouth. One cry, and she'd have shut him up for good, too."

"Different times, Mr. President," Nat noted, and asked his questions.

Frowning, Johnson gave him his answers, sufficiently quotable, and the barber, possibly relieved to have his subject thus distracted, did his work. When he snapped the sheet off, Johnson stood up, tall in the low-ceilinged room.

"Nat, come on upstairs, something you should see."

"Yes, sir."

Loping upstairs and through the West Wing, Johnson burst into the Oval Office.

"Morning, gentlemen," he called airily to the men waiting on the sofas. Nat saw the Secretaries of State and Defense, the Chairman of the Joint Chiefs, several aides. But the President took him over to his desk, the mighty *Resolute* desk, and picked up a notebook lying on top of it.

"Just take a look at this, *tell* me it's not good for business," he said, thrusting pages marked EYES ONLY FOR THE PRESIDENT at him. Nat scanned them as quickly as he could—they appeared to concern build-ups in ship, aircraft and armaments production—while in the background the Cabinet and Pentagon visitors looked askance, stirred impatiently and checked their watches.

"Mr. President—" called one.

"Hold your horses, Mac," the great man growled.

As it happened, the President had more to show Nat Handler, and it was 20 minutes before, with a last sanctifying squeeze of the shoulder, he let him go, having put in their places his seething, too-big-for-their-britches officials.

Nat went by the Bender Building to type up his notes at a borrowed desk and, after lunch at Paul Young's with old colleagues, caught the shuttle home.

# II.

# *Colorado*

**20.**

IN SEPTEMBER OF 1941, Nathan Micajah Handler, 17 years old, transported himself and his personal mysteries from Krux, New Mexico across the country to Ithaca, New York. Having won an engineering scholarship to Cornell University—he was still 16 when notified of it in May—Nat was off to fulfill a glorious destiny.

Krux huddled at the base of the Lakachukai Mountains on the Navajo Indian Reservation in the state's northwest corner. A mission church and a handful of houses for Indian Service personnel surrounded Krux's Trading Post and the high school that Nat's father, David Duncan Handler—Mr. *Tall Man American*, the Navajo called him—served as principal. It drew its 300 students from a territory of some 30,000 square miles.

Goodbyes had been said in a series of round-robin dinners given by teachers at the school, three years later still mourning the death of his mother, their colleague, so Nat's actual departure felt anticlimactic. After breakfast on a Wednesday morning he wandered out back to smoke a Camel. It had rained overnight, so freshness reigned in the desert. Usually its colors were muted, its sparse vegetation gray. Today, sands shone yellow below buttes and chimneys painted gaudy reds, the shrubby mesquite and creosote were tenderly green, and tiny, intensely-colored flowers—purple clusters of verbena, the swollen golden spikes of burroweed—sparkled like glass. The scene approached the super-saturation of Kodachrome photographs in *Arizona Highways*.

Nat was seeing Krux through new eyes. Though a metropolis compared to his earlier homes—the one-room schoolhouses his parents for years manned across the Maricopa, Zuñi and Hopi Indian reservations—like them Krux was remote, drab and ramshackle, battered by sun and dust. Dogs roamed the unpaved street. Navajos waited in wagons in front of the trading post for Mr. Krux to open up, the teams stamping their feet.

Flicking the butt sizzling into a puddle, and shaking his head at the thought he'd ever lived *here*, Nat stepped back inside the bungalow. Soon he was bringing his Gladstone bag out front and helping carry the trunk to his father's ancient Plymouth sitting next to the black government Ford never used for personal trips. The tops of both were shiny with rain, sides daubed with red mud. Securing the trunk as best they could, they left for the train station in Gallup, 50 miles away.

Wrestling the car through the mire, his father declared (quite unnecessarily) how proud Nat's mother would have been of her youngest's scholarship, and Nat turned aside to the glistening landscape. Little else was said, apart from a few impatiently received paternal injunctions and sorrow expressed at the time that would pass before the following June—there was too little money to think of bringing Nat home for Christmas. His father was not looking forward to being alone. His eldest son, Junior, was off at Ohio State doing graduate work in chemistry, and the middle child, Dan, had started pre-med at the University of Colorado a week earlier; Dan and Nat were in the same grade, having first been tutored by their mother, later by both parents, before being sent to Escalante Hall in Utah, destination of many Indian Service brats.

By the time they came down Thirteen Mile Hill into Gallup's smoke, the sun had leached the landscape of moisture, restored its dun-colored grittiness and coated the roads in dust. They were early, so had coffee on the plaza before crossing to the Atchison, Topeka & Santa Fe Railway station.

The big headlight rounded promptly into view — pallid as a tin platter until, the track straightening, it smote out, blinding, even as diesel horns blared silver plumes of sound — and four locomotives painted in war-bonnet reds and yellows glided down the track. The train briefly stayed its momentum to perch shuddering beside father and son. The trunk flew into the baggage car. Where they stood a porter stepped down with a stool, Nat stepped up in his horn-rims, shiny and determined face, herringbone jacket, sharp-creased chino trousers and glossy brown shoes, his father handed up the Gladstone bag, for a moment Nat felt confused and uncertain as he looked across the low dusty town and at his father, tall in a white Stetson and smiling tightly, but already beneath his feet the train was sliding, the landscape shifting.

The porter nudging the small of his back, Nat stumbled into the car and found a seat.

## 21.

CORNELL WAS A DISASTER.

Nat was a smart kid who won his scholarship without feeling particularly committed to an engineering career or liking its mathematical component. His interests and ambitions were literary. Younger than his classmates by a crucial year or two, he came, moreover, from a part of the country they looked at askance.

Nor did they scruple to let him know they found him odd. It made Nat burn with solitary resentment. Until now, he had enjoyed a prestige based on his father's position in the Indian Service. That vanished, in fact was held against him—he was mocked for being his father's son.

"You an Indian, Handler?" his roommate Wilkins liked to ask. When Nat faithfully demurred, Wilkins would add, "Still, not exactly one of *us*, are you?"

"*Us*" were Easterners, often with money in the background—or foreground—and reflexively scornful to meet anyone from so unlikely a place pursuing the same things they did. Although no one had ever before suggested that he was an Indian, Nat in response to the charge was as impassive as a Navajo.

*Indian?* His nose's acute angle, relic of a sturdy English, German and Scotch-Irish heritage, precluded the possibility, made it absurd. Nat bore a nose so precious that the rest of his face — strong chin and brow, big open eyes protected by glasses — served, as it were, as its candleholder.

And he of sensitive inwardness had never dreamed engineering to be a pursuit so rowdy, so entirely external in thought and deed. His classmates loved fart jokes! Whereas to Nat passing gas was an act requiring furtiveness and, if detected, the opposite of comment. No, one of *them* he decidedly was not.

Thus he disdained to participate in the life around him. Worse, he flailed academically, by mid-semester was flunking Calculus. He was depressed, could learn nothing, took to roaming the plain old town and drinking Cuba Libres in a half-timbered tavern.

Then there was that roommate. Wilkins was a self-assured graduate of the famous Massachusetts school Middlesex. His major was undeclared; not so his sexual desires. With those he was vocal and direct. At first Nat thought it was funny; a boarding school product himself, he was not unfamiliar with the trend of Wilkins's suggestions. But he found insulting his roommate's conviction that leaving photographs of himself on Nat's bed in their Dodge Hall room would seduce him. The first, a glossy black-and-silver glamour shot bearing the stylized signature of a New York photographer, resembled in its lighting and soft focus a portrait of Garbo, save that its subject was Wilkins gripping his erection.

When Wilkins asked, "Did you see my nude photo?" Nat sassed back, "Didn't see a *nude* photo, but did find a perverted *naked* one."

Wilkins was *charmed* at the distinction his pedantic roommate made: nude for display, naked for use, erections in the latter category. He presumed it an arguable point. But Nat refused to argue.

Then came the date that lives in infamy, December 7, 1941. Nat had returned to bed with the Sunday *New York Times* and his roommate was at his desk when shouts erupted in the hallway and their door opened to half a dozen of Wilkins's friends all talking at once.

Shrewdly assessing their excitement, Wilkins silenced them with an open hand and asked, "All right, who's *engaged?*"

A few days before Christmas Nat transferred to the dorm where Cornell housed those with no place to go for the holidays. He spent his time reading William Faulkner and Rex Stout—this when exams in Mechanical Drawing and Calculus loomed. Also he strolled the snow-covered campus and town. Boots crunching, he might as well have been on Mars. On New Year's Day he found himself looking down from the bridge that spanned the deepest ravine, speculating where someone inclined to jump would be best advised to do it.

The next day, Friday, he ended both his Ivy League and engineering careers by boarding a Short Line bus with his Gladstone bag—he left the trunk behind—and heading for New York City to become a writer.

## 22.

THE ALL-DAY BUS RIDE took Nat over white hills and past gray woods where bare branches telegraphed somber but unreadable news. The door gasped pneumatically open at towns and hamlets. After a long course down the Hudson River, enfiladed by hills and studded with mansions, not to mention West Point, the bus passed through close-packed towns of countless frame houses across the river from a glittering growth whose silhouette reminded him of Monument Valley: slender stone towers and tapered masonry masses that rose hundreds of feet. Manhattan's highest point — the silver dirigible mooring atop the Empire State Building — shone in the sunlight. But even as Nat looked, dusk was sliding up the spire and quenching it.

The Lincoln Tunnel abruptly swallowed them and, after a humming passage of its tiled corridor, they ascended, went two blocks down 42nd Street, and turned into a mid-block bus station. The door gasped open.

Nat retrieved his bag, walked out and emerged onto 42nd Street. It was like being hit by six million people, everyone sprinting for buses and cabs or striding along and jostling him as they made their wants known at the top of their voices.

He stood stunned on the sidewalk. Used to the desert's terrible stillness—frozen expression of geologic time—he found unsettling the activity of every quantum of his field of vision like a dead sheep crawling with maggots and the fact that no notice was taken of his awful personal dignity. Lights blinked in sardonic commentary. Up the street he recognized the dynamic blue-green profile of a skyscraper, the McGraw-Hill Building, temple to the printed word. Emboldened, reminded of who he was, he turned into the glare and din.

Striking for the marquee of the Dixie Hotel, he walked safely across the street in the one-time-only manner vouchsafed new arrivals, marked by shrieking brakes and the most vulgar curses he ever heard. Pushing past an indifferent doorman, he went through a passage that was quiet until towards 43rd Street it opened onto a double-storied lobby that in miniature re-created the chaos of the streets: a reception desk busy with clerks assisting patrons and summoning bellboys, a luggage desk, newsstand, restaurant entrances, a wide doorway open to the Planters Bar, ship models under glass, people milling on patterned carpets beneath intricately-starred, if dusty, chandeliers.

He asked for a room. The issue hung as the desk clerk's face went slack. Suppressing the thought that possibly he was too young, Nat bulged his jaw, and the clerk acceded, collecting two dollars and handing a Bakelite paddle dangling a key to a bellboy. This evil-looking old man—costumed as a juvenile clown in red and black—took his bag, and Nat, scowling, put out at making himself liable for an unneeded service, followed him to an elevator, scowling the more as he apprehended a look of amusement pass between bellboy and lady elevator operator.

On the eleventh floor they got out, and down a narrow corridor found a tiny room. For a moment, before the bellboy flipped the light switch with what Nat took as a sarcastic gesture, the city on fire out the window made the room garish. By lamplight it was worn and threadbare. Nat paid over a quarter and ignored the bellboy's leering, "Just step off the bus?" He closed the door, locked it, slid the chain on, used the bathroom—little bigger than a phone booth, outfitted with miniature sink and tub—washed his face, took off his clothes, got in bed, gave himself his urgent goodnight pull, wadded the result in tissue and fell asleep.

To his surprise, he slept the night through—apparently throwing your life away exacts a toll on the unconscious—but his dreams were laborious. The one that lingered after he clenched awake at 7:00 in the morning had him being chased naked—*nude*—back through the Lincoln Tunnel to Jersey.

He opened the window and stuck out his head. He'd never been so high up in a building. It was Saturday, and even without any points of comparison he realized the streets were subdued. The occasional honk of a taxi seemed as haunting as the call of a mourning dove across Cornell's campus, or that of an eagle circling the New Mexico desert. He looked across 43rd Street at the crackled terracotta of what looked like an English castle keep, and with a shock realized it was the New York Times building: Vertical neon spelled out the name in gothic type. Thrilled, he looked through a row of windows giving onto a room of desks. It had to be the newsroom. He saw a woman sitting atop a desk, kicking her foot as she talked to the man in the chair, her shoe teetering on her toe. They looked as though there was no place else they wished to be.

Nat was not certain that he could wash up, descend to eat breakfast and return to his room before the domestic staff reclaimed it. Of prime importance was that he move his bowels, but the challenge of doing so knotted them. Still, he showered, dressed, went down to the lobby, selected *Times* and *Herald Tribune* from the riches of its newsstand and stepped into a restaurant. Soon he was drinking coffee from a heavy queensware cup and spreading marmalade on a toasted English muffin.

Afterwards he went upstairs and hung the *Do Not Disturb* sign on the knob to stave off the wheeled carts already moving down the hallway. Listening apprehensively as one trundled past his door, nevertheless he experienced the miracle he feared would not occur, packed his Gladstone bag and sat on the bed, staring out the window while his courage slowly welled up. Finally sufficient had collected that he could come to his feet, hoist his bag, go downstairs and drop off his key.

He left by the 43rd Street doors so he could gape at the Times Building and the frosted globes painted with the great name. The globes reminded him of the Ithaca pub where he'd studied the delights of rum-and-Coke. At the end of the block he emerged into Times Square, a chasm in the city's fabric shaped like a stretched bow-tie. He craned up at the gigantic Chevrolet billboard—driver and passengers gaily navigating the Great White Way—and directly overhead at the original, ornate Times Tower, and began walking down Broadway.

The shafts of sunlight were cheering and, though a brisk January day, it was so much warmer than Ithaca as to feel balmy. The sky was different, too, higher and lighter, striped with chevrons of vapor drifting in from the sea, whereas at street level the light was refracted and brittle.

Scrupulously stopping at red lights (even when it meant getting bumped from behind), and witnessing several hair's-breadth escapes by pedestrians apparently unaware of the vehicles bearing down on them, Nat slipped down Broadway's slant. The dense tapestry of buildings shifted with every step he took under turn-of-the-century hotel parapets. At Herald Square in front of Macy's bronze Moors gonged the hour under the lighted eyes of bronze owls. Turning left, Nat saw the fins of the Empire State highlighted in the sun as he entered the Sloane House YMCA.

Heads snapped and eyes swerved as he asked about rooms by the week and month. Handing over $7 for a week's lodging, he received a key and found his way to the eighth floor, where a tiny room, smaller even than the one at the Dixie Hotel, was his. Furnished with narrow bed, narrow bureau, narrow desk, its window framed the neighborhood's familiar landmark, the Empire State Building, at what Nat considered to be about ankle level.

He unpacked, counted his money—$47 in bills, $2.30 in change—then sat on the edge of his bed for a quarter hour, raking up enough courage first to find the men's room, then to make his plunge to Manhattan and his new life.

## 23.

FOR DAYS NAT MARVELED at how New Yorkers withstood the nonstop assault on their ears — the roars of traffic, of the el overhead, the subway below. And the variety of streetscapes constituted visual assault. In a given block he could walk past storefronts of bronze-framed plate-glass, a gothic stone church and a tower of 15 stories — or 50 — whose façade recapitulated the classical principles of a three-story Renaissance palazzo. It required keen, exhausting attention to navigate sidewalks that streamed with troops of blank faces alongside free-flowing rivers of cars, trucks and buses.

The key to winnowing the cacophony of sounds and sights was to focus on what concerned immediate survival, and day by day Nat sensed his body learning to do just that, unconsciously selecting which stimuli to attend to, which to ignore. Also crucial to the defense of his personal mysteries, lately so battered and bruised, was his stance and the proper set of his expression. He tried for a clenched *Touch me and I'll kill you;* a winning expression on one so young.

However, his deadpan failed to rebuff the friendly assumptions of his fellow YMCA residents. It was like living in a corps of Wilkinses. One guy padded back from the showers pushing at every door on his way, until one opened. All night long the knob of Nat's bolted door turned — lying in bed he could watch it go back and forth. It was unsettling.

But thanks to the war, Nat got a job on his first try. Responding to a typed index card tacked to the Y's bulletin board, on Monday morning he found the loading dock beneath Wanamaker's Department Store in Cooper Square, a great stone cube said to be — pending completion of the Pentagon — the world's biggest building.

Walking into the shadows of a delivery bay, he found himself ignored by the burly types unloading trucks, but under scrutiny by quick eyes at an elevated desk.

"Need work?" barked their possessor.

"Yes, sir."

"See Mac. *Mac!*"

Mac, a UPS supervisor, hired him on the spot, in fact asked if he could start that *minute*, but Nat promised to show up at 8:00 o'clock the next morning.

He returned to the Y with new purpose to his step. Not so bad, this city! True, he saw himself in the not-distant future writing novels high in a turret commanding a wide lawn — he had admired Ithaca's Victorian piles — but writers, he knew, must take what comes, and anyway for the time being he was safe; safe until August, when he would turn 18 and have to register for the draft.

Next morning, he found that although the job required an irritating physical effort, it would be fine, even fun. UPS handled the store's shipping from its cavernous, clangorous subbasement. Packages wrapped in brown kraft paper, tied with twine and bearing delivery labels came off conveyor belts and into bins devoted to neighborhoods in each borough, Long Island, Jersey, Connecticut and Westchester. Nat and the other "Stuffers" had to stuff the packages into wheeled boxes that would then be loaded aboard trucks. It was fast, rote labor, and got him in the back, for all that the bins' height minimized stooping. But he was paid $18 a week, and that was enough to live.

And there was even a certain satisfaction to finding himself, between the hours of eight and five, at a complex system's pivot point, emptying bins, loading boxes, laboring amidst chutes slanted every which way in a space that reminded him of Piranesi's prison images (which he now realized are actually abstractions of department-store subbasements).

At lunchtime most of the men adjourned to a back room with food brought from home, but Nat escaped to the streets, wandering them the whole hour, save for the ten minutes it took to duck into a lunchroom and gobble something. Lunchrooms crowded with working men and women were everywhere, on the street, off lobbies, in basement vaults or the backs of drugstores, and he fearlessly sampled new foods — hero sandwiches, teriyaki, chop-suey, gyros, pizza.

At Wanamaker's, as at the Y, he resisted camaraderie and none was forced upon him. But every day one co-worker smiled at him, persisting even when Nat's face tightened and his eyes narrowed as he gave a clipped nod of acknowledgment. The smile came from a huge young blond guy with rolled-up sleeves who worked at a nearby station of chutes and bins, tossing boxes all day long as though they were nothing, clearly taking pleasure in movement, whether going up on his toes to launch a package or stooping to lift a carton. He was good looking, if very large, but Nat thought he didn't look too bright.

At 5:00 o'clock, exhausted, aching in every limb and joint, Nat walked home like Frankenstein's monster. He was too fastidious to press himself into the human meat of the subway back to Herald Square, but the streets were filled, too, with the whole circus of mankind. Once he crossed 14th Street in the wake of a fierce old man stumping his cane along while holding a badge out to the honking drivers with, *"Put-ya in jail for ten years-ya!"* There must have been a school for the deaf near Union Square, because he was liable to come across knots of teenagers signing to one another while laughing uproariously in utter silence. He passed Madison Square, which was bounded by the stone cliffs and ziggurats of the New York Life and Metropolitan Life buildings. On 23rd Street, he was sometimes caught by an importunate vendor in overalls selling *The Daily Worker*. Walking through Manhattan's printing neighborhood he might find street doors open to ranks of Linotype machines, and would pause to watch the operators at work, their hands pressing at keys and pulling at iron stops.

He ate dinner downstairs, alone at a table for two, or went out to Chock full o'Nuts or the Automat, until he discovered a diner on Ninth Avenue where he could fill up cheaply on meatloaf or goulash.

Evenings he spent in the Y's utilitarian library, where he found enough Kipling and Hemingway to keep him amused. Sometimes he had to give in to his aching muscles and have a steam. Disrobing in the locker room, he wrapped himself in a towel, descended to the steam room and sternly found a place apart on the slatted-wood shelves. He left his glasses behind so as not to see the ranked bodies, terrycloth carelessly dropped, glances subtly directed, touches ventured; they would have fogged up, anyway. He sat sweating into his towel, its closure's overlap secured by his fist, until his soreness relented and let go. He showered (eyes kept strictly to himself), returned upstairs and bolted his door.

There followed the day's luxurious interval, reading the

bouquets of newspapers he brought home—broadsheet *Times* and *Herald Tribune* or *World-Telegram,* tabloid *Daily News* and *Post.* Later he might study city and suburban maps for expertise that would earn promotion to "Sorter" and a raise of $5. Sometimes, in for the night, he turned off the lights and pushed the curtains aside to sit on the sill and take in the city's irrepressible roar to the glow of the meerschaum pipe he bought at Nat Sherman's on Broadway. It beseemed a writer to smoke a pipe.

In the course of an evening the roar resolved itself into a high-tension hum, while day by day the night sky grew darker as the Army-ordered "dimout" against German bombing took effect; against bombing or, as was thought more likely, shelling from U-boats or disguised merchantmen. Apartment and office lights winked out when the sun sank, and stars, those rare birds of the Manhattan sky, began to glimmer. Just as in the daytime, the Empire State Building dominated the view, a looming shadow of itself drawing a towering blank shape against the stars. On moonlit nights it dimly disclosed the corporeality of its stone, cut by windows reflecting slivers of light.

It was the loneliest Nat had ever felt. Odd, perhaps, that a boy who grew up in empty corners of remote Indian reservations could feel so lonely amidst New York's millions, but he did.

On weekends he took long walks roaming the flower district and Chelsea and down to Wall Street, or else up through commercial loft neighborhoods to the midtown office district and beyond. Exploring Rockefeller Center, the engineering *wunderkind* perceived how its cunning layout of cut-throughs exploited the Bernoulli principle just like a carburetor: By compressing pedestrian and traffic flow between Fifth and Sixth Avenues, it increased its pressure, thereby heightening, vivifying, *charging* the experience.

One particular tower, near Paul Manship's bronze *Prometheus* overhanging the skating rink — the Orbs Building, a well-proportioned slab of limestone impressed with shell fossils — was abuzz on Saturdays when others were empty, men and women purposefully breaking away from sidewalk crowds of shoppers and tourists to enter the magazine empire's headquarters. When Nat finally dared enter its lobby — his heart fluttering, aware of wearing dungarees and a pea coat and of being a boy who had shamed his family and himself — he found himself invisible to the stylish men and women walking rapidly about, crowding into elevators, tossing *bon mots* as at, he imagined, a high-speed cocktail party. He didn't take time to try to solve the lobby mural, but shot outdoors again through a revolving door ahead of a woman who was saying to her companion, "Just a quick one," the man answering, "There's no time."

Close by, what Nat thought of as the club neighborhood entranced him. Guarded by liveried figures who specialized in giving him the beady eye, elaborate stone façades disclosed glimpses of luxury within. The New York Yacht Club bulged stern-like windows over the sidewalk, transforming it to a storm-tossed sea as seen from a snug quarter-deck. The University Club occupied a mighty Fifth Avenue *palazzo*, walls of rusticated stone enclosing rich interiors. There were also the Harvard Club, Yale Club, Princeton Club and Columbia Club; by comparison, he thought the Cornell Club distinctly dowdy.

But one club did admit him and other readers: The Grolier Club. There Nat felt at home browsing displays of incunabula in a library like an English country house's, two stories of walnut with balconies and circular staircases.

Sometimes he strolled the greenswards of Central Park, too, though the public grumbled that it was excluded from a large tract where behind canvas-shrouded fencing everybody knew concrete was being poured for a top-secret antiaircraft gun emplacement.

And everywhere on his wanderings Nat saw *girls*—every day, girls were more visible as they took jobs abandoned by men entering the services. They were pretty, confident things who might, for an instant, rest speculative eyes on him, even giggle, and then—winning a flash of interest—move on forever. It incensed him, even as it excited him, but he had no way to break through the barriers.

Loneliness brought him down day by day, until by February—New York's longest month—he was in that stage of depression that as he walked past a bank after hours, he sought comfort—company, sociability—from its order and tidiness. He peopled the Jacobean armchairs in which no one ever sat, was warmed by the sight of officers' desks fenced off by railings, sidechairs arranged in supplicant fashion. At the wall stood marble counters hedged with bright brasswork, pens angled at the ready.

One noontime, Nat was coming out of Wanamaker's basement when a hand grasped his shoulder. He turned to find grinning at him the young man-mountain, who, saying one word—*"Lunch"*—guided him to the Horn and Hardart Automat at the corner.

After they pushed through the turnstile and plucked plates of turkey and gravy, mashed potatoes, stuffing and rolls from behind the glass doors, gushed coffee into cups at the end of the chromium counter and found a table across the black-and-white tiled floor, Gus introduced himself and asked, "Where do you live?" His wide face, smiling and eager, reminded Nat of a puppy's.

"Sloane House Y," Nat answered.

Gus's eyes lighted up. "My roommate was just drafted, I'm

looking for a new one. In the Village, $10 a week, breakfast and dinner except Sunday. Come see it after work, have dinner."

Nat said, "I'll take a look."

At 5:00 o'clock they joined the throngs on sidewalks so crowded Nat was amazed they didn't have to march in step. Passing the Astor Library and Louis Sullivan's Bleecker Street tower where angels' wings support the cornice, Gus plunged along, leaving Nat working to keep up, so they exchanged hardly a word. At an old brownstone near MacDougal, Gus vaulted up the stoop and went inside, shouting, "Hello, Mrs. Gallagher!" Nat brought up the rear. Upstairs, Gus opened a door to a room with double bed, desk, chairs, fireplace and a bureau pushed aside from a space given over to barbells and weights. He tore off his shirt and began doing curls.

"Well, this is it," he said. "Mrs. G.'s cooking isn't bad, if you like hash."

Nat looked at the bed.

"Choose your side," Gus told him. "I'm not picky."

Gus was huffing as though nothing but curls existed. The physique swelling his undershirt was magnificent—the male idea simplified and exaggerated past reason. He was a Michelangelo, a Manship, every movement rippling minutely through his musculature.

Kneeing out of his pants, in boxer shorts Gus addressed a barbell. Squatting, he lofted it with a grunt—it came to within an inch of the ceiling—and lowered it. This he repeated 24 times.

Mrs. G.'s chicken and dumplings managed to remind Nat of his mother's. Afterwards, Gus lay down to observe an hour's strict digestive immobility, and urged Nat to do the same. Lying down, he was immediately enclosed, spoon-wise, by Gus's massively larger body. It was warm and very comfortable and, wriggling into a tighter fit, he promptly fell asleep. He woke up, refreshed, when Gus, after tenderly placing a hand to his brow, sprang up to lift more weights.

Nat moved in the following Saturday.

That first night they staggered home supporting each other, full of beer from the corner bar, and Nat modestly pulled on pajamas in the privacy of the hall bath. He got into bed, where Gus already lay on his back, eyes closed, said, rather remotely, "Good night," and found himself, not exactly against his anticipations or his wishes, under wordless assault. Gus pulled off Nat's pajamas and stripped himself with columnar arms, as Nat, urgency flaring, pressed back.

It was, to Nat, not remotely sexual. Sex would be when he was with a girl, on top of her and in control, directing her to do things, *making* her do them, *occupying* her. With Gus it was abstract and accidental, tussles, touslings, thumpings, lickings, comical little gestures, riding, bucking, and if, after a series of suppressed cries, it climaxed with jerks of the bedsprings and semen flying, it felt good, gave relief, was something two guys—*friends*—could do; but it wasn't *sex*. Anyway, nobody's business.

They turned their backs to sleep, but when the alarm clock rang Nat awakened in Gus's arms. They didn't greet each other until after he freed himself.

# 24.

THERE FOLLOWED A HAPPY interval. Divorced from his own or anyone else's expectations, Nat felt freer and more himself than ever before. All day long, he and Gus stuffed boxes, Nat meanwhile attending to whatever story he had in his head, Gus attending to Nat. Then they went home for dinner and a rest.

Afterwards, while Gus worked out, Nat wrote at the desk by the window, first with pencil on yellow legal pads, later, after a foray uptown to the pawn shops under the Third Avenue El, on a fine old Woodstock typewriter. As exhaustion gradually engulfed him, he punched away trying to write decent sentences and build good paragraphs, and do it in a style all his own (*Good Lord!*). Sometimes he had to shake himself awake when Gus, luminous with sweat after hundreds of reps, dozens of sets, put on his shirt and announced he was thirsty.

They stepped around the corner to some bar on MacDougal, or farther down Bleecker, sometimes going as far as the tough dockside taverns on West Street where floors were strewn with reeking sawdust and, as doors banged shut behind them, heads along the bar might lift rheumy eyes and eroded features. In Gus's company Nat felt safe even when fights broke out among drunken stevedores.

Gus's drink of choice was beer because it fed his physique's ferocious need for starch. Nat thought beer déclassé, but doubted rum-and-Coke would do for the big city. So he experimented. One evening he ordered bourbon. It came in a shot glass. Touching it to Gus's stein — "*Chin-chin,*" said Gus — he threw back his head and swallowed. Wiping his mouth, he exhaled contentedly. He hadn't expected to like it, but he did, finding the taste, despite a certain antiseptic wash, vivid and rich, and glorying in the serenity that succeeded the taste. Gus watched with pleasure as the tight facets of Nat's face melted and he began smirking with the beguiling insouciance of a boy.

But bourbon was his father's drink, so, on consideration, it wouldn't do either. He next tried gin and, after a flirtation with gimlets, settled on the martini as his usual libation — the urbane, sophisticated, vanishingly dry martini. Its refreshing taste belied a wallop that lifted him to realms enlarged and congenial.

As winter broke up and a blowy, blowsy spring followed, Nat became moody. Sometimes as he worked on a short story he had to make clear to Gus that he was *de trop.* Gus took it cheerfully.

Nat wrote a story about a bodybuilder who lifted so many weights he attained the circumference of a balloon and floated away. He felt guilty making him so stupid, but what could he do? *The New Yorker* returned it with a letterpress card of rejection crisply engraved with a mysterious, possibly Masonic numeral. He started another about a sissy weightlifter who could have any girl he wanted but wanted none. He wrote stories about predatory Ivy League roommates, about an Indian Service teacher who failed in myriad ways and about a put-upon white boy growing up in an exotic and closed world of Indians.

Whatever he did, Gus looked on with pride, an attitude Nat began to find grating. Also he became kissy. Nat would turn his face aside, but Gus innocently persisted in sticking his tongue in his mouth. Perhaps the kisses offered and refused — the closed lips — was the mechanism that began to cleave them apart, even as Nat continued to work at the jungle gym of Gus's body.

One evening they were drinking at the Cedar Tavern on West 8th when Gus found his attention seized by a conversation on his other side. Two men were celebrating the check *Esquire* had sent one for a short story.

Gus broke in. "My friend's a writer," he announced, leaning back to afford them a view of Nat, who, taken unawares, was curled atop his stool like a half-blitzed infant.

"Looks like a writer," said *Esquire*'s contributor, and called over, "Where do you publish, kid?"

Nat's face froze. That day's mail had brought a rejection slip from *Collier's*.

"*The New Yorker*," Gus answered proudly. "He's had stories rejected by *The New Yorker*."

The two found that hilarious. Guffawing, one called over the bartender, who bent his mouth in an anticipatory smile, repeated it to him. He guffawed, too, and carried it to customers down the bar. Laughter spread. Nat got up and left, Gus trailing behind, surprised.

Then in early June the Teamsters abruptly called a strike. Their drivers refused any longer to pick up or deliver UPS packages because UPS recognized no labor unions, so Wanamaker's dismissed UPS and UPS laid off its staff there.

Gus took it in good part. He knew he would be drafted soon, anyway, so that evening over beer proposed to Nat that they enlist together.

"Enlist, and you can choose your service," Gus mildly pointed out. "Like to be a Marine? Old enough. We could fight together."

Nat snorted.

"Well, what're you going to do, then?" Gus asked sadly. For the first time, Nat saw unexpected depths to his eyes.

"They can get me after I turn 18," Nat told him. "Not before."

In Times Square the next day Gus signed up, was kissed by the curly-haired brunette congratulating that morning's enlistees and a few days later reported to Pennsylvania Station for the train to Parris Island, South Carolina.

Nat saw him off. They waited against a great Roman pier beneath the vaulted ceiling, Gus repeating, "Nat, what're you going to *do?*"

"Gus, don't *worry*," Nat said.

"You have to *choose*."

"When Fate's at work?"

After an uneasy interval Nat pointed across the vast room to a uniformed figure marching some boys in ragged lockstep. With a final, bruising grasp of Nat's shoulder, Gus ran across the marble pavement—ran as though two seconds saved would stick it to Hitler—and joined them. As the line began to descend to a platform, he held it up by turning around, eyes awash in tears, giving Hitler back those two seconds so he could wave at Nat.

Nat stepped into Western Union off the waiting room. The station's roar ceased as on a yellow form he scrawled:

```
PLEASE SEND MONEY SO I CAN
COME HOME NAT
```

Adding his address, he directed the telegram to his father

in Krux, New Mexico.

Saturday morning's mail brought a check folded within a note:

> Good to hear from you, son. Wire your
> train and I'll meet you at Gallup.
> Love,
> Dad

Nat's money had not held out; he had to get going *that day* if he didn't want to be thrown out on the street. But how to cash on Saturday in New York City a check drawn on the State National Bank of Gallup, New Mexico?

Payday lunchtime Nat had always rushed with his crew to the Wanamaker's branch of Chase Manhattan to cash his paycheck. Once, seeing the line already long, he'd sat down beside a desk in the middle of the floor and inquired about opening a savings account. In the end he hadn't done it, but he retained the business card of the personable banker he'd spoken to.

He looked in the telephone book, found an East 52nd Street address for that name, dialed and found himself speaking to the selfsame Mr. Sharman.

Mr. Sharman said — though Nat thought it improbable — he remembered him, then proved it by reminding him he'd mentioned New Mexico. After hearing him out, he asked Nat to meet him at the bank in an hour's time. Nat got there first. Wanamaker's was busy, but the closed bank's marble lobby had the hallowed air of a President's tomb. He stood against its bronze gate, while near by a guard yawned in his chair.

A little distracted, Mr. Sharman appeared and shook Nat's hand, his eyes not exactly meeting the younger man's, unlocked the gate and brought him inside the bank, inspected the check, had him endorse it, and took it behind the scenes, leaving Nat in the company of empty seating arrangements and cleared desktops—a bank interior of the most soothing type, complete unto clipper-ship prints on the walls. Someone passing along the sidewalk peered indoors for the companionship bank fixtures could offer, and their eyes met. Nat sneered.

Mr. Sharman returned, counted over bills, shook his hand again and wished him luck. Nat thanked him, returned to Bleecker Street, said goodbye to Mrs. G., hoisted the Gladstone bag containing his typewriter and the duffel bag with everything else, and walked to Grand Central, waylaid by unexpected emotion as he passed landmarks of his New York life. He bought a ticket through to Gallup and wired his father.

Waiting, he smoked his pipe on 42nd Street's sidewalk, noticing how sunlight filigreed the iron of the Park Avenue viaduct overhead (*write that down*, he commanded himself). Soon he was homeward bound—though he had to stand until Poughkeepsie—rolling, rolling, rolling out of New York, at first like a rat in a tunnel, then bursting into the sun and heading up the Hudson.

## 25.

THAT SAME DAY—Saturday, June 13, 1942—the Garrett clan was enjoying lunch at their favorite restaurant, The Promontory, perched atop a foothill of the Rockies above Denver.

It was a special occasion that warranted consuming tires and gasoline—both rationed—on the stately approach from town at the wartime speed limit of 35 m.p.h.: The Garretts were celebrating that morning's graduation of Vivian Garrett and her cousin Buzzy from Our Lady Academy (though happily mindful, too, of that week's victory at Midway).

Our Lady was a select school, and their girls were going on to college, sharing a dorm room that fall at the University of Colorado in nearby Boulder. As valedictorian, Viv had given a speech, her black gown crowned with an effusion of ash-blonde hair escaping her mortarboard, her face beautifully animated as she gushed gratitude to the scowling nuns standing sentry one last time over her and her classmates. Her eyes teared up as she spoke, which those who knew her attributed less to emotion than to the agony of her contact lenses—first generation instruments of torture, glass hemispheres that cupped the eyeball, a bubble at the cornea giving her eyes an other-worldly glow.

Now she and Buzzy sat across from each other exchanging furtive giggles about the new busboy. Service being of a high standard at The Promontory, the waiter had immediately set him on rounds of the table. The youth filled water glasses, placed butterballs on bread plates, brought rolls and more rolls. He was comely as well as efficient, bending on the fulcrum of his rounded little bottom with a skewed secret smile for Buzzy as he worked one side of the table, from the other side another for Viv. The cousins giggled at each other and at their mothers' obliviousness.

"*Cute,*" Buzzy lobbed across in a voice none but Viv could hear.

"Mm-*mmm,*" replied Viv, equally covert.

The five sisters were born Garrett, but none now bore the name; Viv was the sole Garrett at table. Her mother, the formidable LaCinda, second of the sisters, had substituted her own maiden name for Viv's after Harry Halderman divorced her, but retained Halderman for herself, for the sake of the *Mrs.*: married still and forever in her own eyes and in those of her Church.

The sisters and their daughters—each had one (and four of them husbands, too, to assemble at Alice's for that evening's celebratory wienie roast)—sat looking upwards at snowy slopes drenched in purple and downwards past the city at wheatfields gilding the horizon. A western gale made the plate glass windows waver, but giant fieldstone fireplaces were blazing. The sturdy restaurant featured steep shake roofs, towering chimneys and cantilevered terraces.

"You know being up here makes me uneasy," Violet remarked. "Always expect to take flight."

"Don't you *love* it?" replied LaCinda, toasting the waiter with her empty glass for another Bloody Mary before the food came. One sufficed for the rest of the Garrett gang; LaCinda required more.

"You're braver than we are," Mary informed her. It was family lore that LaCinda was the one who would drive anywhere, day or night—into the mountains, even across Yellowstone sleeping with Viv in the open trunk of her car despite the bears; the one who returned from Cuba with a souvenir photograph taken at Sloppy Joe's Bar showing her sitting next to a vulpine man she denied acquaintance with and memories she refused to speak of, though subject for a long time to silent, nostalgic moods.

The five sisters—Violet, LaCinda, Alice, Mary and Ida—were one another's best friends and spent much time together. Hence conversation was sparse, largely devoted to correcting their girls' deportment. Though Violet was older by eighteen months, LaCinda dominated, sitting in censure and disapproval, sisters ranked around her speaking in businesslike tones like bank officers rejecting loan applications. All smoked, so occasionally picked at their teeth, shaking the abundant hair that flowed to their suits' wide shoulders.

Their daughters—Henrietta, Viv, Buzzy, Annie and Martha, three still in high school—had hair even more abundant, and conversed on two levels, chatting openly about the school year just past, covertly about the busboy. The sisters pretended not to notice. LaCinda was stately in her moodiness, feeling joy at her daughter's graduation, but pangs, too, at the sudden aging such an event signalizes. Lifting her fresh glass, she saluted the peaks.

The cousins giggled as the busboy circled the table again, concentrating his soulful looks on Viv. Having refreshed their water glasses, he brought yet more warm rolls.

Buzzy said resentfully, "He likes *you*."

The same age as they, he was freshly emerged from the feminine wrappings that can enshroud boys until late adolescence. His lean face sported features that probably had a girlish cast a year earlier, with precisely cut lips, a dimpled, out-of-balance smile and short, light hair. When he placed a bread basket in front of her, Viv thought she'd never seen anything so beautiful as his long tapered fingers.

Meanwhile their mothers and aunts sat there discussing — what? The view, as always. The view didn't change.

Alice launched a new topic. "LaCinda, dear, what's Viv doing this summer?"

"She'll be very quiet. She needs to prepare for classes in the fall."

"Buzzy's thinking of getting a job."

"A job!" LaCinda's scorn put that notion to rest.

"We're so proud of you girls," Mary called, lifting Viv's and Buzzy's heads from private conference over the floral centerpiece.

"Father wouldn't let *us* go to college," declared Violet.

"He thought we only wanted to go so we could find husbands," added Ida.

"And he always said there's nothing easier for the daughter of a rich man to find than a *husband*," said Alice.

They tittered, until LaCinda gravely pronounced, "He wasn't wrong, either."

The silence that followed was rueful.

The sisters were not wealthy. So they told everybody, and it was true. But each had a competency from their late father, a Kansas wheat king. Rawboned and enormous, after youthful forays to California — where he found the laboring jobs already filled by Chinese — and Nebraska, where an Indian raid rousted him from his first homestead, he settled along the bend of the Arkansas River. Annual floods silted his land, which in the 1890s enjoyed a freakish succession of rich harvests, and he acquired more and more farms, until he held six fertile sections. Thereafter he stopped buying land and instead plowed his profits into shares of American Telephone & Telegraph Company. At 40 he retired and moved to town, raising to an imposing height the first brick house in Great Bend. Later he moved to Colorado Springs, where he liked to play cards or plunge his Maxwell over the Garden of the Gods, daughters teetering in the backseat.

One day in 1927 he figured his net worth—farms and Telephone together—at a total exceeding one million dollars. What the Depression did to that sum depressed him even unto the grave. Though not himself Catholic, by a bishop's dispensation he was laid to rest in Christ Commander Cemetery, where his widow now slept beside him.

"I don't know," LaCinda said, toasting the waiter again as he distributed Salisbury steak and pork loin. "I just don't know."

Despite Viv's professed gratitude to the nuns, she and Buzzy, her dark, small-featured cousin around whom boys buzzed like bees around honey (hence her nickname), were glad—ecstatic—to be out from under them, rejoiced at never again having to stop on the walk home to unroll the hated lisle stockings. Six years' attendance away from the eyes of males, doing rigorous academic work plus enforced devotions plus field hockey, eight-and-a-quarter hours a day, Monday through Friday, Saturday mornings, too—only on Sunday did Our Lady let go its grasp, but Sundays took care of themselves—amounted to an eternity of purdah. Naturally they were excited at the prospect of finally dating boys.

Of course, three times a year young men did penetrate Our Lady's spike-topped wall for dances in Rubart Gymnasium, but a squadron of nuns patrolled the floor with rulers; when the space between two dancers impeded free passage of any of the twelve inches, down came the ruler on knuckles and keisters. But now the long sentence had expired at last.

The busboy came around again. Awareness of his attention, not to mention the allure of his backside, stirred Viv as he plucked a butterball from ice water with silver pinchers and placed it just so on her bread plate. She went beet red.

LaCinda frowned. A boy, *of course.* She had monitored Viv's secret looks, but disdained looking at their object. Graduation meant the stopper that Our Lady put on the girls was pulled out with a *pop!* and the deluge was upon them. She pressed her lips together.

Viv was telling Buzzy, "I think he has charm."

Buzzy giggled. "You could call it that."

"I mean that sparkle in his eye. I'd like to talk to him."

Buzzy giggled again. "I'd like to — *you* know. Not that he's any Tyrone Power."

"Well, who is?" countered Viv.

"Tyrone *Power,* that's who."

After recovering from the giggles, they began to eat. Chewing her food in the unhurried manner of an only child, Viv patted at her lips so as to preserve their bright red lipstick.

"Such a nice-looking young man," murmured Alice (she of the vivid instinct for life) to LaCinda. "Our busboy?"

"I'm sure," LaCinda said, twisting her fork and torturing her roast, her mouth screwed up in displeasure. Alice began to add something, but the way LaCinda crushed a peppercorn silenced her.

When the food was finished, including wartime's ubiquitous bread pudding, and the sisters and nieces were smoking, LaCinda artfully signaled for the check with a nonspecific gesture in no way meant to imply she was going to take care of it. Thus when the waiter proffered it to her she took no notice. He proffered it to each sister in turn, but such were its repellent properties that a silent ballet of snapped-back heads and dropped shoulders ensued, until he laid it in the middle of the table, where it reposed undisturbed while cigarettes were finished and coffee cups leisurely drained.

Viv took advantage of the check's arrival to excuse herself. It seemed the crucial moment of her life. She hustled through the room so quickly no cousin, query or reproach followed.

The restrooms were off a corridor past the swinging kitchen doors, Ladies' to one side, Gentlemen's on the other. For a scary half minute she pretended to search her handbag, until, drumming a tray against his thigh, the busboy walked out of the kitchen and swerved her way—smiling that irresistible smile, one side up, one side down—and went past her through a latticed glass door to an empty terrace. He held the door for her.

Viv's knees wobbled as she ducked into the cold outdoor shadows, drawing blonde curtains over her face. Peaks cut jagged lines against the sky.

He said, "Hello, Beautiful," and before she could reply put his arms around her and kissed her.

Viv was shocked, but instantly thought, *Yes, how right,* and pressed back. Eyes closed, he was blushing furiously. Her fingers found a nascent curl in the close-cropped hair and crushed it like a grape. His lips opened and something—his tongue!—emerged. She pulled back then, and his head dropped, nudging at her shoulder like a puppy its mistress's. Not counting occasional darts thrown by dance partners, it was her first kiss. When his blue eyes opened they watered in sympathy with the agonies her contacts caused.

"Oh, I'm sorry," she confessed. "My eyes—I have to—I wear glasses."

"What's your name?"

"Vivian. Viv."

Slumping against the wall and crossing his arms, he watched as she lit a Lucky Strike, intending that her sophistication impress him.

"Come on, I've got a car."

"Oh, no, I couldn't!"

"Just to sit. For a minute."

"Oh no."

His warm fingers put a card in hers. "Call me later?"

She snapped it into her purse and turned to the door. "Can't tonight. Having a wienie roast."

"Can I come?"

"Don't think so," she said. "What's your name?"

Someone opened the door and called: "*J.T.!*"

"Tomorrow, then," he said, and hurried off.

In the Ladies' Viv took out her contact lenses, which she could wear for two hours at most. After rinsing her red and aching eyes, she returned, blind, glasses in her hand, to the dining room. As she passed a table she heard, "Viv! *Vivian!*" and, squinting, greeted a classmate and her family, and apologized for walking past.

"Didn't see you," she explained. But as she went on again she knew they were calling her stuck up.

Her mother and aunts were sitting rigidly, purses pulled onto their laps, while their daughters maintained an apprehensive silence.

Sighing, LaCinda reached for the check. She found the entries for what she and Viv had eaten, added them up, silently withdrew bills from her billfold, plucked coins from her coin purse, carelessly set them down and leaned back to regard the view. The only fair way to split a check, the sisters agreed, was for each to pay for what she and her daughter consumed; that way, there could be no mistakes and no hard feelings.

Violet was the next to subject the check to an examination worthy of a sacred palimpsest, then Alice, then Mary, then Ida. Judiciously, reluctantly, they opened their purses and probed the silk-lined recesses, withdrew billfolds and coin purses, took out bills, pulling at them, stretching them in drawn-out goodbyes, loath to see them go, with subdued clinks built stacks of coins and pushed them across the tablecloth like losers at cards.

When all had contributed, Ida, the youngest, counted the money and announced that $2.57 was yet wanting.

Negotiations began. Each strove to remember what she'd eaten, but found it easier to remember what the others had.

"Violet, dear, don't forget your iced tea."

"Oh, thank you, Alice. And Buzzy had sausage, I believe?"

"The stewed carrots were yours, Ida?"

They sought to reconstruct a meal already eaten and to reconcile small items they were reminded of (bleu cheese dressing, coffee) with the grand total. It took time, and the waiter's initial relief at being asked for one check gave way to dismay, which would deepen when faced with what the sisters thought a sufficient tip.

LaCinda snapped, "Put on your glasses, Viv. You're driving me home."

As they left, J.T. was standing at the waiter station. He signaled Viv invisibly with a minute rise to one corner of his mouth. She signaled back, pulling her hair free of her face. Buzzy, refusing to see anything of their transaction, flounced past.

As they emerged into the sunshine, Alice said, "When I exclaimed at what a nice-looking busboy? *Thought* I recognized him. He's that Pelletier boy from Christ Commander — the one who went to reform school? Remember, it began with drinking Monsignor Flynn's communion wine when he was an altar boy?"

"*Pelletier?*" LaCinda said. The father was a printer on a large scale, the Archdiocese his client, its weekly newspaper and parish bulletins his handiwork. "Then that's the son that's gone to the bad. No wonder he reminded me of Harry Halderman. Wouldn't trust him far as I could throw him."

Viv sucked in her breath at mention of him who divorced his wife and abandoned his child years earlier.

"Just graduated from military school," said Alice. "Could go to Officer Candidate School, but they say he refuses — prefers to be a busboy. Won't even work for his Dad. A bad seed."

"Even so, the Army will get him," LaCinda said. "And that'll fix him."

**26.**

RETURNING HOME FROM Mass and brunch the next day, Viv pulled LaCinda's yellow Pontiac convertible into the garage, and they stepped through the jalousied breezeway and into the light-filled kitchen. Only five years old, the house was of blonde brick with sections of glass brick and big picture windows. Its lawn, graced by flowerbeds, a bird bath and an elm, was tended one day a week by a Mexican father and son.

Viv took advantage of the cheerful mood getting home put her mother in to ask, "Mother, do I *have* to go to Aunt Mary's?"

Sunday supper always took place at one of the sisters' in their neighborhood east of Colorado Boulevard.

"Of course you must, Vivian," LaCinda said, detaching her pearline earrings as she admired her glass-topped table in the bay window, the teal counters stretching beneath matching cabinets and the wall array of shiny copper Jell-O molds—a shrimp, a wreath, a fish, a rooster. "Everyone will be there."

"Told you, Mother, I might go out."

"Yes, so you said, but it's Sunday. You can't go out on Sunday night."

"Not a school night any more."

"Viv, while you're under my roof, I'll *tell* you whether you may go out or not."

"I'll be at C.U. this fall."

"Yes, and I'll be paying your tuition and your room and board, so I *think* — "

"I'll pay it myself if I have to." Viv, too, had inherited money from the wheat king.

"There's an idea," allowed LaCinda. "I'm going to lie down."

As Viv changed clothes she heard the mattress complaining through the wall. Because she wished to make a call and the telephone sitting in the living room niche had an extension at her mother's bedside, she went quietly out through the kitchen and breezeway, walked a few blocks down Krameria to a row of brick storefronts on Colfax — a Piggly Wiggly, a dry cleaners and the Ritz Drug Store.

Behind the Ritz's newsstand and soda fountain was a bank of telephone booths. Viv slipped into one and shut the wooden door, folding herself into darkness until the little light snapped on. Phone booths reminded her of confessionals. Inserting a nickel, she dialed J.T.'s number.

After three heart-stopping rings, he answered.

"Hello?"

"I don't even know your name."

"John-Thomas Pelletier, if you can believe it," he said. "But everyone calls me J.T."

"My mother says you're bad."

"To the bone," he replied. "Believe it. Look, let's figure out a movie."

"Movie?"

"Want to go out tonight?"

"I *can't*. Well, I *could,* except for Mother."

"OK, but look, I don't have a car today. Meet me on Colfax,

we'll catch a streetcar downtown? Colfax and Colorado?"

"Colfax and Krameria's better for me."

"Fine. Seven o'clock?"

"That's late."

"Big high school graduate like you?"

"Six?"

"Six o'clock it is." The line thrummed faintly as they lapsed into silence. "OK then, Viv?"

"OK, J.T."

Saying no other goodbyes, they hung up, Viv thought, like two crooks planning a heist.

When LaCinda emerged from her bedroom, refreshed, Viv was lying on the couch turning the pages of *Life* magazine while Woody Herman played on the radio.

"Wearing *that* to Mary's? That blue she gave you would look well, and please her."

"All right."

Viv changed, and as soon as LaCinda finished her 5:00 o'clock double Manhattan they left, in concession to gas rationing walking the few blocks to Grandview.

Climbing the bungalow's steps, they entered without ringing. After calling to the menfolk in the basement—Mary's husband's lair, where a St. Louis Cardinals game on the radio obviated the need for conversation among the brothers-in-law—LaCinda went into the kitchen while Viv continued upstairs to her cousin's bedroom.

"LaCinda, did you notice Monsignor Flynn *wobbling* on the altar steps this morning?" asked Violet, scandalized.

"*Tipsy*," LaCinda declared. "As usual."

The kitchen door closed and Viv heard no more. Buzzy's phonograph blasting Glenn Miller, her cousins were dancing, and she joined in.

Half an hour passed with nothing more monumental

happening than two cousins going downstairs to make lemonade. While lemons were squeezed, the aunts sat back and contemplated the table's centerpiece, a ceramic ashtray painted with sombreros and saguaros, Mary's souvenir of Tijuana. They never complained about the thumps and rumbles from upstairs; it told them where their girls were.

A little later, crumpling an empty pack of Luckies, Viv looked into the kitchen to announce she was going to the Ritz Drug Store for cigarettes. Her mother was holding forth at the table—division of labor meant leisurely cooking, and each sister had a drink in front of her—but cut herself off to say, "*Do* wish you wouldn't smoke, Viv." Aunts meanwhile offered theirs.

"No, thanks, should have my own," Viv said. "Be right back."

Buzzy and Martha insisted on accompanying her, heels clicking on the sidewalk. When Viv failed to turn into the Ritz, Martha called, "Viv, *this* way."

"Be right there," she called.

The others entered the drugstore, but Viv clipped a few doors down to the closed drycleaners at the corner, where J.T. crouched, smoking. Seeing her, he flicked his cigarette at the curb and came economically to his feet by shoving his rear up the wall, a move lazy and sensuous. He drew her back from the street.

"Hello, Beautiful."

"Hi, not-so-bad-yourself."

"Those your sisters?"

"Cousins."

"Pretty. But not half so pretty as you."

"J.T., is there even a *streetcar* Sunday evening?"

"Streetcar?" he asked, leading her down the block and peering into parked cars. "S'pose there might be, but why do you ask? Oh, the *idiots*," he added, darting down to open an unlocked Dodge's passenger door and urging her, "*Get in! Get in!*"

She folded herself into the front seat in a quick but lady-like way, giggling to see him scramble in on the other side and press the starter. The car screeched into the street, the motion closing her door, and she saw her cousins at the curb, cigarette packs in hand, watching with dropped jaws.

"Slow down, J.T.!"

"Not much gas." He shook his head at the gauge, then regarded her full on. "God, Viv, you're so pretty."

She wondered at her calm as she brushed hair over her shoulders with both hands. He was ruddy, handsome and believably bad.

"This your car?"

"So suspicious! No, baby, don't got a car. Don't got nothing but what I take — so ain't it lucky I got what it takes?"

He said it with a sidewise roll of his eyes, angling his face and smiling to show he was joking, even to the bad grammar. She laughed as at an epigram.

"Viv, what do you want to do?"

"Thought a movie?"

"It's the gas that's the problem. This one, can't risk more than a few miles." He turned the wheel and stepped on the accelerator. "But I know a place."

"I bet you do," she said, but was terrified. Repartee is safe — nothing safer — but speeding off in a stolen car?

"City Park," he said, his grin hinging open his jaw at the dimples. "Like City Park?"

Passing without comment his family's house — she knew the big Spanish Colonial — they entered the park, curved along the lakeside, went over low rises and shallow dips softened by trees and pulled up within a thicket of pines beside a picnic table. He switched off the engine and with a smile put an arm around her.

"J.T., *what* are you doing?" she asked, shaking it off.

"Let me hold you, Viv. You do feel good," he reported, replacing his arm. She fought it off again, so he dug his face into her neck. "Smell even better!"

"Well, so do you. As if you didn't know."

Dimpling, J.T. waited until he saw the ghost of a smile flit past her face. "Come on, baby," he murmured. He pushed his arm along the seatback, and this time she leaned forward to accommodate it. They sat like that for some time before his lips began brushing her ear, nibbling her hair and she started sighing.

His lips found hers and gently rested against them. When hers fluttered, his pressed and opened, and his tongue pushed out. After due consideration her lips parted, too, and their tongues began to screw forcefully into each other's, bringing their heads together with a seashell's ocean roar. Breathing became gasping, and they groaned as from pain *in extremis*.

J.T. lowered his hand from Viv's shoulder to her breast. She slapped at it, but as in a dream couldn't remove it. His breaths were coming right in her face, unexpectedly intimate. His other hand began delving at her skirt. She slapped it away. In probing her cardigan and blouse, trying to get at her brassiere, sweeping aside her skirt's pleats, he was pulling off the wrappings that protected her so completely. *About time*, she thought, even with both hands busy slapping his away.

His leg under hers, his fingers were creeping up her thigh, but she had hands sufficient to counter him, though exertion made both pant and his grunts of frustration came more and more frequently.

"Come *on*, Viv. You know what I want."

"I have a general idea."

"Let's get in the backseat."

"No!"

"There's nothing wrong with it. I would never hurt you."

"J.T., we're not *married*."

"Please, Viv, *please*."

"*No!*"

She continued to counter him, and in a show of disgust he abruptly let go, brushed his hand over his head, sat up straight behind the wheel and started the engine. Looking over his shoulder with features bland and unreadable, he backed the car out.

"J.T., are you all right?"

"*Fine,*" he said. She could see he was seething.

He drove back towards Colfax, again passing his family's house. Viv made the mistake of saying, "J.T., isn't that where you live?"

Wrenching the wheel, he steered into the driveway and braked hard. Viv had to fend off the dashboard with both hands. The house was one of the city's finest, a long stucco block pierced by an archway, with two rows of casement windows, numerous chimneys with distinctive finials and a patio with a stone balustrade. The headlights flared into the interior.

"Like to meet Mom, Viv? Sure, she's in her chair bombed out of her skull, but we'll just shake her awake and have a nice chat. Or care to make Dad's acquaintance? Don't know, he's either at the plant or the girlfriend's."

"Just asking, J.T." Though she thought she could understand his moodiness, it wasn't what she liked about him.

He backed out of the drive. "Where should I drop you? Drugstore?"

"Where are *you* going?"

"Leave this where we found it."

The *we* registered with delightful complicity.

"Take me home, J.T. I'll call over that I got a headache and came on back. You're not mad, are you?"

"No," he said.

As they pulled up across from her mother's he managed a smile, and they parted with a kiss wonderful for its matter-of-fact quality.

"Call me," she said, and chanted her mother's number.

He chanted it back, and she slipped across the street and into the house. The lights were off, she was pleased to see; her mother wasn't home yet.

# 27.

MEANWHILE THE TRAIN carrying Nat Handler westward rocked his crotch to irksome tumescence as he sat sneering out the window. Changing in Chicago, he claimed a seat, but gave it up to a lady; it was nearly Missouri before he had another.

Telegraph poles marked off his disgraced homecoming with a counting-out-the-measures-of-life rhythm that matched in quality the trackside wastes, alleys, backs of sheds and garages. Those moments of deflected crash, when another train passed shrieking an arm's length away, sucking at the windows, excited him, but he hated waking up haggard next to the same foul-breathed man he'd gone to sleep beside.

In early evening three days out of New York, his train glided into Gallup and he stepped off into cowboy hats and bright shawls.

"Welcome home, son," said his lean, weathered father, shaking hands and picking up the duffel.

Nat sneered from one horizon to the other before following after with the Gladstone bag. They drove west in the Plymouth beneath a billowing development of clouds in dazzling silvers, serenest pinks. In resistance to the joy radiating from his father, Nat leaned his head against the window frame.

His Dad was pleased to have him home. Cornell had sent a letter revoking Nat's scholarship on account of his leaving without taking exams, and for months that was all he had. Imagining him to have gone to New York to be a writer, on Saturday marketing trips he stepped into the Gallup public library to scan magazines that published fiction, but never found his name.

But his conviction was that Nat had a right to live his own life, even prematurely, and was smart enough — sufficiently his mother's son, was his modest thought — that with ordinary luck he'd be all right, and would get back in touch when he needed to. When he needed money.

The sun clawed the sky bloody as it sank behind buttes.

Nat was grateful at least for his Dad's habitual (Snopesian) silence as he pushed the car over the road, eyes creased against the setting sun. In New York, reading Faulkner's analysis of the Snopes family had led Nat to discover that his father *was* Snopes. "That's Dad *exactly*," he'd told Gus. "As if Faulkner *knew* him!"

As the perspective shifted among hills and chimneys, Nat thought over his time in New York, his losing fight to be a writer. Return of the prodigal; if with an entire lack of success, he'd survived. Not that New York cared one way or the other. But surely no place else could be as tough?

He'd seen how poorly his innate (paternal) diffidence had served him; no help in a city or world where confidence rules. And that observation helped spark to life the long-dormant self-confidence instilled by his mother: *That* had to be what he presented to the world from now on, what he lived off.

He regarded his father — miniature against the Lakachukai Mountains, *nothing*, sawing away at his jalopy's wheel, for God's sake perfectly content!

Disgusted, he turned the other way.

# 28.

J.T. CALLED JUST AFTER 5:00 o'clock Thursday afternoon; he'd warned Viv he was pulling double shifts until then. When the phone rang, Viv—eager not to appear anxious—let her mother reach from her wing chair to answer it.

"Hello? *Hello?*"

LaCinda hung up.

"Who was it, Mother?"

"No one there," she said. Lifting her cocktail from the Moderne table at her elbow, she drained it. "Another Manhattan, please, Viv? *Light.*"

Viv took the glass of crackled blue and went for the refill. The hang-up electrified her: *Had* to be J.T. She needed to get out of the house and call him back without letting her mother know.

LaCinda lifted the lid to her music box—Lucite in the shape of a grand piano—and it was tinkling *Claire de Lune* when Viv brought her drink. She took a pacifying sip.

"Mother, I'm going out for bread."

"*Bread?*"

"Piggly Wiggly. Back in a jiffy."

A little later when LaCinda got up to heat leftover

meatloaf—*just too bad if Viv didn't get any!*—she was thinking about having a daughter *versus* having a son; she might as easily have had a tall, rangy boy, strong as an ox like her father, handsome like Harry Halderman. Viv was athletic, tall and pretty, but a girl. And her weak eyes offended LaCinda. Where had *they* come from? Her own mother had worn spectacles—from that line?

Her mother had been a strong woman in every other respect—no choice, raising a son and five daughters on a primitive farm on the Arkansas River—but forever lessened in LaCinda's eyes because she'd had to get married. Not on her own account, to be sure, but when her family still lived in Pennsylvania her sister got pregnant before—*without*—getting married. In their German Catholic community, there'd been nothing for it but to load up and trek west; remove themselves from the community of decent folk. And when a farmer near their new home wanted a wife, they reached an agreement—a business agreement providing for her and any children's eventual inheritance, she meanwhile to be in all things his wife. Hence, six children; their son still worked the home farm.

LaCinda surveyed her living room. In its careful way, it was inviting: robin's egg walls, a suite upholstered in silver-gray fabric that felt like velvet, with a hassock covered in slick, expensive new stuff called *plastic,* a round birch coffee table and matching side tables. Plus the lamps her sisters found so flamboyant, of rose-red glass, extra bulbs glowing inside the base.

Not to mention the mirror over the mantelpiece, a gilded confection of innumerable tiny panes surrounding a projecting boss. She'd paid a fortune for it in Havana, shipped it home at ruinous expense, but *had* to have it. It probably came from a Spanish palace of long ago. Her sisters shyly shuffled past it with admiring glances, not at themselves, but LaCinda swung into its plane with confidence, challenging her own large eyes with the assurance that, when Viv was six, took them to Hollywood for a year.

LaCinda found it a lark to parade the haughty cheekbones around Tinseltown. She was a handsome woman, with eyes she knew how to liquefy like the sirens of the silver screen, well-framed brows and glossy brown hair.

Hollywood led to nothing—she met several men in positions to discover a star, but refused their demands. Meanwhile she put Viv into Catholic school in Santa Monica, where she became best friends with Loretta Young's youngest sister. But ever since, LaCinda had followed the careers of Joan Crawford and Bette Davis as though they were more authentically her sisters than Violet and the others.

*Hollywood men!* LaCinda was an authority on men, hers a hard-earned authority. That was what made her mouth, once a rosebud on a pretty farm girl named Lucille, such a short, severe line. Under the glaring sun of Ellinwood, there in the Arkansas River's fertile bend, she invented a spicy, passionate, veritably Mexican name for herself: *LaCinda*. And though LaCinda married for love, the rosebud withered.

At first she appeared to marry better than her sisters. Whereas Alice married a car salesman, and Mary a postman, she snagged Harry Halderman.

Harry was a lively and prosperous fellow, big and dark-haired, built something along the bluff and handsome lines of Franklin Roosevelt. He'd had a harrowing war as a corporal fighting in the 89th Division until, gassed at the St. Mihiel salient, his war ended. LaCinda felt overwhelmed when he began to court her. In rapid succession they married and had their daughter.

At first Harry sold insurance, but one day when he recommended a whole-life policy to a farmer rocking on his porch, the farmer said, "Nope. Not interested. Tell you what, though. Got a hundred twenty acres I'll swap you for that car."

Harry turned around, looked at his gleaming brown Hudson, made a rapid calculation, and said, "Done." Had to walk home, sunburned and footsore, but — deed in hand — very satisfied.

Thereafter, he was a landowner and employer of men, buying more and more acres as prices fell through the Twenties. Unlikely though it was to prosper with Kansas farmland in the 1920's, Harry did it.

But he became so alarmed by what he perceived as threats to the values he'd fought for in France that he joined — nay, locally *led* — the patriotic reaction: Helping found a branch of the Ku Klux Klan, he donned the scarlet-embroidered white robe of its Kleagle and Exalted Cyclops. His mother, Kentucky-born, was proud.

With an adorable baby at home, Harry spent more and more evenings with his Klansmen. And when he *was* home, he found marriage increasingly a thing of fights and arguments; every one of which LaCinda won, except the last. Her mother journeyed out and removed daughter and granddaughter to Colorado Springs. No one imagined the exile would last — inconceivable that Harry wouldn't come to his senses!

But months later, while LaCinda awaited their reconciliation, Alice sent home a clipping from the Kansas City *Star* classifieds stating that Harry Halderman, having dissolved the marriage between himself and LaCinda Garrett, would no longer be responsible for her debts; announced it as if divorce in the Midwest were as simple as in Islam. The following week his wedding announcement appeared. Her humiliation deep, LaCinda quietly took care of the Colorado legal niceties.

Her mouth was the index of how things had gone, that

blossom, that pink flourish compressing itself to an embittered, closed valve that, as time wore on, pulled down and marred her other features. Thereafter she maintained her surveillance from a bastion to which nothing human—at least, nothing of vulnerability or desire—could be attributed. No; the lids to the large eyes could lift sufficiently to express judgment, but not so far as to show need.

Her sole concern now, she told her sisters, was her daughter. Every aspect of Viv's life came under her supervision. She was a good girl, but LaCinda thought her Garrett inheritance of intelligence and sweet temper counterbalanced by her Halderman legacy. She had a pretty Garrett face, but also "that lank Halderman hair"—lately teased into a Veronica Lake peek-a-boo—and had to be watchful against "that Halderman tendency to fat" (though Viv was very slender; it was her mother who fought the roll at her waist with extra cigarettes); and especially, LaCinda proclaimed, Viv had "that Halderman willfulness."

An after-dinner Manhattan? Why not? But wasn't Viv back yet? Or had she said she was going to Buzzy's?

LaCinda worked to her feet, traced the wall to the kitchen, made her drink—a double, to save steps—traced her way back to her chair and sat down with a suddenness that startled her.

Having been born and baptized a Catholic, for her there could be no question that any Protestant maneuver of Harry Halderman's could actually dissolve their marriage. Church teaching was as plain as it was sensible: If marriage doesn't endure until death (and past it, too, for the eternity Catholics toss around rather lightly), then what can be its meaning? Harry may have "remarried," but LaCinda, his bride still, resumed a virginal state.

Oh, she went on dates occasionally. Sisters or friends might come up with some eligible man who duly took her out to dinner, but the ones who reminded her of Harry Halderman — attractive, charming, successful — she tongue-lashed mercilessly; the basic questions anyone has to ask to get to know someone came out inquisitorial, adversarial. And the others bored her, and realized it, too, as, chain-smoking, she offered perfunctory conversation and perfunctory thanks. In either case, one dinner sufficed.

But then it was so nice not to have a man in the house — she could keep a neat home with assurance it would stay neat. The bathroom she shared with Viv — bad enough — at least was never sprayed yellow (those days she entertained her sisters and their husbands were a trial). Though she had a recurring dream that Harry's big shoes were paired up neatly beside the furnace underneath the floor grille, she retained nothing of his, save for his wartime Colt .45 automatic, her sole protection.

With a jolt she remembered that she hadn't tested it in a good six months. Going into her bedroom, LaCinda retrieved the gun from the drawer and, clicking the safety off, teetered to the front door, opened it, aimed for the sky and squeezed: *Bang!*

Satisfied, she scrupulously added a bullet to the clip and put the Colt away. Refreshing her drink, she regained her chair, lifted her glass and sipped it dry.

Eventually, she got up and, caressing the wall, moved carefully towards her bedroom. At the mirror she hesitated, seeing in it someone she didn't recognize — some dour woman past 40 (who let *her* in?) — then went to bed.

There she closed her eyes, awaiting the slowing of her head's orbit to deposit her in the still center of sleep.

## 29.

MEANWHILE VIV HAD SLIPPED into a booth at the Ritz Drug Store and called J.T. He was waiting by the telephone, promised to run right over, they again hung up without goodbyes and, as she loitered over the magazines, there he came, breathless.

They moved to the counter for a burger and something called Pepsi—a substitute for the rationed Coca-Cola—so Viv could show him off. A master judge of the envy that makes the world go round, she took pleasure in looks bent their way, the way shoulders down the counter rounded forward as girls exchanged remarks *sotto voce*.

Afterwards they took a lemon-colored streetcar down Colfax and at the Ogden Theatre saw *This Gun for Hire*. Talking it over with Buzzy and Martha, Viv had learned she'd better not get in another car with J.T. if she cared what people said about her. But she nestled happily under his arm, both too engrossed in Veronica Lake and Alan Ladd to do more than hold hands; he was on his best behavior.

"What time's your mother expect you back, Viv?" he asked as they left.

"No time," she giggled. "Told her I was going to the Piggly

Wiggly, but I'm not sure she heard."

"Like to go for a ride?"

She clung close. Yes, as a matter of fact; it was getting dark and no one would see. As they walked up the street he tried door handles on cars parked curbside. Unexpectedly the door to a Buick roadster opened — he took a false step as it swung outward, making Viv stumble, too — and they got in.

"J.T., there's no key!"

"Show you something." Clenching his teeth, J.T. worked his fingers beneath the dashboard. She saw sparks as the engine cranked to life, and laughed and laughed as they pulled into traffic and sped off.

"Where'd you learn *that?*"

"The Wayward." He grinned. "Learn a lot in reform school, Viv."

"Well, you shouldn't oughta, you know."

"Oh, I know, I know."

"J.T., why aren't you in the service?"

"Well, ma'am, I'm waiting."

"For what? The draft?"

"Not just sure I want to go off and kill Germans, *or* Japs."

"No? My father did, in the Great War — Germans — and his *grandfather* came from Trier. And couldn't you go in as an officer? Military school?"

"*Hip-hip-hooray!* Sixty days at the Home for Wayward Boys makes that —"

"*Oh!*"

"Drink?"

Now she *was* startled. He pulled a flask from his pocket and unscrewed it with one hand while changing lanes.

"What is it?"

"Gin. Like gin?"

"I don't know."

"Try it."

"I don't know about *any* of this, J.T."

He smiled and took a slug, and looked so happy, cares so completely cast off, long-lashed eyes so shiny, that she reached for it, too. It smelled like something you'd find in a garage, but she swallowed some. It burned and made her cough, but also made for an additional bond.

Pulling into City Park, he eased beside the same picnic table as before, did something under the dash that killed the engine and slowly leaned into Viv. Their lips pressed, rubbed, scraped and opened, and their tongues began to orbit much as their hands meantime were doing, until J.T placed one on her breast. This time Viv looked away with an intake of breath before removing it.

For some time they were joined at the mouth as their hands continued slow-motion combat. J.T.'s breathing intensifying to near-sobbing, with his left hand he pulled at her right as in a foxtrot, her hand wavering in the air in resistance, until his strength prevailed and both their hands came down squarely on his crotch.

Viv gasped. Beneath the cloth she felt an unexpected solid of fascinating quality. Pressed by his fingers, hers stretched and closed, avidly gauging that hardness, and to her astonishment the corresponding place between her legs quickened and liquefied. Groaning from the depths, J.T. scrubbed her hand into his groin, twisting his face into hers as he reached seeming heights of pain, and she moaned back.

"Love you, Viv, *love* you," he breathed urgently, and she breathed back, "*Love* you, J.T."

After a prolonged cry of agony, he went suddenly still— ceased to move, his grip so tight she couldn't move, either.

Loosening his hold, slinging his face from hers like a nursing infant's, eyes brimming with merriment, he said,

*"Oops."*

She giggled, jittery and of course mystified. For a long time, he held her even as cars nosed up and brushed their heads with headlights. Had they been doing so all along? Finally disentangling himself, J.T. climbed out. She heard a splash against a tree; the physical frankness made her feel close to him. He zipped up with a pull that took him to his toes, and shoved in his shirttail.

Getting in again, he struck a match and lit their cigarettes. The tops of the cottonwoods around them flared gold even as molten metal edged the mountains. His arm held her while they attended to their smokes, tapping off ashes.

"God, you're going to have beautiful children," he said.

She blushed. "I will if I have them with you."

"Not me, Viv." Something dark churned across his eyes and he took back his arm. "Won't live long enough for that."

"You mean the war?"

He snorted. "Can't escape your fate, isn't that what they say?" Flipping the butt far into the darkness, he sparked the engine back to life.

They were homeward on Colorado Boulevard where the siren they heard was no rare thing, but then a police car pulled up right behind them, its spotlight projecting the shadows of their heads on the windshield as its siren keened.

"Oh, J.T.!" Viv said, horrified.

*"Crap!"* The police car was pulling abreast as J.T. mashed the pedal, urging, "Come *on*, come *on!*"

Thrashing, the engine gradually gave them speed. Viv sat quietly, of course worried about getting caught, but also *thrilled*. A moll to the manner born, she inched closer to him. Caught up in his own incredible joy, J.T. smiled dazzlingly at her. For a minute, it was like a movie: Streets flashed past, and as they turned into Colfax cars honked and brakes squealed and people on the sidewalks stopped to gape. The siren wailed, but slowly the police car lost ground.

"Viv, I'm going to do a left, very tight, into the Sixth Avenue Parkway," J.T. told her. "Have your door open, and when I say, *jump*. That's where those fir trees are? Get right in the middle and sit tight. Don't come out till it's quiet."

"J.T.—"

"Don't want to hear it, Viv: Safest thing for you."

The spotlight no longer reached them, though the siren did, along with others in a call-and-response coming inexorably closer by the time J.T. made his turn and slammed on the brakes.

"*Go!*" he commanded as the car lurched forward on its springs.

"J.T., I *love* you!" Viv yelled as she tumbled out the door.

"Love you, Viv!" he called.

She scrambled into the stand of firs, crouching on the soft needles as police cars blurred past, sirens playing an extended aria before reaching a gaudy crescendo some ways off.

Stepping out, Viv briskly walked the half mile home, glad to find her mother already in bed.

She cried herself to sleep. She didn't know *what* had happened, what to *do* but weep.

## 30.

FOR 36 HOURS VIV lived in suspense.

All day Friday, LaCinda seemed to patrol the phone, and from supper at Alice's Viv had all she could do to get away and dart into the Ritz Drug Store to call J.T.'s house, where a voice, possibly a maid's, told her he wasn't home and no message could be passed on.

But on Saturday morning Viv woke up to find the front page of the tabloid *Rocky Mountain News* splashed with a high-contrast photograph of J.T. in handcuffs, sullen and defiant, teeth bared, wrenching away from a policeman. He wore a T shirt; his sedate plaid sportshirt was gone. She studied the photograph, passed her hand over it and tried to read the story, but was drawn back to the picture.

LaCinda arose late on Saturdays, a day devoted to shopping with her sisters. This morning she cleared her head with coffee at the bay window, followed by orange juice and Rocky Ford cantaloupe — good, though too early in the season to be midsummer's aromatic marvel. Then came eggs and bacon. The radio, tuned low, played big band music.

Relinquishing the paper, Viv went to get dressed. LaCinda intended to scan the war news and the May D&F ads, but the headline caught her eye:

# JOY RIDER NABBED!
## Charge John Pelletier, Jr.
## with Grand Larceny

With alarm and vindication she smoothed it flat on the table.

The telephone rang. It was Alice with the Denver *Post*'s page three story, and they discussed the shock of having had their table bussed a week earlier by a criminal who smiled at their darlings.

Finally LaCinda hung up and called, "Viv-*yan!*"

She showed her the miscreant's photo, reminded her who he was and forbade contact. "He's a disgrace to his family, and a threat to any decent girl. I expect you to obey me, Viv."

"Yes, Mother, but I don't even *know* him."

J.T. was lucky not to have gotten shot, but the officer who took him was a cool-headed veteran, and J.T. not too proud to follow orders when the man giving them had a gun and he had none.

Viv's name never passed his lips—silence was all he could give her. On principle his father declined to bail him out of jail or hire a lawyer. Arraigned on charges of grand theft auto, evading police and resisting arrest, J.T. heard from his public defender that he faced up to seven years in prison, though as a first adult offence it might work out to as little as six months. But if he agreed to enlist, the lawyer told him, the prosecutor would urge the judge to remit the prison time. That was the common-sense solution. Since the war was going to get him anyway, why not now?

But J.T. refused the deal. No one understood why, and he disdained to offer any explanation. In July he was tried, convicted and sentenced to six months in the Canon City Penitentiary.

Consequently, Viv's summer was a sad one of daily trips to the pool club with her cousins for sunning, swimming and dancing. It was the swing era, when dance steps were strenuous, precise exercises which, executed with the right partner, lost their gymnastic exhalations to become liquid solutions in joy. It excited her to be with a boy (or cousin) moving in rhythm with other couples on the dance floor, stretching, kicking, the flow absorbing all. Viv was a terrific dancer, quick and graceful, with wind that never failed, and boys flocked to her. She met a lot of new ones that summer — good dancers, some of them, if uninteresting as *boys*. None compared to J.T.

As a bookworm, she had other consolations, too, especially stories about people falling in love and enduring every ordeal so as to be with each other. That summer she read *The Foxes of Harrow, Kitty Foyle, Lorna Doone, The Count of Monte Cristo* and, shivering, *Forever Amber*:

> Amber, inexperienced but not innocent, returned his kisses equally. Spurred by the caresses of his mouth and hands, her desire mounted apace with his. . . .

She'd cut out the newspaper photo, folded it into squares and hidden it in the lining of her purse. Taking it out and ironing it flat with the heel of her hand was like unwrapping an origami lion: J.T. sprang to life, twisting, fighting, his jaw awry, arms flexed, trunk torqued, gripped by forces bigger and stronger.

How did they goad him to such fury? If only she'd let him have his way, that police car would never have come upon them, and she'd have more intimate memories of him to cherish, too. It was her fault, then, partly. The whole thing was tragic.

Soon she had creased the picture so many times the squares began to tear along the edges and fall away.

# 31.

NO ONE ALL SUMMER mentioned his failure to Nat, though his father, in between doing the multifarious tasks required to run a school, regarded him with an insufferably softened expression: *Had hopes of him, but our mistake, taking him for more than he was. Like him the way he is, though.*

What people did want to talk about—school staff, trading post clerks and his brother Dan, home from a stellar freshman year—was his New York City experience but, aside from a few set pieces, Nat was not inclined to speak of it. Sure, he'd visited the Statue of Liberty, but neglected to recall how he raced up the steps with Gus's broad hand propelling his rump upwards. Yes, he'd gone up the Empire State Building, but didn't mention hanging over the 86th-floor parapet with Gus's arm locked around his midriff, secure even as he *flew*.

A few days after Nat's return home, Dan left to man a Grand Canyon fire lookout tower for the summer, and Mr. Krux, the trader, sent for Nat. He ducked into the trading post—the polished logs overhead were low for him, festooned as they were with sheep-shearing equipment, wagon and riding tack, blankets and rugs in geometrical motifs. The walls featured canned goods and racks of dead pawn—cords of silver bugles weighted by chunks of turquoise.

The upshot was that Mr. Krux hired Nat to drive his one-ton Ford stakebed truck six days a week on the Holbrook loop. His supplies—supplies that helped feed and service an area larger than some Eastern states—came in on railcars that were shunted to a siding there.

It suited Nat, driving the 70 miles of dusty track, Krux's Navajo helpers Hosteen Kani and Hosteen Begay sitting beside him in silence. It took five hours or better to get there, load up and come back. Depending on the perishability of the goods waiting in barrels or crates, they would do it again the same day.

Nor was it always routine. After rain anywhere within 200 miles, in edging the truck down one side of an arroyo and gunning it up the other Nat had to watch out for flash floods—walls of water that could come out of nowhere—while judging where the quicksands lay.

Sometimes, though, he got stuck anyway, when there was nothing for it but to wait for the trader to miss them and come out in his other truck with a tow rope; Nat always had a book in his pocket against such an eventuality. Sometimes, when Krux's Dodge finally showed up, it too would bury itself in the mud and they had to await rescue by local Navajos.

Nat acquired a lifelong skill that summer. Liquor was forbidden by law on the Reservation, and his father observed it to the letter, though trips to Gallup included a visit to a saloon. So did Nat follow the law, but in Holbrook he would fill the silver-plated flask he'd bought in a New York pawnshop and drink it half-empty by the time he hid it while peeing behind a saguaro just short of the Reservation line. The next day he'd retrieve it and between the Rez's border and Holbrook drain it dry.

Nat could stay sufficiently watchful for coyotes or wild horses or jackrabbits scurrying across the road, and for the occasional oncoming vehicle (announced long in advance by dust plumes), and meanwhile enjoy the enlarged outlook liquor gave him. Certainly it helped him endure his companions' silence. It had never bothered him before, but after his Eastern experience the way Hosteen Kani and Hosteen Begay declined every conversational gambit got on his nerves.

Home of an evening, father and son would read in Morris chairs in the pine-paneled living room draped with rugs, pinyon pine snapping in the fireplace against the chill night air, Nat tending to his pipe. If the radio should play a tune from a musical he'd second-acted, the orchestra soaring over the chugging accompaniment of the Kohler in the shed around back, he might lay his book flat for a moment to say, "Oh! I saw this show," and his father would cock his head and grunt acknowledgment.

It was arranged that Nat return with Dan to Boulder that fall, a few weeks after his 18th birthday, and matriculate at C.U. The brothers would share Dan's boarding-house room on College Hill near campus. Their father would pay tuition, but to defray living expenses Nat would find a job to augment his summer savings. Dan drove a cab weekends, and thought Nat probably could drive one, too.

# 32.

THAT SEPTEMBER VIV moved into Sewall Hall, C.U.'s women's dorm above the ravine bordering one side of campus. Spreading with the grandeur of an Italianate English country house, courtyard wings embraced a five-story block on whose fourth floor was Viv's and Buzzy's room. Sewall Hall coeds lived as locked-away virgins, retired from the world, particularly from the temptations of The Hill. However oppressive, there was no alternative for freshman or sophomore women.

Nat rode to Boulder in Dan's proud acquisition, a rusty '33 Chevy. They looked like a couple of Okies, they agreed, bags and packages tied to roof and fenders or sticking out the window. Climbing Wolf Creek Pass, Dan laughed at his brother's gasping for air, but for a minute Nat felt on the verge of blacking out.

The campus he discovered disarmed his pre-emptive sneer. Founded under the Morrill Land Grant Act, the University of Colorado built its first building, Main—soon and forever *Old Main*—tall in stripped-down Second Empire brick on a plateau high over town. Old Main now presided over neighbors built in gothic and Georgian styles along a mall of mature elms. But newer buildings — like the grand Norlin Library that closed the mall, *Who Knows Only His Own Generation Remains Always A Child* carved across its pediment (George Norlin's elegant Englishing of Cicero's thought; Nat approved) — were built to a master plan mandating a "Tuscan" style: walls of sandstone struck into oblong bricks, with recessed casement windows and red tile roofs. Every new structure rising in pleasing proportions and placed in careful relation to the others, the campus was becoming one of the most attractive in the country.

Nat got the job Dan proposed. Shorthanded, Yellow Cab was glad to have him drive flexible shifts in one of their dusty-smelling '38 Fords. As provider of an essential service, Yellow Cab got the gasoline and tires it required even as rationing thinned civilian traffic.

Menial though the work was, it helped fill out Nat's new sense of freedom. At C.U. nothing was expected of him; he was disburdened of the high-flown predictions that had followed him to the Ivy League. Meanwhile he found his courses congenial — survey courses in English, journalism and various liberal arts. His existence was less solitary than at Cornell, too. He had Dan and Dan's friends, became friendly himself with several classmates.

Not that he was unaware of girls, especially given how severely askew the war was putting the sex ratio. Girls abounded; between the end of one class period and the beginning of the next, for ten exciting minutes 4,500 undergraduates hurried over the walkways, an unprecedented proportion of them female. Nat gawked into girls' bright faces as they walked together in bobby sox and sweaters, skirts swishing, barrettes in their long hair, giggling as they pretended not to notice him. He longed to possess one, a pretty one he could show off as his own, but they seemed as untouchable as in New York.

He complained to his brother, but Dan pointed out that the war would so soon derail any plans they could make that they should make none; lucky if they made it to the end of the school year.

Nat conceded the sense of what he said, but still gawked at passing coeds.

Viv, enjoying the same new freedoms, was studying English, French and Biology, without for a moment forgetting the drama of her love life. She was in love, but her love was locked away in prison.

# 33.

THE DENVER PARENTS of a friend invited Dan and his brother for Thanksgiving weekend.

They waited that Wednesday on Broadway for the 5:00 o'clock Flatiron Trailways amidst some two dozen students. Seeing how many there were, they regretted not trekking downtown from The Hill to where the schedule originated. The setting sun whipped the sky full of creamy clouds, but it was chilly. Dan happily kibitzed with his friend while Nat hid his chin in his inadequate pea coat and shoved his hands in his pockets, bumping a foot against his Gladstone bag.

Thanksgiving at Cornell a year earlier was the most homesick he'd ever been. On a slate-gray afternoon he'd found his way to the one dorm whose kitchen remained open to eat thin slices of turkey slathered with gelatinous gravy, sitting by himself amongst strangers who radiated unfriendly shyness, as befit those left over. The only comfort he found was the mincemeat pie. Not so good as his mother's, and the hard sauce was laughable, but he had seconds.

Now, standing apart from his brother, he felt a pang of loneliness even as he scoffed at those around him laughing like excited children. *Kids*, he judged, none staking exclusive claim to an identity, but fluidly exchanging them; while he stood apart, a figure of personal dignity.

The bus came, a line formed and, Dan bumping him from behind, Nat worked his way aboard.

Already the seats were filled. At the driver's urging, they edged towards the rear. When the pressure eased Nat found himself three-quarters of the way back, and turning towards him a tall blonde girl whose beauty, for all that she wore glasses, instantly set him aflame.

He gripped a leather strap. As a glasses-wearer himself, he could look past the frames to the soft and pretty flesh beneath. As the bus set off, causing them to sway in unison, the girl brushed back her long hair and looked out the window.

So did Nat, stooping. The couple in the seat below shot him a look of distaste, then angled their heads together. The bus passed the last of the fraternity houses, gas stations and a roadhouse, and took the road for Denver. Frozen in place, Nat was glad his coat covered his crotch. Discreetly, he checked to make sure that it did. Was it at this the girl smiled?

Foothills passed in procession, tracing, as Nat couldn't help but notice, a sine wave against the sky. What to say to her? He could catch no more than a whiff of her own personality, though hints of Hollywood ones — Veronica Lake, especially — abounded.

He reflected how seldom girls seem to *have* personality. Their mothers certainly do, so he supposed the daughters must possess the germ of it *somewhere*.

But Viv, too, was flagrantly aware of standing next to this *boy*. Having long mastered the arts of focusing and unfocusing, of seeing without being seen to look, she confirmed that the young man standing beside her was as good-looking as he was tall, even granted his intense air and the pointy nose supporting horn-rimmed glasses. He looked intelligent, she thought as she sculpted and smoothed her hair.

Nat thought her hands like fluttering doves (*write that down!*). Heart pounding, he turned and asked pointblank, "Are you at C.U.?"

"Yes, I am," Viv answered as if delighted. "I'm a freshman." She liked the timbre of his voice, low and reverberant, full of saw-toothed energy.

"Me, too. My name's Nat."

"I'm Viv," she said, and put out her hand, albeit at a funny angle — they were so squashed together that just shaking hands made them sway.

"Do you live on campus?"

"Yes, in Sewall Hall. Of course. Do you?"

"No, on The Hill with my brother. He's behind me." Nat nodded vaguely aside. He could hear Dan chatting with some acquaintance, old or new.

"Oh, that's nice." She thought he looked like a young professor.

"What's your major?" Nat asked.

"Not sure. Maybe English. I love to read."

"Me, too — I mean, I do love to read — I'm a writer — but my major's going to be journalism. Think so, anyway."

They talked books. Nat recommended Faulkner, Wodehouse and Waugh. Impressed, she promised to sit down to them in Norlin.

At some point she remarked that, because her 18th birthday was the following week, her family was celebrating it that weekend along with Thanksgiving, but that her boyfriend couldn't be there —

"*Boyfriend!*"

"But I haven't seen him in a long time. He's away."

"Oh? Where?"

"Canon City."

"Not the *prison?*"

She bit her lip. "As a matter of fact, yes."

"Oh! What did he do?"

"Nothing, really. Took a car. Borrowed it for an hour, or not even. Just his bad luck they caught him before he could return it. Actually he's a *charming* young man, from a *very* good family."

"What did your parents say to *that?*"

"My mother forbade me to see him. My father. . . I don't have one." It came out in a little girl voice.

"No *father?*"

She pulled at her curtain of hair. "My parents are divorced. We haven't heard from him in years."

"That's terrible!"

"They divorced when I was two. He used to see me, but his new wife didn't like it, I think. Haven't seen him since I was seven. Last year, turned out my classmate's father works for him, so I got his address and wrote a letter."

"That was brave."

"No, not brave, just asked how he was doing, told him Mother and I were fine and I'd like to hear from him."

"What did he say?"

"*Nothing.*" It came out a sob.

"Oh Viv, don't cry," said Nat. His hand momentarily perched on her shoulder. "He's just a bully. Oh *Viv*. My mother died."

"*Oh!*"

"Four years ago."

"Oh, Nat, I'm so *sorry*."

They fell silent, but a current had started up between them, the hollows of their losses gripping with unbreakable suction.

As Denver abruptly declared itself beneath the Capitol's golden dome, Nat did what even a shy person knows must be done in such a situation. "Can I see you some time?" he asked.

"Oh Nat, I *can't*," Viv said. "He's away, but he's still my boyfriend. Thank you, though."

"OK," he said, "but you're awfully young to be out of circulation."

She shot him a look of agreement, and cast her eyes down. "Do you like to dance?" she asked.

"Love it!" he said, although nothing was further from the truth. "Would you go to a dance with me?"

"But I *can't*," she said. Startlingly, they were downtown, the bus making dramatic turns that made them lean to keep their balance. "I truly wish I could, Nat."

"When does he get out?"

"I don't know. They sentenced him to six months last July, and they say they sometimes release them early, but I don't know."

Nat asked for her phone number. She *couldn't*, but heard herself stating her mother's surname.

"Halderman," he repeated, noticing that she didn't ask his; and then the bus was nudging up against the terminal wall like a cow her stall.

From the garishly-lighted frieze of persons moving to and fro, Dan and his friend turned smiling for Nat. But Nat, having carried Viv's bag off the bus and received her grateful smile before she turned to the daunting woman in furs who met her, stood looking after her, feeling a cut on his heart.

## 34.

DAN'S FRIEND TOOK them on a Capitol Hill streetcar to his house on Downing Street. There they were welcomed, established in an upstairs guest room with a dormer and twin beds, dined and, somewhat to their hostess's surprise, wined as well.

The evening passed slowly. Nat was friendly, if reserved; distracted, thinking about Viv. He was eager to get to bed and improve their acquaintance, if only in his imagination. It was a big new project, and he wanted to get on with it.

And finally he was there, his brother's breathing, after an interval of agitation, smoothing out as he fell asleep. Picturing Viv's shy face behind its veils of hair, Nat began to stroke himself, fire in his fingertips, amazed at his swollen contours. *Love at first sight!* He worked faster, anticipating floods of ecstasy as he unbuttoned her blouse, lifted her dress, stripped her *naked*.

But something went wrong. He could feel the cloth—*oh, happy cloth!*—of her blouse, sense the shapely masses it hid, but its buttons defeated him, and he couldn't even reach her bra clasps. Nor would her skirt come up. He could barely fondle a knee! Imagination balked; refused to sully her.

He tried and tried, turning over and assaulting the mattress without mercy. But she eluded him, he got nowhere. Then came a stray thought of Gus and—groaning in powerless misery—he ejaculated and slept.

It was unsatisfactory—torture.

THE SISTERS CELEBRATED Thanksgiving at Ida's that year.

Among her cousins Viv enjoyed prestige for having fallen in love with a criminal, if also ridicule on account of their enforced separation. But when alone for a few minutes with Martha, younger but acknowledged to be wise, she thought back to the boy on the bus and ventured to ask a question on a topic she knew nothing about. She might have asked Buzzy, but somehow didn't want her to know.

"Martha, is it all right to enjoy *talking* to a boy? I mean just talking, without petting or anything?"

"I *suppose* so, simpleton—not that *I* ever met one worth talking to. Why? Meet someone?"

"No. I don't know."

"And what's *that* supposed to mean?"

"Just—a boy on the bus yesterday. Freshman."

"Did he ask for your number?"

"I didn't give it!"

"Remember, you have a boyfriend," Martha said with sparkling eyes, "and he *needs* you."

Back at the house, when LaCinda went on about how having Viv at home made her feel younger, and asked about boys, she said, "Oh, *Mother*. With *school?* There's no time."

THE NEXT DAY, Nat found *Halderman* in the phone book and called.

LaCinda answered, charmed to find herself telling a boy that her daughter wasn't home. She kept her inquisition light, but learned that his name was Nat, he was a C.U. student who'd met Viv on the bus to town and hoped to see her while he was in Denver, too, or at any rate back in Boulder, and wanted to wish her a happy birthday. Something in his voice caught her interest—low and rich, but nervous and somehow congested as he dictated his host's number and asked that Viv call.

Her questioning of Viv that evening netted only the fact that, though she barely remembered him, Nat—*Oh, was that his name?*—seemed nice enough. Her indifference, including crumpling up the phone number, alerted LaCinda to her interest.

BACK IN BOULDER, Nat was too shy to assault Sewall Hall directly, too bashful to go in and ask for Viv. What he counted on instead was a chance meeting—to come upon her unannounced; to find himself with her, just the two of them, the bond formed on the bus re-emerging to enshroud them both.

But he meant to assist chance. Hence he lurked in her dorm's vicinity, peering up at its casements for the glorious fall of her hair, and prowled the reading rooms and stacks of Norlin Library. He wondered if his fellow students were likewise on errands contrived to bump casually into their objects of desire—if that boy so deliberately walking the mall were calculating a meeting at the corner with some certain girl, if that girl hurrying up Old Main's steps was timing it to run into some certain boy. (It gave him an idea for a short story, and *The Student Romeo* appeared some months later in *The Prairie Schooner*, his only published short story.)

One day he did encounter Viv coming down Norlin's steps.

It did not go as he hoped. His eagerly asking how she was drove her to swipe at her hair with one hand, transfer her books to the other arm and swipe at the other side, with the effect of retreat. The gesture's impersonality made Nat feel he didn't know her at all. But she found his barging in irritating, his intensity off-putting: She *had* a boyfriend, and he knew it. Hence her curt refusal of his invitation to the Christmas dance.

When he and Dan journeyed home for the holidays, sitting on their bags at one end of a jammed train car (gas rationing defeated the notion of driving), Nat was morose, silent and unwilling to enter into the reason why.

"Some girl," Dan informed their Dad. Returning from a solitary sunset walk, Nat heard them as he was coming around a corner.

"Thought so."

He went back to work for Krux's Trading Post. His route across the endless landscape allowed Viv's face to supervene no matter what he might be doing. When he inched down an arroyo, he was thinking of the passing streetlights picking out tiny white hairs on her arm, and as he handed up boxes from the siding was overwhelmed with her radiance on Norlin's steps. But the aggravating result was that he could not mar his beloved's image by imagining her sexually; *impossible*.

Since turning twelve, first acting on a hint from Dan, Nat had masturbated several times a day. Now he'd met Viv and, though consumed in flames for her, could not make use of her in his fantasies—could not, even in his mind's eye, compel her to do what he wished her to do, partly because he'd never done those things with any girl, partly from a lively sense of guilt. Thus he wanted Viv, but she remained proof against his imagination. He was stymied, frustrated, nightly kept awake stroking himself sore or rubbing himself raw against the sheets, before necessity brought him to an efficient reminiscence of Gus.

Wallowing in self-contempt, he told himself he was

pathetic: Trying to come across her by accident, indeed!

And he found the Reservation newly foreign. How had he ever fit in with the crew of saints and failures that made up its white population? His father was unbearable, working day to day as though it meant something, accomplished something, when nothing ever changed.

Christmas brought the ordeal of dinner with Indian Service personnel who liked to talk about his mother. He and Dan, showing off a prized boarding-school accomplishment, carved the turkeys. On New Year's Eve came the staff party. Dan had a good time dancing to records with ladies young and old — the youngest years older than himself — even as clouds of dust rose up from the floorboards, but Nat soon took himself and his pipe off to brood in the desert air — to brood about Viv and her bad boyfriend as the moon rose through sunset's last burnt offerings.

## 35.

EARLY ONE EVENING after returning to Boulder for the semester's rump end — a last week of classes, followed by two weeks for finals — Nat nervously entered Sewall Hall.

Walking through the loggia and a forecourt filled with giggling maidens, he presented himself at the counter. After grilling him, its hellhound directed him, under escort, to the large living room opposite, the only room where males were permitted. He opened the door to find some 40 or 50 girls sitting in chairs and couches, sprawled on the floor or gathered around the radio at one end.

With one accord, they turned to look at him.

"Viv?" he called, after swallowing to get some moisture in his mouth. "Is Vivian Garrett here?"

"Oh, hello, Nat," Viv called from the Atwater-Kent, pulling a thicket of hair off her eyes. Nat's crotch pulled.

He walked across to her, a stir of interest following him.

"Viv, the end-of-semester dance is at Balch Field House this Friday, and I wonder if you'd like to go with me?" She combed her hair with her fingers. "Glenn Miller's leading his band. Didn't you say he's your favorite? It's just a dance."

Viv had no intention of saying yes, looked mournful as her

mouth opened to say she wished she *could*, but he knew why she *couldn't*, but—as if wiping hair from her face had changed her mind—heard herself say instead, "Thank you, Nat, that would be lovely." She was startled, but let it stand.

"And dinner first?"

She looked troubled. "Well, no, I don't think so," she said. "I get dinner here."

"Oh! OK then, pick you up out front, Friday at 8:00?"

"All right, Nat," she said. "Thanks."

He closed the door on a sea of giggles. Only when he emerged from the loggia did triumph give him, for a few paces, the knees-up steps of a conqueror.

NAT HATED TO DANCE, hated everything athletic—anything that put his body or his use of it up for comparison with anyone else. Moreover, though given dance lessons at Escalante Hall, his practice had been with other boys; no one there (well, almost no one) learned to dance really well.

So for the next week he practiced with Dan, grimly throwing his weight around in obedience to Glenn Miller's trombone on Dan's phonograph; Dan was taking a nursing student to the dance. The thundering alarmed their landlady until they explained.

That Friday, Nat met Viv at Sewall's forecourt amidst young women flooding outdoors to meet their dates, most risking the walk to the field house without wraps. Everyone was going; except for May's end-of-year blowout, it was the best-attended dance of the year. Viv wore a frilled, wide-shouldered dress in puce, Nat his blue serge suit with padded shoulders. During the walk to Balch they could hear drums beginning to pound and woodwinds to lick. Viv skipping in anticipation, they entered to find the vaulted ceiling crawling with balloons and the floor filling fast. Pulling Nat into its middle, Viv began to solve the music's driving, propulsive rhythms.

On stage, Glenn Miller, in double-breasted plaid, turned the big smile on his big face this way and that beneath glasses and slicked-back hair. His wrist whipped clarinets to keening over saxophones and trumpets in luscious textures and harmonies. Occasionally he untucked the trombone from beneath his arm and contributed its sound to that of his red-jacketed players.

Nat felt stiff, looked stiffer, but as song followed song, his excitement mounted, and when Tex Beneke and Paula Kelly stepped out to sing *Chattanooga Choo-Choo*, thought — *hoped* — he was loosening up. Regardless, grimacing, he danced on.

Skirts twirling, smiling deliriously, Viv happily followed his lead, and when the band took a break crowded up with him to buy the single Coke apiece that rationing permitted.

"You look a little like a young Glenn Miller, Nat," she said. "Handsome, isn't he?"

"You're a wonderful dancer," he answered.

"Thank you."

Refreshed, they resumed to the antic *Pennsylvania 6-5000*. Viv was amused at the pile of stiffness that was Nat. Willing, but *stiff!* It kept her from showcasing her own grace and command of rhythm — kept her from showing off — but she thought him sincere and endearing, even cute. Grimly hanging on while Viv bounced joyously, Nat was shouting about having *been* there, when he lived in New *York* going into the Hotel Pennsylvania *lobby*, when he noticed a young man in dungarees and leather jacket making his way towards them smiling maniacally, lips drawn back to reveal a missing front tooth. Putting out his arms, he brushed past Nat, and to Nat's horror Viv's face lighted up and she screamed with delight. They embraced and kissed, instantly were moving together, dancing, leaving Nat standing there with no idea what to do with his arms.

"J.T., what happened to your *tooth?*"

"Little disagreement inside."

Viv thrilled with horror. "How have you *been?*" she shouted, then remembered Nat. "Nat, this is my boyfriend! J.T.'s *here,* he's *out,* I can't believe it!"

Nat went over and finished Dan's Coke for him.

On examination, J.T. exemplified so many qualities Nat despised that he couldn't list them all. Handsome, for one thing—a big strike against him. Chiseled features, smiling easily, with obvious (Nat thought *cheap)* charm; light brown hair, short as an Army recruit's; a frame shorter than his own but broader at the shoulders, slimmer at the hips.

Worse, a hell of a dancer! Easy, flexible, unself-conscious, instinctively twirling Viv, kicking the opposite way, visibly loving it, her perfect match. Showing off now, Viv was an altogether different dancer, blossoming in motion to the sustained blare of brass over a driving beat, the boy's face joyful, hers *radiant.* Nat had the dispiriting realization that other couples were watching, even falling back to applaud: Viv and her partner were the stars of the floor. They moved fluidly through the song's transformations and variations, until it ended in an extended scream from the band that left everybody shiny and panting.

Nat felt biting frustration. Why was it so easy for the other, so hard for him? He was too shy to do what would take, after all, an unusually confident person to do—cut in and reclaim her—but as the next song began his hands fisted, his feet stepped towards them. His intention noticed, couples cleared a way for him, and for a long moment he stood paralyzed with longing. There was tittering. Viv noticed the stir, noticed *him,* and missed a step, which made J.T. look around and raise his eyebrows.

"My date," she shouted.

He laughed. Nat receded as J.T. pulled Viv through a series of turns, her cries of joy carrying over the music. Backing up until he hit the wall, he stood in shadow. Soon he saw J.T. steering her by the shoulders out the door.

He went up to Dan and his date, held out his open hand. Dan dropped his car keys in it, and Nat hurried out to the parking lot.

J.T. PULLED VIV to a spectacular car, a red Oldsmobile convertible, canvas top up. As she got in, she was thinking how he'd changed. Despite the tooth, he had a new, somehow different element, arresting and provocatively masculine.

"Let's go park somewhere?" he murmured, and she breathed, "OK."

First he pulled into a Phillips 66 on Broadway and waved gas coupons at the attendant, who got the gas flowing and wiped the windshield, careful not to catch Viv's eye. When he stepped to the rear and replaced the gas cap, J.T. started the car and gunned it into the road.

"*Hey*, come back here!" yelled the gas jockey.

"Oh, J.T.," Viv remonstrated.

"My only coupons," explained J.T.

The moon was up, a half moon shiny as a dime. Snow on the ground meant there was plenty of light as J.T. drove west along Baseline Road and turned up the sweeping switchbacks of Flagstaff Mountain. Rather than continue to the summit, where doubtless other cars were parked high over the golden gridiron of town and campus, he turned off at its saddle. Apparently he knew the track that coursed along the snow fields beneath overhanging rock outriggers to either side. No one was in sight as he eased to a stop in the shadow of one, turned off lights and engine, embraced Viv and screwed his face into hers.

But Nat was with them. Hanging a hundred yards behind, he extinguished his lights as he followed the Olds off the road. Seeing its brake lights glow, he stopped in the shadow of a rock, got out and began a stealthy approach by foot. Warm updrafts washed over him, though when they failed he froze instantly. Stars spangled the sky—as is obvious at altitude, they were aflame, burning—and the moon cast shadows. Managing his so that it might not brush over his prey, he moved from outcropping to outcropping.

Meanwhile J.T. and Viv got out and levered themselves into the convertible's backseat.

Nat swallowed hard, parched and suffering, as silhouettes merged in shadowplay on the oval rear window. J.T. put his head back and pulled at Viv's, brought hers lower. But it rebounded, and Nat heard her giggle. After an interval of planetary kissing—their heads going round and round—J.T.'s shoulder did something that Viv's repeated.

Nat, hard, couldn't breathe. After weeks obsessing about Viv, fantasizing about her, if never with success, he was face to face with her carnality. But he couldn't make out exactly what she was doing, what was going on; springs squeaked once or twice, but not in any rhythm, and his impression was that she was pulling back, pulling back.

Then the doors opened, Nat ducked, and J.T. and Viv got out, J.T. complaining, "Oh, Viv, and I love you so much." He sounded very disappointed. They got in the front seat and the doors clunked shut.

Exuberant—*J.T. was disappointed!*—Nat trotted back to his car, lowering his head as the Olds passed. He backed up to the road, achieving the pavement with a slide of the rear end. His watch said it was almost midnight, later than he expected. Viv was late! Even in the presumably relaxed circumstances of the semester's last dance, she was late for curfew!

But the Olds squealed up in front of Sewall Hall while girls were still fleeing indoors as if from a sudden shower, and Viv popped out and joined them. When Nat arrived, the scene was deserted.

# 36.

AFTER EXAMS CAME a two-week vacation before the new semester. Nat spent it in Boulder driving extra shifts and reading Marcus Aurelius. Humiliated by Viv's abandoning him at the dance, he felt further aggrieved that she made no effort to apologize. She had no means of doing so, of course — didn't know where he lived — but Nat thought it would not have been beyond the mind of man to find out; just, apparently, beyond the mind of *girl*. Presumably she was home in Denver having fun with her jailbird. He didn't call; she would think him desperate, when clearly she didn't think of him at all.

Thank heaven for the *Meditations*:

> To be vexed at anything that happens is
> a separation of ourselves from nature.

Such wisdom made Nat laugh mirthlessly, like a character out of Wodehouse.

Meanwhile, Viv effortlessly continued to stymie his fantasies. Every night he lay abed, gripping himself and trying to summon her in the accommodating flesh; but her image remained adamant, unresponsive, ideal and fully clothed. Whatever she might be doing for J.T., she refused to do anything for him.

The start of spring semester brought a brief spell of nearly summertime warmth. Dorm casements were thrown open and portable phonographs hoisted to the sills; turned up loud, they sent the hues and blends of the big bands across campus. It stirred Nat both with joy and the frustrating memory of dancing with Viv.

A week in, he happened to run into her late one morning at Old Main's snack bar. She was having coffee between classes, he breakfast after driving his taxi past midnight. They came face to face as he turned from the counter with his tray. Nat clamped his jaw; both blushed furiously. But they sat down together at the only free table.

"Oh, Nat, how grand to see you!" she said, lifting her face from tresses obscuring as a nun's wimple *(write that down!)*. "I feel terrible about what happened. I'm so sorry I left the dance without saying goodbye, or thanking you for taking me. I had such fun."

"That's all right," he said, thoroughly mollified.

"No, it was *rude,* but I was excited to see J.T. after— Anyway, I *am* sorry."

"It's OK," Nat repeated.

Suddenly it was as though they'd been friends for years. He couldn't resist asking if she had fun after the dance, too.

"Oh, yes," she said brightly, and left it at that.

In fact, she'd had a harrowing time of it in the Olds that night, subjected to needs beyond what she was prepared to fill. Rubbing J.T.'s head, she'd yelped, "What did they do to your *hair – ?*" But the brushlike stiffness excited her, and when their tongues met she lost herself. Breathing hard, he pressed a knee against her lap, urgent and specific, and pushed her to the leather. Alarmed, she tried to distract him.

"J.T., now that you're out, what are you going to do?"

Angling his head, eyes and dimples spilled shadow. "I'll be OK."

"Are you — on parole?"

"Nope, served my time. No crossing *i*'s or dotting *t*'s for *me*, I'm a free man. Draft might get me, though. Might *try*." Then he got serious again, and it was all she could do to plead her curfew. It was a near thing. She didn't like to think people subject to such paroxysms of compulsion, and felt half-relieved not to have seen him since; LaCinda had taken her to San Diego for a fortnight's sun.

Nat intended never asking her to another dance, but as she humorously complained about the snack bar's brew — rationing halved the amount of coffee available; made it half as strong but twice as expensive — he told her that Flattop's on The Hill had the best java in town, and suggested they meet there.

But she declined. "You know why," she said.

Then, forgetting his resolution, he asked her to the new semester's first dance that Saturday, again at Balch Field House, this time featuring Woody Herman and His Thundering Herd. She explained she'd already accepted an invitation "from someone else."

For Nat, solo sex that night was particularly frustrating. He wanted to punish her, but Viv's image, though hovering closer than ever, permitted not the least liberty. No one had any fun. But this was love.

OF COURSE NAT couldn't let her go to the dance alone and unprotected.

He parked his cab outside Sewall Hall to watch and wait. Fresh snow was on the ground, and the air was freezing. For an hour—as dusk fell through blues, lilacs and violets in skies vivid as a theatre's cyclorama—he fended off student fares. Then an Oldsmobile convertible pulled up behind him and honked. Indignant heat went through him. *Honked!*

In the mirror he saw his nemesis shouldering into a sheepskin coat as he loped for the loggia, and moments later come out with Viv. She buttoned her coat as they came down the walkway, smiling in dark lipstick, eyes glowing like a cat's—she wasn't wearing glasses—then took his arm. His smile displayed a new front tooth. Nat shielded his face as they passed. He'd been running the engine for the sake of the heater, so was ready to pull out after them. But they took the Olds only a short way, parked in the field house lot and hurried inside.

Nat parked, too. He sat gritting his teeth, frozen, sustained by sips of bourbon until, past 10:00 o'clock, he saw them trot down the steps, run to the Olds and rush off campus.

He followed. Taking the same route as before to Flagstaff Mountain, they roared up the switchbacks. Nat let them go; he knew where they were headed.

And was right: He found them parked along the same track as before, snowfields to either side. Easing the yellow Ford, lights off, into shadows, he turned off the engine and watched the rear window's silhouettes. Viv's gave Nat the impression of unrelenting resistance.

HER HAND REGISTERED something hot and alive, as if an animal were trying to burrow out of his pants and in zipping them open she was abetting its nosings for freedom. His hand closed on hers and made her squeeze, which forced such piteous moans from him that she was reminded of her grandfather's dying gasps.

Squeezing at least staved him off from between her legs,

but there was nothing of *her* in the action, for nothing of *her* seemed wanted. His hand moved hers up and down as he registered a pain so intense he apparently could endure it only by closing his eyes and groaning as though she were stabbing him in the heart. At the crisis, even as he cried out that he loved her, *loved* her, something warm splashed her wrist and the car filled with an organic aroma, not unpleasing, and J.T., moaning contentedly, finally settled down.

BEHIND THEM, NAT grew alarmed as the hands of his watch swept onward. Eleven-thirty passed, 11:45, and he was muttering warnings when the doors opened and Viv and J.T. dived into the front seat and the Olds roared to life. It was 11:50 — surely cutting it too close?

Nat scrambled back to the pavement first. The Olds passed him on the downhill and sped onward. He followed at a more moderate rate, and it was ten past midnight when he cruised up to the front of Sewall Hall. The dorm's gates and doors were closed, the carriage lights off and the Oldsmobile roosting beneath a bare cottonwood in the circular drive, dark and its occupants assessing the situation. Clearly every grace period had expired.

"DON'T WORRY, VIV," J.T. was saying. "We'll get you in the back way."

"The back door? Is it open?"

"Never done it? No, I mean climb up to a window."

"*No!*" She was horrified.

They had pulled up to find Sewall Hall closed and no one around, which confirmed what her watch plainly said, that she had missed curfew and was in trouble. Latecomers were summarily dispatched to a bed in the guarded infirmary, suspended and their parents notified.

The known way around this, what the sluts and slatterns did to get indoors undetected, was to go around, climb up the back of the building and tumble through a window. Sandstone jutted out several inches from the mortar, making the wall climbable. Practice helped, but anyone who kept a cool head could do it.

J.T. led Viv around to where the ground fell away to the ravine and, ten feet overhead, a hallway casement was open. Nat got out of his cab and cautiously followed to within a few yards.

"C'mon, Viv, it's easy, you'll see. I know guys who climb up just for the view."

"But I'm a *girl*."

"I'll give you a boost."

Seeing that he had to intervene, Nat called, *"Don't,* Viv: It's dangerous."

She didn't ask where he'd come from, only said, "But I missed curfew."

"Not the end of the world. Not worth breaking your *leg*. We'll tell your mother tha —"

"The hell's *this?*"

"It's *Nat*, J.T. You met at the dance a few weeks ago."

"Viv, don't be silly," Nat persisted. "We'll get your mother on the phone and she'll square the dragon at the door or, if they send you to the infirmary, we'll —"

*"Asshole!"* J.T. said and — to Nat's utter shock — launched a fist at his nose. "She's with *me*, you bastard."

Gushing blood, Nat reeled backwards and fell. Cold and *wet*, he found himself blinking up at the stars as he pressed his handkerchief to his nose.

J.T. stalked to the wall and interleaved his fingers. "C'mon," he urged. "Take off your shoes."

Bending backwards, Viv looked up the terrifying

stonework, stepped into his hands and was flung upwards. Her fingers scrabbled into jutting rock and found purchase. Her feet likewise gaining toeholds, she pulled herself up, every limb working. After a few seconds, she tumbled through the window.

For a moment, as Viv put out her head to wave goodnight and caught the shoes he tossed up to her, J.T. looked ready to spring upwards, too, Romeo going after Juliet. But she vanished, and J.T., pausing only to spit in Nat's direction, regained the Olds and drove off.

Nat was alone, flat on the ground, trying to stanch the blood, overwhelmed by the sight of Viv's hips pumping her upwards. He lay there wanting to masturbate, before deciding he'd better not; he was freezing, and also he needed to retaliate. But when he scrambled to his feet, his antagonist was gone.

Indoors, Viv went to wash her face and hands, but at the row of washbasins first sniffed at the fish scales that pungently varnished her wrist. She caught a deep-earth essence before letting water grizzle into the edges and wash them away.

WHEN THE BLEEDING finally slowed, Nat, keeping his head back as far as he could, found his cab, faked his run book, added to the till what he had in his pockets, turned in his receipts remarking, "Slow night," admitted he'd caught a drunken customer's fist and delicately carried himself home.

Dan sleeping noisily, Nat addressed himself to his nightly project, reviewing the sight of Viv tackling the wall. Sexiest thing he'd ever seen, that laboring, vulnerable backside? No matter, she remained proof against his lust.

In the morning Dan peered over and asked, "Hell happen to *you?*"

"Fight."

"Who with?"

"Viv's jerk-off boyfriend."

"Sorry to be the one to tell you," Dan said, "but the bastard broke your nose."

Nat got up and looked in the bureau mirror. Turning his head aside to test his profile, he contemplated his image with the first stirrings of joy. The family heirloom was *ruined*. Discolored, swollen, squashed, the Old World treasure gingerly carried across the seas and handed down through generations of Appalachian farmers was now the blunt nose of the Indian chief on the buffalo nickel. Gone was the pensive air of a sensitive and questing soul. The new nose gave Nat gravitas. Made him a new man—his own! Bruises the color of bad meat striped both sides of it, and the blood seeping into his eyes gave them a vampire aspect, but Nat at last was the man he wanted to be.

"I'll make him pay," he told Dan, caressing his nose with veiled delight. "Count on *that*."

"Dad's going to kill you."

It took weeks for the bruising to disappear from his heroic proboscis, but the next time he mentioned to a classmate that he lived on the Navajo Reservation, the response was, "Yeah, I can see the Indian in you."

## 37.

VIV'S CLIMB UP Sewall's wall of course was seen and reported. The next morning Mrs. Wilt, the dorm supervisor, telephoned LaCinda to demand she take Viv home to serve a two-week suspension.

Alice accompanying her, LaCinda immediately drove to Boulder, gas coupons be hanged. She expressed her displeasure in screeching around corners, accelerating like a demon, braking abruptly. Her sister philosophically grabbed hold of the door strap.

"Drama unto the newest generation, Alice!" LaCinda fulminated. "Neither *you* nor *I* nor our *sisters* ever went with a *jailbird*—"

"True, dear, but I believe the light's red."

The car squealed to a stop.

"Why she won't listen, *I* don't know."

"Remember how *we* were, LaCinda?"

"We did whatever Father said!"

"But remember how sweet the Powells' watermelons were? Just like ours, but theirs tasted better because we *stole* them? It *is* a stop sign."

"Thank you."

After a brief, unsatisfactory visit with Mrs. Wilt, they went upstairs, where Buzzy sprawled across her bed, legs keeping time to the radio's swing. Viv's suitcase lay open on the other bed.

"Where is she, Buzzy? Where's *Viv?*"

"In the lav," Buzzy remarked complacently. "Back in a mo."

Indeed, Viv had scrutinized her face in the mirror, refreshed her lipstick, brushed her hair and gone down the corridor. In Sewall Hall, girls primped before visiting the lavatory.

Returning, she opened her door on a frightful scene: her mother, somewhat awry, shouting, "Never in my *life*, Vivian, have I been so *humiliated!*" Buzzy shot her a triumphant look.

"Hello, Mother," Viv said.

"*'Hello, Mother,'*" mocked LaCinda. "If she cared about *Mother* or Mother's peace of *mind*, *Mother* wouldn't have to come all this way, would she, Buzzy?"

"Oh no, Aunt LaCinda."

Sitting down emphatically, LaCinda pushed and pulled at her ensemble. Viv soon found the Pontiac similarly askew, with a smashed headlight and scraped fender.

"Mother, I'm sorry," she said. "Sincerely."

"Who was it, Viv? Who made you do it?"

"What difference does it make?"

"*Who?*"

"Well, if you must know, it was my boyfriend, J.T. Pelletier."

"Knew it!" said LaCinda. "Come on, we're putting you on the train for Kansas."

"You can't do that, Mother!"

"Try me! Can't trust you, evidently. *Told* you I didn't want you seeing him, yet now I find you're *inseparable.*" She peered at Viv with X-ray vision. "Probably *worse.*"

Viv shot scarlet and began to cry. Closing her suitcase, she picked it up and, flanked by mother and aunt, took a walk of shame down the hall, the stairs and out through the forecourt. She could see eyes brimming with speculation and mouths going crosswise, LaCinda meanwhile upright as if not associated with the hunched figure dragging the suitcase. Viv couldn't pretend she didn't care about being regarded as a girl whose body and private uses of that body were community trash.

Asserting herself sufficiently to insist, Viv drove them home (Alice was glad). Nothing more was said about Union Station.

"When I forbade you to see J.T. Pelletier, it wasn't any whim of mine," LaCinda declared. "Not any whim of your witchy old *mother's* who was never young *herself.* He's fast, he's unreliable, has a criminal record and been in *prison.* Just *which* of these qualities is so very *irresistible?*"

"Though we can see why you find him attractive, dear," Alice put in.

"Why can't you be a good girl like Buzzy?" LaCinda asked severely. "She never gets into these scrapes."

Viv looked at her sharply, but apparently LaCinda spoke sincerely. In fact, Buzzy emphatically was *not* a good girl, a fact celebrated among C.U.'s men. For Viv to room with her risked her own reputation.

At home she vanished into her bedroom.

## 38.

THE SISTERS CONVENED at LaCinda's that evening, going into emergency conclave at the kitchen's bay window while their husbands waited in the living room and their daughters in Viv's room.

They made sandwiches and iced tea, carried a tray out to the husbands, another to Viv's room, and returned, closing the swinging door. The husbands knew the rules, squelched discussion about their wives whenever the door opened, laughed heartily after it closed again and never, under any circumstances, complained.

In Viv's room the cousins shrouded themselves in Artie Shaw's woodwinds and percussion, though one or another went out from time to time for more iced tea. Whenever that happened, the sisters fell silent.

LaCinda looked around her pretty kitchen before laying out the evening's topic for discussion. It was papered in daffodils and hung with flower prints; even the linoleum featured squashed yellow blossoms. The sisters sipped iced tea from rose-painted glasses, which they replaced on rose-printed placemats. But LaCinda's powder had all it could do to fill the creases of displeasure around her mouth.

"I forbade her to see him," she said gravely, "which only made her determined to see him more than ever, thank you very much. That's what she thinks of *me!*"

"Remember when Father told me not to see Frank Austin ever again?" Alice asked. "Not under any circumstances?"

Frank Austin's offense—lounging in the sunny altogether on a fence beside a pond where he *knew* farm girls would come upon him—could not be mentioned in mixed company.

"Point is, I went on seeing him behind Father's back. LaCinda, forbid Viv to see J.T. and I *guarantee*—"

"Alice, he's a *convict*. Been in trouble already, and headed for worse. Remember the picture in the paper? That snarl? That *undershirt?* Viv's my *daughter*—"

"Henrietta says Martha says Viv says he told her he loves her," said Ida.

"*Love!*" scoffed LaCinda.

Violet said, "Martha says Buzzy says Viv says he has a *tattoo.*"

LaCinda went white.

"Eagle on his calf," Violet added comfortably. "Got it in prison."

"My God," muttered LaCinda.

"He's *wild,*" said Mary.

"But so good-looking," said Alice. "I like him myself."

LaCinda smiled grimly to signify the ill-advisability of a woman's liking a handsome man.

"This war, LaCinda," said Mary. "It'll either straighten him out or kill him. And whatever comes, Nature will take its course, you can be sure of that."

"*Nature!*" said LaCinda. "I know about Nature. Nature just wants *babies.*"

That truth sobered them all. Having delivered to Nature a girl apiece, each had quietly—without notice to the priests—

prevented Her from making further ravages.

"No, my mind's made up. It's time to send Viv to Brother at the farm. I hope you all agree."

They did not. They knew that farm—knew its demands, its loneliness, the yearning to be anywhere away from it. Her sisters protested at length, and in the end LaCinda remitted her decree. Viv would not be exiled unless she saw J.T. Pelletier again.

Then they discussed how to let Viv know of their final, unanimous, unappealable decision.

"I'll tell her," said LaCinda, pushing back her chair. "I'll just *tell* her."

"Let us," said Alice, restraining her. "Let Ida and me do it."

LaCinda sat back as they got up to deliver the edict. It was a quite usual method in the family. The messengers crossed the living room while their menfolk fell silent and looked serious, and knocked on Viv's door.

Unsurprised, Viv opened it and the aunts stepped into the bedroom, loud now with Glenn Miller. Two cousins sprawled atop the bed, another in the chair, another on the rug. One turned the music down.

"Viv, can we speak to you, please? Alone?"

"This is fine, Aunt Alice. We know why you're here."

"Then you'll understand your mother's concern," said Alice, sitting down on the bed beside her and taking her hand. "She's decided *not* to send you to your uncle Earl, not unless you see J.T. Pelletier again—even one more time, mind. You can continue at the University, but you're to concentrate on your studies the rest of the semester and not go out."

Her cousins gasped, and looked to see how Viv took it.

"But I love him, *I love him*," she shrieked.

Everyone started crying.

"Well, if he loves *you*, he's just going to have to wait until you're both 21," said Alice. "That's how old you have to be in Colorado to marry without parental permission. It's less than three years."

"Oh, Aunt *Alice*. Everyone says J.T.'s so bad, but what's he ever done that's *bad?*"

Ida sucked in her breath. "He stole a *car*, Vivian. They *caught* him and sent him to *prison*."

"Why can't people go easy on him? He'll be going off to fight one of these days."

"Oh Viv!" keened Alice. "*Viv!*"

When Alice and Ida returned through the living room, patting Kleenex to their eyes, their husbands rattled ice in anticipation.

LaCinda asked, "How did it go?"

"We could hear some of it in here," Mary added.

"Viv's a good girl, LaCinda," Alice said. "Go easy on her."

Soon the husbands were glad to learn they could collect wives and daughters and go home.

Viv's home stay was dismal. She kept to her room, doing her class reading and studying, but had hardly a moment to herself, for LaCinda took to opening her door at frequent intervals to peer in disapprovingly, before stalking off in the marked manner of One Who Knows.

At first Viv hoped for some kind of thrilling intervention — for J.T. to come through a window and carry her off, something like that. But no such thing happened.

Her only excursions were to attend the aunts' usual brunches and dinners, the identical event wherever held, each the replica of that the day before and the image of that to take place on the morrow. In after years she could not abide the taste of potato salad.

Having learned of her suspension — he'd gone by Sewall Hall in search of her — Nat called the house. LaCinda spoke rather warmly, remembering her impression of him from Thanksgiving, but did not call Viv to the phone. Instead she told him, "Viv's not going on any dates this semester."

"Oh, Mrs. Halderman, *none?*" He sounded so crushed LaCinda smiled. But she did not relent.

Though to her cousins Viv proclaimed defiance and love everlasting, in fact J.T.'s backseat importunities had scared her, and her hands-and-knees climb up the wall humiliated her. Having to do what bad girls did?

The day before she returned to campus, a postcard dropped through the door, fortunately while her mother was in the bath. On textured paper, it pictured a red-tiled adobe church, figures in sombreros and serapes napping on the steps. On the other side, next to a gaudy stamp, was a scrawl:

> *Hi Viv! Missing you down here Old Mexico way.*
> *Know they're neutral? Might sit out the war!*
> > > *Love, J.T.*

Fingering the postcard, she didn't cry, but it felt like a blow—felt *mean*.

## 39.

WITH ALICE'S HELP, LaCinda re-installed Viv in Sewall Hall. Viv unpacked her things under Buzzy's skeptical gaze, then joined her cousin on her bed paging through *Life* magazine. They ran fingers through their hair with a vast indifference.

Viv resumed the life of the wartime coed. There was some catching up to do but, as before, she found her classes enjoyable and absorbing. Meanwhile, she held up her head and, like any seven days' wonder, her infamy began to wear off.

One evening Nat again braved the females of Sewall Hall, his nose sporting its last yellow bruise.

"Oh, *Nat*," Viv said. "Did *he* do *that?*"

"It's nothing."

"Not that it looks *bad.*" And in her sympathy, when Nat suggested coffee at Flattop's, she agreed.

They met there the next day, and enjoyed themselves. The java good by comparison, Nat comported himself like a perfect gentleman and Viv found herself contrasting his behavior favorably with J.T.'s.

She wanted his reaction to something, she said, and handed him J.T.'s postcard. What did he think it meant?

Gravely, he studied it. "Off with the *banditos,* I expect."

She started to say, "That's what *I* thought!" when she saw he was kidding.

At least they shared a smile.

"But sitting out the war," Nat said, shaking his head. "Don't know about *that.*"

"I *know.*"

After lingering over their empty cups, they made a date to meet again a week hence. Neither felt that meeting for coffee violated her mother's edict against dating or could be construed as being unfaithful to J.T. *Coffee?*

So it was a regular thing. They met every Thursday at three o'clock. Nat might grab an hour from work, arrive in the cab. If she beat him there, Viv would feel anxious, though she knew it was silly. Then he'd run in, doffing his brimmed cap, and they would share a brilliant smile, before reverting to companionable quiet. If he arrived first, he would return to the sidewalk and peer up and down 13th Street for her, to Flattop's consternation wringing his cap. And when she got there, he'd be so happy, and she'd return his smile, and they'd sit down, silent until Flattop took their order. Grateful for the chance to say something, they'd ask for coffee, perhaps bread pudding, then fumble for some topic to talk about—the war, classes. Both knew it would be wrong and a mistake to express any interest in, much less any claim on, the other.

With the last crumbs scraped up, silence would fall again until, bringing out money to pay the bill—he insisted—Nat suggested, "Next week?" and Viv said, "All right."

So through March and April, Nat and Viv saw each other regularly. She didn't feel it right to speak of J.T. to Nat, but he always asked if she'd heard from him. The answer was no. Whenever she said no, Nat suggested he'd be a better boyfriend than J.T.

She didn't dispute it; after all, it was true. J.T. wasn't even around, and when he *was*, he took advantage. Being pawed at in his car, involved in his closed-eyed clenches and spasms? Causing her name to be bandied about? Sometimes in Sewall's dining hall or living room or bathrooms she still intercepted knowing looks of the kind that hurt. Then he leaves the *country?*

And meanwhile she was in school and so was Nat, serious people studying for serious futures. While J.T. was off in Old Mexico with his *banditos?*

His *señoritas*, more likely.

ON APRIL 25 the sisters enjoyed Easter brunch at The Promontory, for once without their daughters. There was a new busboy, 40 years old. After they had quizzed their waiter about the previous one — he refused even to remember whom they were talking about — conversation centered on Viv.

"Martha says Buzzy says Viv says *he's* in Mexico," said Violet. "She got a postcard."

"Good, hope he stays there!" said LaCinda, to whom this was news. She scowled outdoors, where snows reached deep into the valleys.

"What if she goes down *there?*"

"Never! And he's a fool if he thinks she'll carry his torch forever."

"*Such* a dreamboat, though, LaCinda," ventured Mary.

"Don't be silly, Mary. Yes, *now*, looks nice *now*, grant you, but in a few years' time? *Bald.* Soon he'll be *bald,* and *soft,* and *thick,* and *stiff*—what other men are. Nothing to write home about."

Mary blushed; as it happened, her bald husband's belly was bulging as though he'd swallowed a bowling ball.

"Martha says Buzzy says Viv says she has coffee sometimes

with another boy."

"Oh, really?" This also was news.

"Buzzy's met him. Name's *Nat*. Very serious. Wears glasses."

"Coffee, eh?" But LaCinda was thoughtful. "You know, I might have spoken on the phone with this young man."

"After you told her no dates!"

"Something tells me it's summer on the farm for Viv!"

"Coffee?" repeated LaCinda.

Viv was surprised when, on the phone that evening, her mother said she wished to meet Nat.

"*Nat?* How do you know about *Nat?* He's just a student, Mother. Mother, I'm busy with *papers* and *exams* and –"

"Nonetheless, let's find the time, shall we? Say, dinner on Friday?"

# 40.

NAT BROUGHT VIV in his Yellow Cab to the bus station to meet LaCinda and whisk her off to dinner at Normandy Farms, the town's fine French restaurant.

Coming off her bus, LaCinda saw her daughter holding hands with a tall young man in spectacles. Viv looked nervous, but he in his herringbone jacket struck her as, if ludicrously young, confident and determined.

He stepped up but waited to present his hand until she put hers out (she noted the good manners) and presented her with a Whitman's Sampler; that hit the target. She had to look up to thank him; he stood taller than six feet, though skinny, with dark hair swept back from a good brow and good features. His strong nose reminded her of photographs of Geronimo.

LaCinda had taken cool care with her own appearance: the gray suit, pearl necklace and earrings, blue coat and hat, fox stole, powder pressed veil-like over her features. She thought Viv, by contrast, unnecessarily insignificant in a cotton print, eyes aglow behind the weird contact lenses.

Nat handed LaCinda into the back of his cab, and Viv slipped in beside her. At a stoplight on Pearl Street he was astonished to find in his mirror a magnificent Lincoln

Continental convertible, top down, black but so begrimed with red clay as to seem transported from the Navajo Reservation. On the bumper he could make out a Texas license plate.

The instant the light turned green, the Lincoln honked. Startled, Nat looked again, and saw J.T. Pelletier smiling lopsidedly, fingers splayed on the wheel.

Nat flicked his eyes towards Viv in the mirror, and she caught on right away. Sneaking a backwards look, she turned around again gripping her purse with a shocked, "*Oh!*"

"What is it, Viv?"

"Nothing, Mother — a new store there. Dress store."

"This town always strikes me as being well-off."

"Oh, it is."

The drive was not a long one. Nat pulled up under the restaurant's porte-cochère, the Lincoln taking a space near by.

Doffing his cap, Nat opened LaCinda's door. "Ma'am."

Favorably impressed, she said, "Thank you. What do I owe you, young man?"

Nat was shocked. "*Nothing*, Mrs. Halderman. Dinner's my treat, too."

"No, that *cannot* be."

"Mrs. Halderman, you're my guest," he repeated firmly. "Ladies, if you'll please step inside, I'll go park."

Nat ran the Ford around near J.T.'s car. Smoothing his hair as he trotted back, he ignored J.T. and J.T. ignored him.

"Now, then," Nat said proprietarily, offering LaCinda his arm.

The atmospheric room had a beamed ceiling and rough-plastered walls. An enormous fireplace dominated the far end. Red-checked cloths covered the tables, which bore candles stuck in wine bottles covered in rivulets of parti-colored wax. Nat had never been before — too rich for his pocket — but liked what he saw: the Faience-ware and copper platters and bellows hanging on the walls, the painted tiles inset into them, bowls filled with flowers, the well-dressed diners scattered about.

A hostess in Norman peasant costume greeted them and escorted them to just the table beside the fireplace LaCinda would have chosen, positioned so as to survey the room. On the table minefields of cutlery flanked brightly painted cover plates. LaCinda looked around approvingly as Nat pushed in her chair.

The menu, too, elicited her gratified murmurs. Its cover was a charming sketch of buxom peasant lasses in a farmyard teeming with plump animals vying for a place at the table. The inside was printed in red type resembling a copperplate hand and ornamented with Norman motifs.

The waitress — garbed as a milkmaid — took drink orders: one Manhattan, one Shirley Temple, for Nat a martini.

"The *canard à l'orange* here is good, they say," Viv remarked.

"Too fattening," LaCinda declared tunefully.

She continued her perusal, trying to penetrate Nat's demeanor. Though good-looking, he lacked the fatal beauty of a J.T. Pelletier or Harry Halderman; the mere sight of him did not quicken the pulse. But that was good. *Beware the handsome man.* Meanwhile his serious mien amused her.

LaCinda ordered escargots, a salad with bleu cheese dressing, filet mignon (medium) with roast *pommes de terre* and creamed spinach. Viv had the same, while Nat ordered *joue de boeuf* and — as behooved him who was paying — *teurgoule* as dessert for the table.

He saw LaCinda's eyes flash with pleasure at his open-handedness (although reading in them also the continued intention of paying). Viv sat between them placidly offering supportive chirps while Nat attended to her mother exclusively.

Who quite enjoyed herself. LaCinda felt born to the role of grande dame, and though lacking some perquisites of the class—namely the dead rich husband (hers being alive and remarried, her grandeur in fact derived from a receding status in a Kansas farm town), it was fun to have at hand a susceptible youth to impress. And that youth quite enjoyed playing up to her.

"Tell me about your people, Ned."

"*Nat*, Mother."

"Nat."

"Nathan Micajah Handler, ma'am. Well, my father's principal of the Indian Service high school at Krux, New Mexico—"

"Are you an Indian yourself?" she asked.

"No, ma'am. Scotch-Irish and English, on his side. He was born in Tennessee, moved to Texas as a boy. On my mother's side English and some German. I'm named for her father: blacksmith, Indian fighter, buffalo hunter and rancher. She was born in Texas, where her brothers are marshals and sheriffs. She was a schoolteacher, too, ma'am, but she died."

He couldn't say it without tears welling up and looking in confusion at Viv, who put a hand to his arm. His answers were good, but even better the way he and Viv glanced at each other for guidance and support. On the surface the man dominated, but LaCinda sensed room in their relationship for the woman's contribution, that Viv helped fuel the intensity with which Nat looked back at LaCinda. She apprehended something of their bond.

"And what are your plans?"

"I'm a writer, ma'am."

"That's a *plan?*"

"Last year I was at Cornell University on an engineering

scholarship, but discovered that's not what I want to do. Taking different courses now. Probably going to pursue journalism."

"Do you have brothers and sisters?"

Nat told her about Dan's being pre-med, and how Junior at Ohio State had already been co-opted by the Navy for top-secret research on specialty waxes for aircraft-carrier radars; when he tried to enlist—Junior felt he *had* to enlist—M.P.s escorted him back to campus.

"Will *you* enlist, or wait to be drafted?"

"Ma'am, I'm already eighteen, so they can draft me any time they want, but at least I'll have this year of college under my belt. Keep going till they take me, I expect."

He told her about Escalante Academy, knowing she'd like the boarding-school note, and how his mother had been friends with the famous "two Ruths," the pioneering anthropologists Ruth Benedict and Ruth Bunzel, and also with Mabel Dodge Luhan of scandalous Santa Fe and Taos associations; when LaCinda expressed uncertainty as to whether she knew the name, he said casually, "You know, D.H. Lawrence's lover?"

"What religion do you follow, if I might ask?"

"Well, I'm Protestant, I guess, but don't belong to a church. Neither does my father. His people were Cumberland Presbyterian. Mom was Methodist."

"Well, *we're* Roman Catholic. If Viv has children, she's to raise them in the Church."

"Oh, yes, Mrs. Halderman, I quite understand." What Nat understood was that she had made an essential concession. He shot Viv a smile of triumph. She almost choked.

Meanwhile she kept putting in, "He's very smart, Mother. . . . Works hard, Mother, but never complains."

The food was exceptionally good, the conversation

reassuring. LaCinda, having had two cocktails, and wine with her meal, displayed a vivaciousness her daughter found alarming.

When her mother excused herself to go to the ladies room, Viv lagged behind for a moment. "She likes you, Nat, I can tell."

"Viv, I know how to deal with her, if you wouldn't always be butting in with your little, *'He's such a darling, Mother.'*"

"I'm just trying —"

"Will you please just dry up? Tonight's *important.*"

LaCinda apparently noticed nothing amiss.

When, after *teurgoule* and coffee and, brandy suggested and declined, the check at last was lodged at Nat's elbow, LaCinda with perfect timing — waiting until he lifted his hand — picked it up with a flourish.

"Believe me," she told the chagrinned young man, "I can afford it better than you."

Viv beaming, Nat graciously acceded.

LaCinda and Viv lit cigarettes and Nat, asking their permission, his pipe; he hoped it gave him distinction.

The light was finally failing when he brought round the taxi. Twenty paces off, J.T. lounged against the Lincoln's fender — the top up now — arms and legs crossed, torso crooked as his smile. For Viv, seeing him there was as jarring as coming out from a movie matinee and finding that ordinary daily life has been going on the while.

"Viv, surely that isn't J.T. Pelletier over there?" LaCinda asked primly.

"Gosh, what's *he* doing here?"

"I wonder," her mother said dryly. "Back from Mexico?"

"I guess."

Nat offered to drive LaCinda home, but she wouldn't hear of it, and he had to parry her shrewd questions about how he had the cab for personal use, anyway. After first, at LaCinda's request, driving past his boarding house ("Very nice"), he ferried them to the bus station. On the way, Nat's mirror told him that J.T. was following.

They waited in the terminal's harsh light, which made the yellow Ford distinctly blue. When the bus, green by day, pulled in, the lights made it violet.

Having bought for LaCinda the latest issue of *Orbs* magazine—General Patton glared from the cover—Nat and Viv saw her aboard. They waved as the bus huffed away, Nat putting a hand to Viv's waist.

"*Whew,*" he said. "I'm tuckered out. But went pretty well, considering. Come on, run you back to campus."

## 41.

VIV WAS GETTING INTO the cab's front seat when a Lincoln Continental cut in front. From ten feet ahead J.T. called, "Hey, Taxiboy! Tell my girl I want her."

"She's with me, dammit!"

J.T. jumped out, opened Viv's door and yanked her out of Nat's grasp.

"C'mon, Viv," he ordered. Tapping his hip, he told Nat, "Get you *good* next time, Taxiboy."

He stuffed Viv in the driver's side of his car, never letting go. She scooted across to the other side and sat up straight. Nat rushed up to her door, but J.T. gunned the engine and, tires squealing, the car charged ahead, gouging the turfy verge and going over the curb as he turned it north on Broadway.

Nat followed, foot to the floor.

"VIV, YOU'RE MY LADY, remember? *Love* you. Told you that, right?"

"Yes, J.T."

"Love *me?*"

"You're *trouble*, J.T." It came out in a small voice. But *there*, she'd said it at last. "You've been in prison—"

"All over now."

"*Over? How?*"

"Saw a judge today."

"A judge!"

"Getting tired of it. Said it's jail or enlist."

"Oh, J.T.!"

"Have till tomorrow noon to live it up." The car swerved as he touched his lips to hers. Sneering, he asked, "Why isn't Taxiboy in uniform, anyway? Flat feet? Hernia? The four eyes?"

"Draft hasn't gotten him yet, that's all."

"Know there's a dance at The Elks tonight?"

"I don't feel like dancing, J.T."

"Don't feel like *dancing?* You *OK,* Viv?" He placed cool fingers to her forehead.

"I'm fine, just. . . *last* time. . . ."

"Yeah?"

"Nice girls don't park. Mother would be *horrified.* I'm not allowed to see you, anyway—not since you got me *suspended.*"

"But for my last night?"

"Oh J.T.!" Her face caved with concern.

"Viv, I'm in love with you. Didn't know anyone could be so beautiful, and nice, and smart. Know I'll never meet a better girl."

"Oh J.T."

"And, look, we're all in the same boat. Between Hitler and Roosevelt, who knows what's going to happen? Have to work things out, hope for the best. That's why before I die. . . I want. . . just *once*. . . with *you.*"

"J.T., I'm not in love with you any more."

"*No?* Who with, then? Not *Taxiboy.*" He looked over, grinning.

"As a matter of fact, yes, I think I am."

His grin faded when a car honked behind them and, startled, he glanced into the mirror.

"Jesus, *chasing* us? Good for Taxiboy!" Flinging hair from his eyes—it was longer now, had a dashing life of its own—he sped up. "Let's see what your *boyfriend's* made of. Not much, I don't think."

Careering through a red light, he headed up Mt. Sanitas into a sedate bungalow neighborhood, powering through stop signs and without difficulty losing Nat.

But soon a red light was revolving in his mirror and a siren blaring. J.T. came alive. Ignoring half a dozen more stop signs, he maneuvered back to Broadway and through downtown towards campus. Near Pearl another cruiser joined the chase. Past Arapahoe yet another intercepted the Lincoln, making J.T. skid it across four lanes and steer up Baseline Road for Flagstaff Mountain.

"They're after me now. *Shit*, nice car but too damn *showy*. Kiss me, Viv."

"J.T., slow down!"

He didn't, but took his kiss anyway as they roared up the first long switchback, seeming to hang right over the town and its slew of sirens. Tires shrieking, they rounded onto the next. From behind the mountain the sirens seemed echoes from out of the past, muffled, meaningless, moot. The air smelled of pine, and the sky was clear and starry.

But on the next switchback a police car, probably a juiced-up one, came into view.

"Viv! Steer for me, OK?" said J.T., staring into the mirror.

"No, how can I—?" But when he took his hands off the wheel she reached over and managed to keep the car on the road while J.T. pulled a .38 automatic from his waistband.

"J.T.! Where'd you get *that*?"

"*Steer*, dammit!"

Aiming rearwards out the window, he pulled the trigger. The recoil made his hand fly, but he cackled with delight at the muzzle flash, cones of red and yellow flame. Viv was screaming as he took the wheel back.

The police car fell away, and J.T. wrestled the Lincoln, lights out, off the road onto the mountain's rocky shoulder. After jouncing several hundred yards, he turned up the slope, leaning forward to urge the car *up up up* until it faltered and, its rear working sideways, stalled.

"Let's go, Viv!" he said, pulling her out and slamming the door. "Won't be needing *this* any more."

"J.T.! You're scaring me!"

"Hurry up!" He yanked her up the talus slope. Their feet dug down twice or thrice for every step they gained. When the slope evened out he pushed her to the ground and, breathing hard, got on top of her and kissed her. She turned her face away. "Come on, Viv," he said. "Just once, while we can."

But to his surprise, she fought back, mute but fierce, scratching his face and pulling at his hair and, as a siren howled, scrambled out from under him and fled downhill. Before finding her footing she fell on her seat, then got up and skipped downhill as in a fairy tale, each giant step releasing little landslides. Headlights were rushing up, and revolving red lights.

"Run for it, Viv!" J.T. yelled. Another cruiser rounded a rock formation, its siren dying in a slow whine as, guns drawn, men clambered out and came running, or trying to: The scree that covered the ground made everything take place in cartoonish slow motion. Overwhelmed, Viv fell on her seat again and sat there not moving.

Several cops made attempts at J.T.'s outcropping, but slipped back down. New sirens keened, an ambulance arrived and more police cars. From one a lieutenant aglitter with brass got out. First one and then a second searchlight found J.T. When he dodged behind an outcropping, his shadow was still projected onto higher rocks behind.

Nat's cab pushed up to the group, and he came out of it with arms raised. Nodding up to where Viv sat hugging herself, crying, he said, "That's my girl." But they wouldn't let him go to her.

J.T. emerged against the sky. Legs angled, both hands holding the gun away from his body, he reeled against the stars. Turning to watch, Viv was reminded of the newspaper photo after his arrest. He aimed at the stars and aimed at the cars, twisting, flipping his hair, enacting a kind of dance, fluid, expressive, graceful, as searchlights swerved after him.

"Son, throw down the gun!" yelled the lieutenant. Handed a megaphone, he repeated: "Throw it down, son!"

"Make me, you fat old man!" came the response. *"Make me!"*

"Come on, son, don't do anything stupid!"

*"J.T.!"* yelled Viv. *"J.T.!"*

J.T. drew himself up and, looking overhead, fired at the stars, a bouquet of flame lighting up his face as he emitted the high-pitched squeal of a boy having fun. Rifles and pistols were brought to bear, but the lieutenant muttered, "Hold your fire."

Then J.T. sighted down his gun at them.

*"Pow!"* he shouted. *"Pow! Pow!"*

Though everybody flinched, no one took action.

Gurgling with joy, J.T. aimed at the lieutenant and pulled the trigger. The shot missed, but a ricochet struck sparks on a rock inches away.

"Oh, shit," said the lieutenant.

Sighing, he rested his revolver on his upraised forearm, aimed and fired. Half a dozen other policemen fired, too. Their hits registered in J.T.'s improvised choreography as he jerked backwards and forwards, shuffling as he tried to keep his balance, ending in an extended moment of equipoise, his expression one purely of surprise. Stretching his arms out to the side, he pulled the trigger again in a single blossom of flame, and crumpled into shadow. Viv cried out, and Nat broke away and—feet rapidly stabbing the scree—climbed up and folded her in his arms.

"Careful, guys," someone said as everyone moved upwards.

Soon a cop came down again to ask the ambulance to advance as far as it could and bring a gurney. Attendants scurried up the slope—their feet going into the talus sounded like they were digging a grave—and lifted J.T.'s body onto a stretcher. His head settled comfortably against his raised shoulder, eyes upturned to the stars, one side of his mouth open in a bloody smile beneath the scratches in his cheek. They carried him down the slope, past Viv and Nat—standing together as if carved from stone—and loaded him into the ambulance, where they closed his eyes and mouth.

Nat watched the proceedings dry-eyed while comforting the weeping Viv. "So that's death," he thought. "Stupid to *want* it. *Stupid.*"

Viv's arms tight around him, what *he* wanted was to sink into her, merge with her. As he hugged her, his erection mistimed but sincere, Nat felt his personal mysteries dissolving, eroded and worn away by every ordinary thing it would take to love her, keep her and raise up her children. In the end, though you have to rely on yourself, you can't rely on yourself *alone*.

Without haste the ambulance drove to the hospital morgue. Behind it a cop drove the Lincoln to the police station and, as ordered, Nat and Viv followed in the Yellow Cab.

## 42.

A LONG NIGHT FOLLOWED. "What a waste," cops told one another. At dawn, eyeing her with sympathy and him with disdain, they turned Viv and Nat loose. A policeman drove her to Sewall Hall and quelled the doorkeeper's remonstrances. Too tired to return his cab to the depot, Nat drove it home, not caring whether he was fired.

J.T.'s funeral was held at Christ Commander, a big, barn-like space paneled in blond wood, with stations of the cross in blue and gold and a rouged Jesus lolling on a big crucifix. Against custom, the children of Christ Commander School were *not* brought over to fill up the church. Aged Msg. Flynn made short work of the requiem Mass, taking pains in his eulogy to exempt Mr. and Mrs. Pelletier from responsibility for their son.

"What is written on the heart we cannot know, after all, so let us think the best," he urged, "that John-Thomas, had he lived to fulfill his Army obligation, would have redeemed his youthful mischief. God saw fit to take him to Himself, however, so we shall never know. Let us pray."

Burial was private, cousins lugging the coffin to its hole while his parents looked on. Fortunately, Catholics are better equipped than those of some faiths to lose their young.

Viv did not attend the funeral. For weeks she wandered in a daze. Dormmates tittered when she passed; having her boyfriend shot to death in a gun battle with police enhanced her notoriety by an order of magnitude. It was fortunate she had her studies to help her ignore the whispers and pointed fingers. Buzzy cattily asserted that Aunt LaCinda was jealous of the romantic passion her daughter had inspired. Nat did lose his Yellow Cab job, so was with Viv every possible moment—in Old Main, Norlin, Dan's car, at Flattop's. In spring's surest sign a late blizzard whitewashed the campus.

They never really talked about it. Though young people, contrary to reputation, often are more vividly aware of death than they will be again for a long time, there seemed nothing to say.

Classes ended, and on the first day of exams, midway through coffee at Flattop's Nat broke off his discussion of latest events in the Pacific to suggest they get married. Viv agreeing, Nat went on to analyze the European theatre.

The day exams finished, Nat borrowed Dan's Chevy, as well as gas coupons from their friends, and drove for Nebraska with Viv. Night fell before they made the border. In the event, they got lost, and the border they finally crossed was Kansas's. Looking for a town of sufficient size to boast a justice of the peace, they came across a courthouse in the middle of a town square.

At the only business still open, a diner called the Manhattan Cafe—a two-story devil snaked up its wall in red neon, complete unto pulsating horns—they got the address of the justice of the peace. He was in bed—it was past 9:00—but good-naturedly got up and agreed to perform the ceremony if Nat recruited witnesses from the diner.

He did so, the JP filled out a license, collected fees for it and his services and, yawning, married them on his parlor's Brussels carpet. It was as well they'd gotten lost, for in Kansas, unlike in Nebraska, marrying at 18 required neither parental consent nor a blood test.

A grandfather clock struck its intimations of doom as rings were called for. There were no rings. Cigar bands were resorted to as the usual expedient, and the ceremony completed with a kiss.

Back at the diner, bride and groom enjoyed cherry pie on the house, and Viv lifted her contacts out of her aching eyes. Then, the cashier urging haste, as it was past closing time, she fed nickels into the pay phone beside the counter.

"Hello?"

"Hello, *Mother?*"

"Who is this?" LaCinda demanded.

"Mother, it's *me*. I'm with *Nat*. We're in Kansas, Mother, and we just got *married!*"

Silence, and a gush of breath.

"Married," confirmed LaCinda. "Well, you might have waited, Viv. You're so young."

"Mother, I'm *18!*"

"But Nat's a good man. Congratulations and all that."

"We'll see you tomorrow, Mother."

"Call first."

The diner customers lamented the town's lack of a hotel — in harvest season, the general store rented out rooms upstairs, but it wasn't harvest time, and no offers were forthcoming. Accepting a fresh Thermos of coffee, Nat and Viv said goodbye and turned the Chevy around. They were in sight of the Flatirons as the sun struck them red beneath mountains frosted pink, and almost home when it began to burnish the wheatfields.

Nat rousted his brother and went to bed with his wife. Although they were both exhausted, he took immediate possession.

# III.

# *New York*

## 43.

VIV HANDLER WOKE UP in the muffled, tall-ceilinged stillness, and for a moment hugged to herself the unlikely characters and combinations of her dream. Then the clock-radio buzzed. She and Nat both reached blindly to silence it, their fingers twining each other's, familiar and dry. A modulated voice began speaking. Time and date flashed unseen: *7:15 am Thu 3-31-83.*

Opening her eyes, she registered the dimness, turned — disintegrating the last warmth of something forever irretrievable — and heaved to her feet. Her day began: *now.*

She walked through bedroom and dressing room to the bright bathroom, whose frosted windows fronted an airshaft. They hadn't renovated it; she loved it as it was, a fine chamber of white porcelain fixtures, delicately crackled, made for a race of giants in 1929, the year that endowed New York with so many confident structures. Hexagonal mosaic tiles covered the floor and brick-sized white ones went halfway up the walls.

Then out and around two corners to the kitchen. Cigarettes vied with coffee, but she made the coffee first, a drip Mr. Coffee she wasn't sure she liked: Flavor all right, but the first cup cooler than the hot blast she craved. Standing beside the gurgling machine, she lit a Kent and breathed it in as she admired her new cabinets, new appliances, new Corian counters, new pass-through that converted the maid's room to a breakfast room.

Nat was slower. He had a head, felt logy. He was drinking too much—he knew it. Kept pouring through an evening, inured to bourbon's more pleasant effects, but somehow needing the head-hammering quality of a full evening at it as he ended his day trying to focus on his green-screened PC.

Already he'd twice updated the year-old machine, nervously snapping expansion cards onto the motherboard to achieve a massive 256 kilobytes of RAM (from the original 16kb!), and plugged in a second floppy-disk drive to boot. Coaxing its modem to communicate with *Ducats'* mainframe could, in case of success, result in a story chugging in to his study in mere minutes, and allow him to click at the keys, editing, until bedtime, while Viv watched a movie on TV or paged through magazines or read Trollope or Hillerman.

So he lay for a few minutes before deciding he might as well get up.

Coming into the kitchen, he barked, "Morning."

"Morning," she returned. "How do you feel?"

"Fine," he said. The question always annoyed him, and she always asked it.

She took coffee and cigarette out to the dining room—Nat had abruptly stopped smoking eight years earlier, thinking it silly to be still smoking at 50, and after his Herculean if invisible struggles she didn't want to inflict her smoke on him—and sat down at the head of the table. Her face slack, she looked outdoors. The cliffs of the Palisades across the river were topped with thin green beneath an overcast sky. Spring was coming, April but a day away. A tanker draped in rust worked upstream. In this day and age it seemed unlikely commerce could draw ships up the Hudson, but they passed every day.

Nat retrieved the *Times* from the elevator lobby, dropped off the *Arts* section beside her and sat down to coffee at the breakfast table. Viv got up to pour herself another cup but, deeming herself sufficiently awake, drank only half before filling a bowl with Cheerios and slicing a banana; or not Cheerios, but Fairway's house brand of toasted oats.

She was thinking of the day to come, one of the busiest of the year—a group arriving before noon, in advance of Easter weekend, to join the three that had arrived yesterday and the day before that. Four groups in town! Meldover College's itinerary was well in hand—complete, pending confirmation of one final appointment; she'd type it up, take it to the copy shop and give it to Phil, her boss. Thursday of a long weekend? Phil might want to get out of town, have her meet the group and address the kids herself. She'd done it before, and Meldover's leader, Father Donellan, was her favorite client, but—always shy—she hoped not to have to today.

What she didn't worry much about was what everyone else imagined would keep her terrorized 24 hours a day: the dreadful things that can happen to people in New York City. Classroom/New York hadn't lost one yet. Astonishing: Students—teenagers, many of them—coming to New York for five days and four nights in their groups of 12 to 25 and getting out alive!

Fingers crossed. Knock on wood.

Well, there was the professor last year whose purse was yanked off her arm as she walked down 8th Avenue, so was reviewing mugshots of known purse snatchers at the West 54th St. precinct while her group saw Zoe Caldwell in *Medea*.

Nat retired to the bathroom with the Op-Ed page. When he

returned 20 minutes later he was shaved, his hair wet. Expression was stealing into Viv's face now, but Nat's was unreadable as he put bread in the toaster and rummaged for marmalade.

Couldn't do so without remembering a regrettable episode from before they moved to town. The youngest was temporarily back in the nest, and one morning, having tried and failed to halve a frozen English muffin, Jimmy dropped it in the toaster with the knife jammed in it like the sword in the stone. The toaster of course singed and melted the handle of Nat's mother's bone-handled bread knife, one of his few relics of her. His cold anger helped Jimmy decide the next day to hitchhike west, where he'd stayed ever since.

Viv was watching crows in Riverside Park. They reminded her of northern Westchester, where, towards sunset, crows would flock up and down the treetops beneath their view. She understood this supposed mystery of Nature, why they circled and collected in trees, cawing delightedly, before dissolving and flying off, only to engage again: It was delight in being together, celebrating release and relief from the pain of being alone; for there's no place lonelier than a suburb, unless it be a city.

For some reason she thought of the coma she accidentally drank herself into one summer weekend in Katonah, unwarily mixing vodka with her doctor's sedatives.

She lit another cigarette. Here she was now, snug in her New York co-op. The saga of how they found it was a milestone in her life, not only because of the harrowing race to buy before the market could price them out, but because it brought her and Nat the closest they ever came to fighting.

They'd moved to the city in 1977, at first renting in a post-war building on Second Avenue in Kips Bay. But a few years later, finding Manhattan life convenient and interesting, they began to contemplate buying. And woke up to the fact that the market was surging; New York's latest revival was under way.

In those days, no Manhattan residence had yet sold for so much as a million dollars—no 35-room apartment on Park Avenue, no East 60s limestone mansion, no floorthrough overlooking Central Park. But prices were rising fast. Their budget—give or take $100,000—allowed Viv to view properties on Park and Fifth (generally overlooking Lex or Mad), Central Park West or Beekman Place. Not much was on the market at any given moment—as few as three dozen of the newly popular co-ops, which of course helped prices shoot skyward. She and her real-estate agent ransacked the island every day, Viv taking mornings or afternoons off from work, her panic such that when the actor Gig Young shot his wife and himself, her first thought was of the newly vacant two-bedroom in the Osborne.

Nat and Viv didn't fight—never had: *Never.* Instead, they had evolved (of course tacitly) a tensile arrangement that allowed them to live within a bubble of peace, even as their avoidance of conflict could fuel flames around them.

One evening she suggested that Nat, too, take time off work and accompany her to view apartments, or even go without her, as she was so busy.

"I'm busy too," he snapped.

*Fight!*

It marked an epoch. Neither said another word, but within days they put down a deposit on a two-bedroom penthouse on West End Avenue. But when their son Jack, who lived in the city, though not with them, found it poorly laid out and told them, "You don't want to live there," they looked at each other and saw it was true. They lost the deposit without regret.

So more looking while the market exploded, Viv's heart racing as though under bombardment, brought them to a building on Riverside Drive boasting more writers than lawyers, a "classic six" that stretched out over 2,000 square feet. They bought it for $120,000. Renovating the kitchen cost another $17,000, but supposedly the place was already worth twice what they'd paid.

She crushed the butt into the ashtray, stood up and returned to the bathroom. After a shower, moving rapidly around the dressing room she donned a contemporary businesswoman's ensemble, navy blue skirt and jacket with white ruffled blouse, and the sneakers made acceptable street wear for women by the 1980 subway strike; she would change shoes at the office.

In a good woolen suit of blue pinstripes from Syms, Nat had more coffee while reading the *Times*.

Viv entered the breakfast room with a step that dragged, indicating her readiness. But Nat offered her a section and she sat down and for some minutes they read in silence. Then he wiped his mouth, carried dishes to the sink, brushed his teeth, pulled up his tie, shouldered into his jacket, in the foyer helped Viv into her lined raincoat, heaved himself into his epauletted trenchcoat and picked up his briefcase (containing last evening's work) and collapsible umbrella. He thought it looked like rain; she disagreed, but had an umbrella at the office just in case.

She opened the heavy front door. No sound came from the other apartment off the elevator. Their neighbor was an elderly English actress of distinction, still active, though seldom at this hour, just past 9:00 in the morning. Finding the shared lobby rather dingy, Viv had suggested to their neighbor that they re-do it and, reassured by her posh accent, let her choose the wallpaper. Every day now she had to endure its lurid silver blossoms.

Nat closed the door with a definitive *clunk!* They were off.

## 44.

EXPRESSIONS KEYED TO THE scrutiny of the streets, they emerged from the elevator and moved with purpose through the lobby, as always thinking it could use some work—floor and walls marble, but a plain space even so; but could consensus among the owners (and a hefty assessment) improve it beyond some decorator's beaded window treatments or calculated placement of pillows?

"Morning, Rueben," Nat called ahead, and the doorman smiled and gave it back in a Puerto Rican accent with an attractive soft slur, and had the door open for them.

"How are you, Rueben?" Viv asked.

"Fine, Mrs. Handler, how are you?"

Out on 78th Street, choices loomed. They were headed for the OrbsCorp Tower on Sixth Avenue at 50th, 28 blocks south and six blocks east; Viv would continue to her office at Madison and 41st. So, Nat figured, 6 x 28 possible routes to his office? Another 2 x 9 to hers? (Not to mention shortcuts through or under Rockefeller Center?) Not a cold day, but brisk and fresh, so not the Drive, where the breeze could pin one to the wall. Without a word, then, they turned up the steep block to West End, past brownstone stoops and areaways, in hopes of finding sun on Broadway. At the corner, caddywampus (as Viv would put it) from the Apthorp — remembering they'd looked there, but chose a view instead — they assessed the traffic and, the light against them anyway, turned down West End, overtaking boys slinking, late, to Collegiate School.

At 76th they crossed West End in obedience to a green light and continued to Broadway; they often allowed the lights to govern their route, lend it randomness.

On Broadway they were at loose in the bazaar. People were shopping, visiting, ambulating with no easily guessable purpose, no obvious impetus. In the median between racing lanes of cars, newspapers and plastic bags were carried on the wind to be trapped, flailing, against iron railings. The center benches, guarded by parading pigeons, already held a complement of the elderly, who — rather like vampires — infused energy from the action and noise that surrounded them.

It reminded Nat of the Grand Trunk Road that Kipling's *Kim* travels, with

> a troop of long-haired, strong-scented Sansis with baskets of lizards, their lean dogs sniffing at their heels. Behind them, walking wide and stiffly, the memory of his leg-irons still on him, strode one newly released from jail. Here and there they were overtaken by gaily dressed crowds turning out to some local fair, the boys flashing sun into the eyes of their betters from toy mirrors amid a smell of marigold and jasmine stronger even than the reek of the dust.

It was all there, the homeless man sensibly dressed in smelly layers critically assessing trash cans, the blue-uniformed cop on the beat sensibly declining to intervene in a

Korean fruit-market dispute, the couple staring open-mouthed at the fish in Citarella's window, the elderly men in yarmulkes outside a milk bar, the young woman in Spandex dodging along at a proclamatory jog. Shopkeepers plied hoses over the sidewalk, keeping a nominally attentive eye out for the ankles of passers-by, injecting dust into the air and pushing tides of grime and litter to the curb and down the gratings where rumbled the city's lifeblood, the No. 1 train.

Viv and Nat walked in step at that rapid pace seen, in America, only in New York. As they herded each other down the street, bright and alert, speaking infrequently, their passage aroused curiosity.

For they made for rather an extraordinary sight. Nat's hair mostly silver but full, his strong, handsome face lived up to its Indian-chief nose. (One evening at Columbus Circle his son Jack thought he saw him, albeit with a younger woman, and non-judgmentally was about to greet him, when he realized it wasn't his Dad at all but the movie star Kevin McCarthy.) Viv was trim—she credited walking to work more than her chronic diet—her face unlined, her hair without gray, tortoiseshell frames a stylish match for Nat's, purse secure in her grip. Both were 58.

Striding along, Nat curbside to Viv, they seemed very much of the city, if perhaps not native to it; there was some distance to their intimacy more reminiscent of the West or Midwest than of New York.

"Easter Parade," Viv said suddenly. The *Times* had had a piece. "Sunday? Never been. We should do it."

"Sure," said Nat. "Have a bonnet?"

They crossed 72nd and then Amsterdam, staying with Broadway's diagonal through a series of wide-angled crossings that called for extra alertness to traffic. Midtown's mass rose ahead of them, closer at the rate of a block a minute.

For a few moments it sprinkled, but Nat didn't bother opening his umbrella. Newer apartment houses soaring overhead, the sidewalk began to assume a going-to-work air, men and women striding along hauling briefcases. At 65th, accepting the light's suggestion, they turned down a different spoke—Columbus Avenue—passing Lincoln Center's travertine temples, Fordham's bland outpost and a Navajo-patterned orange-brick storage tower that rose like a New Mexico butte. A young man, long haired and beautiful, a dancer perhaps, hurried past, registering amusement as Nat, the observer of people, turned his head to look. The young man smirked.

Columbus becoming Ninth Avenue, they passed the huge barn of St. Paul's, Roosevelt Hospital, Channel 13, thrift stores, pizzerias, an A&P supermarket. At 54th Street the light turned them onto one of the most unnerving blocks along their route. To their left were old tenements and recording studios and a church, to their right an enormous municipal bus garage—converted from stables of horse-drawn-omnibus days—plus the old night court and a precinct house with green-domed lanterns flanking its door.

Crossing Eighth Avenue, they made up the short block to Broadway, passing the old Studio 54, back in business under new management, but its grille at this hour pulled shut. On the other side of the street one morning they saw Spaulding Gray pacing in front of the Hit Factory, steadfastly refusing to take notice of their looks of recognition.

They turned the corner beneath the elderly Bryant Hotel, home to Senegalese street vendors who kept their milk cool on the window ledges, passed the Ed Sullivan Theatre (long dark), and progressed down an unglamorous stretch featuring old towers of modulated massing and sheer new ones that abutted empty plazas. The real hurly-burly began, the outskirts of Times Square—the theatres, restaurants, bars, junky going-out-of-business electronics stores.

Near 52nd, Nat stopped abruptly. Viv stumbled onwards a step before rounding on him in perplexity, panting slightly. He stood meditatively, thoughts frozen by the odd fact, slow to register, that his umbrella's hooked end had caught the cuff-loop of a passing sleeve. The sleeve's owner stopped, too, he knew not why, for an instant turned towards Nat a yearning expression, before realization curled his lip and he snarled, "Be careful."

"Sorry," Nat said to him, and to Viv, as they re-entered the sidewalk's flurry, "Oops."

At 50th Street, they turned east, towards the OrbsCorp Tower, renamed after the company's big bet on cable TV. (Internally, staffers smacked their lips on OrbsCorp's terminal *p*, but New Yorkers accorded it the same *faux* French they gave Citicorp after it completed its slant-roofed skyscraper: *Citicore, OrbsCore*.)

Food carts were being positioned along 50th Street's wide sidewalk. They found their guy and ordered regular coffees. Served with a flourish, they stood in the stream of foot traffic sipping from cups printed I♥NY®. Viv also had a cruller, which she regretted even as she enjoyed it.

"Busy day?" Nat asked.

"*Very*," she replied. "But tomorrow's Friday."

"Long weekend, for some," he said.

"Not for me," she said. "Call me later?"

"I'll call you." They were going out for dinner and a show that night so as to beat the worst Easter crowds.

They said, "*Bye*," and their lips met. He caught a whiff of the breath of a woman who never passed the gas that yet must escape her body; but he was used to it.

He walked to the revolving doors and gravely stepped into

one, with his usual flashback to being a teenaged runaway intimidated by the original Orbs Building across the street and by the spectacle of New Yorkers who knew just where to go and what to do and how to do it. Now he was one of them.

But he frowned, startled, when Viv pushed giggling in after him. The heavens had opened up.

## 45.

THE LOBBY WAS JUMPING. The famous planetary system commissioned from Alexander Calder swooped and revolved overhead and across glass walls in chromium, bronze and papier-mâché, dipping from the mezzanines into the escalators, demonstrating not only *Orbs'* founder's piety but his ambition. (In fact, the solar system deviated from accuracy with the planet Mercury, which one day had bopped an unsuspecting man on the back of his head and sent him sprawling; the orbit's lateral angle was quietly altered.)

Dripping, Viv got on a down escalator that whisked her through an asteroid belt of crystal and painted linen, and she and Nat called to each other, *"Have a good one!"* hanging ironic quotation marks around the cant phrase.

A minute later Nat was stepping off at the 31st floor, greeted in *Ducats'* lobby by oils that had graced its cover. Walking past Arshile Gorky's dreamy oil refinery and Léger's lyrical steel mill, he nodded at the receptionist, turned and continued to the end of the hallway. Panels woven of metallic fibers — very high end, circa 1960 — and more covers alternated with white-oak doors and glass. Overhead fluorescents off, the hallway was dim, lighted by desk lamps and office windows.

Though downstairs at *Orbs* magazine ceilings sprouted forests of pencils flipped into them by blocked writers, *Ducats'* ceilings were clear.

He went past his secretary's empty desk into his office, blinds still lowered against the setting sun of the day before. A handsome room, made personal by a framed note from Robert Kennedy praising his coverage of a civil rights episode, a blow-up of the 1960 *Orbs* photograph showing Nat interviewing JFK over the caption *Handler & Kennedy*, and a Peanuts cartoon on yellowed newsprint, Snoopy instructing the fledgling Woodstock, "Forget the fancy stuff, just fly!" A magazine editor's credo.

Nat bore no title beyond that of member of the Board of Editors—named to it and let in on a happy stream of stock options in the late '60s—but his office was a big one on Editors Row, complete with the two window bays accorded editors, although to accommodate both one wall angled inward so as to give the Assistant Managing Editor next door the square footage merited by such a personage.

Hanging up coat and suit jacket, Nat cruised out to the kitchen at an inside corner of the corridors, where a hush greeted his seniority. With an affable nod, he poured himself coffee in a *Ducats* mug.

On the way back he ran into his Managing Editor.

"Lunch today," Hank said. On the last Thursday of the month, *Ducats'* Board of Editors met for its sole actual function—lunch—to grill a guest of honor in the 50th-floor dining room. Today's was the CEO of computer giant Datality, Inc.; a special day indeed. "Any questions ready?"

"Just the obvious ones, why they missed their earnings, and aren't they missing the boat on the PC business."

"Good," said Hank. "Not that he'll like them."

"We'll see what he says."

"Well—leave it to our Howard Hughes man."
Smiling, Nat carried the mug to his office.

## 46.

THE CONCOURSE WAS already crowded, more joining the pedestrian flood at every staircase and escalator, a fluorescent-lighted world lined by shoe-repair shops, nail salons and fast-food outlets, as well as vacant storefronts papered over with cheery posters.

Viv moved along confidently. There's glamour to cutting through underground Manhattan, finessing the streets as only a New Yorker who knows where she's going can do. At Rockefeller Center's farthest outpost, Fifth Avenue and 47th, she ascended to the ground-level lobby and looked out at rain pummeling the street. Finding a scarf in her coat pocket, she knotted it over her head and, after a wave of rain arced past, dashed outdoors in its lee and crossed Fifth.

Descending damp concrete stairs partway to Madison, she entered the Grand Central tunnel system. No stores, just wet floors as she worked against a tide of men in raincoats. Keeping her eyes straight ahead and unfocused so as not to risk eye contact—those dangerous moments of unintended engagement—a few minutes later she was walking up a ramp into the terminal's glorious chamber beneath the ceiling starscape, galaxies painted, not as seen in the skies, but as in looking towards Earth from deep space; an idea, she thought, that would occur only to a Vanderbilt.

The view under Park Avenue's viaduct showed the downpour continuing, so she went down another ramp, crossed beneath 42nd Street and climbed steps spangled with trodden circles of chewing gum to the Lincoln Building's lobby. Crystal chandeliers overhead, she passed Daniel Chester French's model of the seated Lincoln and telephone booths that her boss told her had served many of the unemployed as offices during the Great Depression, and looked out at 41st Street.

There, although not convinced there was not a final tunnel connection kept locked up for no reason, she had to brave the outdoors again. Awaiting a brief easing of the shower, she crossed and entered the side door to her own building, 295 Mad, a brick Art Deco skyscraper with a ruddy stone top that resembled a ciborium, another of 1929's jubilations.

Going into the coffeeshop, Viv exchanged greetings with the counter girl and, unwrapping her scarf, ordered coffee and a toasted, buttered corn muffin—her secret vice. Warm bag in hand, she found the elevators, framed in bronze with floor indicators glowing under sheets of onyx. Viv imagined the whole lobby to have been originally thus grand, but in the 1950s it apparently seemed a good idea to lay down asphalt tile and string fluorescent tubes overhead.

Upstairs, the 13th floor was leased to a public relations firm with a bankerly name, but most of the space sublet to small operations like Classroom/New York. The PR firm's receptionist handled phone messages for the suite.

"Morning, Jewell," Viv greeted her.

"Morning, Viv."

The closed double doors to Jewell's boss's office depriving her of the perfectly-coifed, clenched-teeth smile usually on offer, Viv stepped smartly down the corridor.

# 47.

OUR HOWARD HUGHES MAN; a sobriquet of course more mocking than respectful, Nat thought as he greeted Hannah, his secretary, and raised his blinds. Gray light oozed into the room from a commanding view of Times Square's tar and gravel rooftops, water towers and backs of billboards.

He earned it in this wise: Long ago in Grand Junction, he'd known a character named Charlie Scone. Charlie was a uranium prospector, a common enough thing in 1950s Colorado, but unusual for that strange breed in that he had a good Eastern education in geology and a theory that flew in the face of everybody else's about where to find ore. Whereas his rivals scrambled across the Southwest randomly applying Geiger counters to weathered rocks in hopes of setting off a mad clicking, Charlie Scone didn't even own a Geiger counter. He couldn't afford one. But he pursued his theory with a prophet's single-minded obsessiveness over the wide-open landscape in a war-surplus Jeep with a second-hand drill rig mounted on the back.

Charlie had a wife, three children and no money. When Nat and Viv met them, the wife and kids were sheltering in a shack of silvery planks in a ghost town on the Utah border and sometimes subsisted on sugar water. Horrified — she thought a mother had no right to subject her children to deprivation — Viv used to take over sacks of groceries.

One day, having drilled in ground that looked promising to no one else, Charlie staked a claim and brought samples to the assay office. Hysterically chattering Geiger counters confirmed his discovery of a vast underground shoal of uranium.

Charlie stopped by the *Daily Item* that gray January morning to tip off Nat to the great find. Nat and a photographer piled into his car and off they sped. An hour later they had the pictures, Charlie Scone photographed in the mud grinning in vindication, and Nat broke the story, his first national scoop. (Of course, when the Associated Press reported in a teletyped paragraph Rosa Parks' arrest for refusing to give up her bus seat, Nat asked for amplification, as any subscriber could, and was gratified when, filled out with additional detail, that story took off, too.)

Overnight, Charlie Scone was one of the richest men in the country; estimates of his worth ranged north of $50 million. Now that he could live anywhere, he built a mansion with columns and swimming pool in Las Vegas, hired servants, settled millions in trust on his wife and children, and commenced living a life of leisure.

What Charlie Scone didn't do was pay his taxes. Hence over the next 15 years the IRS seized all his assets except the family trusts and house. Still, the Scones lived leisurely on, even if Charlie had to skim the pool himself.

Nat assumed Charlie Scone was out of his life until one afternoon in 1967 when he picked up his phone and found himself talking to him.

"Now look, Nat, calling at someone's suggestion," Charlie had told him.

"Who's that, Charlie?"

"Get to that. Point is, they're exploding atomic bombs every damn week at the Nevada Test Site. Know that's not even 80 miles away? Makes Vegas shake like Jell-O."

"Reminder of uranium royalties, I should have thought, Charlie."

"Howard Hughes lives in the penthouse of the Desert Inn? Shakes like shit every time. Doesn't like it."

"You know Howard *Hughes?" Merely the richest man in the world.*

"Wouldn't say *that,* Nat, not really, but we're in touch because he wants you to get the government to move the testing."

Nat was charmed. "Really, Charlie? Howard Hughes thinks *I* could do that? I'm flattered!"

"Publicity, Nat. Point is, it's bad for tourism, this shaking, and if radiation ever leaked —"

"There's nothing I can do. Promise you."

"Now, Nat, Mr. Hughes knows that if *anyone* can do this, *Nat Handler —*"

"*Charlie, Charlie:* Nothing I can do. What you want — what *Hughes* wants — is to get to your Senators, get to the President. Which I have no doubt he can do. But the Nevada Test Site's the only one we have, would take a *huge —*"

The phone clicked in his ear. Scone had hung up.

Still chuckling, Nat went home, intending to write a memo about the call when he got to the office the next morning. He sympathized with Hughes' not liking the shaking. It reminded him of the time his mother took a nursing course in Santa Fe. Whenever an execution was scheduled at the State Penitentiary there, she would sit in the dark rather than have the lights sputter and buzz as the electric chair stole current. Once was enough.

On his way in to work the next morning, he stopped for a haircut from Manuel at the Joseph Cione Salon in the concourse. He admired Manuel's expertise and was grateful not to be chatted up. They merely exchanged friendly greetings and, at Nat's good tip, mutual thanks.

But today, after pinning a paper collar around his neck, tucking a striped sheet over him and taking a preliminary snip of his locks, Manuel said, "Mr. Handler?"

"Yes, Manuel?" asked Nat, startled.

"Did you know I used to live in California?"

"No, no idea."

"Los Angeles. *Hollywood*, to be exact, back when it *was* Hollywood."

"Is that right?"

"Wife was a hoofer? One day she's imitating Al Jolson when the man himself walks in behind her. Everyone holds their breath, but he laughs!"

"Amazing!"

"Bela Lugosi used to come in my shop. Good customer, Mr. Lugosi, and a nice guy. Always came with the Swedish Angel — his bodyguard who kept him off the drugs. *Tried*.

"Before that I was the barber at RKO."

"Really!" Nat was beginning to be interested.

"In those days Howard Hughes owned the studio. Wonderful man, Mr. Hughes."

Nat felt sudden misgivings. "Is he?"

"Asked me to be his personal barber. Would have done it, too, but cutting just one head? Not for me. Like cutting hair, I really do."

"I understand."

"Point is, Mr. Handler, Mr. Hughes needs a favor —"

"Manuel, I can't do it," said Nat.

"About the testing?"

"Nothing I can do. He should call the President."

Manuel reverted to silence.

Upstairs, Nat typed up a memo to his Managing Editor about phone call and haircut. Hence the sobriquet. His somewhat isolated aura — he'd ended up *Ducats'* house gadfly and house liberal — was not harmed by his also being, for one glorious moment, Howard Hughes' go-to guy.

Later it emerged that after Hughes dispatched aides to various politicians, the AEC, in *Project Faultless*, exploded a bomb a hundred miles farther away; Las Vegas didn't feel a thing. But then Hughes moved to Central America and testing resumed at the old site, until it stopped for good.

## 48.

VIV'S WAS THE FOURTH desk down, set end-wise against the airshaft windows, opposite her boss's closed door. Helen was at her desk just past Viv's; theirs were the only ones along the windows in use.

"Got to go," Helen said into her phone, and hung up as Viv arrived. "Oh, good morning, Vivian."

"Morning, Helen."

"Phil's not in yet."

"Thanks," said Viv, putting down coffee and muffin. She'd gathered as much from his closed door. She unlocked it, turned on the light, hung up her coat and surveyed the room: All was in order. Small and square, crowded with filing cabinets, its sash windows looked across Madison at another building whose windows needed washing.

At her own desk—brighter now, with Phil's door open— Viv put her purse in a drawer, locked it, and changed her shoes. The airshaft looked into the next-door offices of Young & Rubicam, the advertising agency, where youthful antics were often on display. One day cries of hilarity carried as men played catch with water balloons, and the frequent office parties were a voyeur's delight. Helen monitored the Y&R

situation whenever she could bring herself to suspend her scrutiny of Viv.

Helen traveled daily to Manhattan from a far-off corner of Queens, whence, according to her, no one but herself was ever known to go to "the city." She carried herself with the dignity of an envoy. Manhattan gave her the opportunity to study such alien species as Viv and, of course, to perfect her appearance to its standards. In her late 30s, she was pretty, if, to Viv's eye, overly made-up.

"Busy day?" Helen asked with the assurance of someone with nothing to do. She worked for a seldom-seen accountant; in four years, Viv had met him twice. On closer view, Helen's desk was half work surface, half dressing table. To one side stood ranked a red/blue/purple spectrum of nail polishes, balanced on the other by flesh/pink/red tubes of lip gloss and cans of hair lacquer.

"*Very* busy," Viv answered, picking up her phone. Wanting to know how things stood with her groups, she called Sherry at the Westphalia Hotel.

Meanwhile, with the care of a duelist offered choice of weapons, Helen selected an emery board and commenced filing a nail while she listened to Viv's half of the conversation.

"Hi, Sherry, Viv Handler. . . . Fine, thanks, and you. . . . ? Bus should be on its way as we speak. How's Dillinger, and Teasdale? And Woodhouse. . . . ? Oh no, *really?* Oh, Sherry, I hate when they do that. They know, two to a room — it's what sets us apart from the competition."

Its competitors assigned three, even four students to a room at the comparatively ramshackle hotels they used, but Classroom/New York put up its groups two to a room at the Westphalia, plus a room for the leader; but Sherry had just informed Viv that three had slept in one Woodhouse College room: They had a freeloader, someone whose name was not on the rooming list, but who doubtless was tagging along to seminars and appointments. Then again, it was clear Sherry wasn't going to charge extra, and at least no one had asked Viv to supply the stowaway with theatre tickets.

They hung up.

"Customers giving trouble?" Helen asked from an acetone haze. She was glazing her nails. Ignoring her, Viv dialed her contact at The Players. She needed to confirm that last appointment.

"Henry? Viv at Classroom/New York. . . . Oh, thanks, hoping it'd come through! Monday morning at 10:00? They'll be there!"

It so pleased her to think of her students touring Edwin Booth's Gramercy Park mansion, agog at relics of the American stage. Turning on her Selectric, she rapidly typed up Meldover's schedule, now complete. She had a format, typing in capital letters the venue—for instance, THE PLAYERS CLUB—plus its address, the appointment's time and the name of the person they were to ask for, followed in italics by a transportation suggestion: *Take 42nd Street IRT Times Square Shuttle (intersection of 43rd St. & 7th Ave., enter NW corner) one stop to Grand Central, transfer to downtown IRT No. 3, get off at third stop (23rd St.), walk three blocks south, one and a half blocks east.*

A phone call interrupted her, the bus company saying its driver was en route to JFK to meet Meldover. She was grateful for the reassurance.

Also interrupted by Helen, but Viv was adept at ignoring her. Generally she lobbed over one or two all-purpose apologies every day. "Sorry, Helen, were you speaking to me? So sorry, I must have been concentrating."

And these sufficed. Did Helen ever feel like the caller to a radio show still talking when the theme music swells for a commercial? Apparently not; she seemed oblivious to hints as she sat grooming herself the livelong day.

When her own phone rang, Helen was greedily breathing dibutylphthalate, but fortunately one hand was dry enough for her to pick it up and in her broad Queens accent say, "Good morning, Trasker Accounting, to whom may I direct your call?"

# 49.

NAT'S MAJOR TASK that day was to begin editing *Ducats'* next cover story, a treatise on the state of the economy by its chief economist, Sidney Bunsen. It had landed on his desk just before he went home the day before; he'd left it until he was fresh.

His task was two-fold. First, he had to follow the argument, buttress and sharpen it where indicated, rein it in where needed, subject it, too, to his trademark skepticism. On a staff of true believers, Nat stood out as a questioner of doctrine, a trait, however irritating, that was useful on thumb-sucking pieces like this one.

And he had to make it English. Sidney was a genius, a legendary business seer, revered in some quarters as postwar American prosperity's chief prophet, and for almost the magazine's entire history the authority behind its Olympian — and usually correct — pronouncements. But his early dry style long since had given way to breezy and sometimes inscrutable formulations. Fortunately, Nat enjoyed tussling with his prose, holding the argument's structure in mind while pulling it into readable form word by word.

Not quite blind or deaf — door open, he unconsciously

monitored the general pace and mood of Editor's Row—Nat started to read. Immediately he was startled: Sidney was announcing that 1983's first quarter—ending that very day—had seen an economic leap forward that promised to make the 1980s a decade of growth to rival the 1960s.

This was not orthodox thought. The economic moment was difficult. The country had fought—no one could remember why—a long, bloody, losing war in Viet Nam that gutted the economy. President Johnson and his successors failed to pay for it directly, through higher taxes; instead they allowed wave after wave of inflation to shield its costs from view while stagnating the economy. After treading water through the 1970s, the economy suffered a devastating recession: In 1980 inflation reached *13.5%* and, in the new Reagan Administration's convulsions to tame it, unemployment by December 1982 surged to *10.8%* and the prime interest rate to *21.5%*. Most people found themselves behind where they were ten years earlier, and the cleavage between the topmost and the rest had begun to widen.

But Sidney Bunsen was proclaiming that stagnation was *over,* inflation *conquered,* the Reagan recession *ended* and economically it was *clear sailing ahead.*

Nat's phone rang. Picking it up, he instantly transferred his full attention. He was the only one on Editors Row who answered his own phone.

"Nat, *Tony Duchess!* How ya *doin'?"*

Duchess' call was an annual event. Every June *Ducats* published a list of the richest Americans—the *Ducats Top Tier*—and its omission of his name year after year was a running grievance with Tony Duchess. The list made lip-smacking reading for those who liked that sort of thing, studded with Rockefellers and Fords, Mellons, Watsons, Basses, Timkens, Gettys, lately Waltons. For several years past

Nat had overseen the researchers who compiled it and, ferreting out the most interesting stories connected to it, assigned and edited a half dozen sidebars.

He brought gifts of his own to the list. When the OrbsCorp morgue yielded only a single fuzzy photograph of D.K. Ludwig—one of the country's three living billionaires—it was Nat who, after investigating, assigned a photographer to capture him pushing a walker from his station wagon into Burlington House; Nat who laid hands on the insurance magnate C.V. Starr's funeral program, from which it was impossible not to deduce that *nobody*—not even (or especially?) the underlings at AIG he made multi-millionaires—had *liked* the man.

Tony Duchess billed himself as New York's youngest billionaire. He was a real-estate developer whose self-made greatness was—in his own mind—not impinged upon by the fact that his father owned 5,000 outer-borough apartments. Certainly he was the city's *noisiest* citizen, every day figuring in the tabloids. His crowning achievement was building Duchess Tower at (he boasted) Fifth Avenue and 57th Street, although one could stand at any corner of that intersection without finding oneself within half a block of it, just as he exaggerated its height by ten stories on grounds no one understood.

For Nat, Duchess with his combover and fat face classed himself for all time very early on when he gave a tabloid interview in a stretch limo he'd rented to go shopping at Barneys. He was a rich kid with mean little eyes and no more breadth than the envy he worked so hard to rouse in others, with a proclivity for debt, lawsuits and bankruptcy.

"Nat, just trying to do ya a *favor*, man," Tony Duchess was saying. "Could call your Editor-in-Chief, ya know."

"He'd just bounce you back to me, Tony." Duchess insisted

that Nat call him Tony.

"Nat, you know and I know, without my name on it your *Top Tier* will *suck!* Reputation'll go right in the *toilet!* No one'll even want to be *on* it, it'll lose so much prestige!"

"Tony, did you know *prestige* is derived from *prestidigitation?* Which, if you think about it—"

"And in the end, Nat—*sorry!*—maybe put you out of a *job!* You like your job?"

"Tony, Tony, Tony: It's simple: You don't have enough money to be on our list. Call yourself a billionaire all you like, we find more *debts* than *assets.* Last year you were in the hole by what, a hundred million? This year—give you that—seems less, but somebody who, when you add it all up, *owes* the banks money—has a *negative* net worth—is just not *Top Tier* material."

Duchess didn't get it. He protested until Nat suggested devoting a sidebar to his own peculiar finances, when he hastily got off the line. Nat hung up refreshed and amused.

Twirling his chair around for a minute he watched the city take its licking from the rain, then returned to Sidney Bunsen's piece.

## 50.

VIV LOVED HER JOB. She'd gone to work after the kids left home just to stay busy. In Westchester she was secretary to a firm of fire-protection engineers, where she read Trollope all day, except when there was a client report to prepare and she had to type like the devil.

She met Phil through mutual friends soon after moving to the city when he happened to be looking for an assistant. The job was a perfect match. It seemed to her a privilege to be discovering and exploring New York City even as she helped student visitors do the same.

Meldover College, for example, was making a Theatre Visit – her favorite – and as she typed up its program Viv thought with satisfaction of suggesting to Father Donellan what shows to see, the kinds of appointments that might prove interesting and educational, then buying the tickets, making hotel reservations and arranging those appointments, which often involved playing phone tag for days and repeatedly having to explain Classroom/New York's mission; but in most cases getting the acceptance.

Meldover had some treats in store. They were to see two Broadway shows – *Brighton Beach Memoirs* and *Agnes of God* –

and three Off-Broadway: *Cloud Nine, True West* and the Classic Stage Company's *Henry IV, Part 1*. Moreover, after three of the performances cast members had agreed to stay on and chat with the group. In addition to the guided tour of The Players, they would make a jaunt over to Eaves Brooks in Long Island City, where costumes from *My Fair Lady* and *Hello, Dolly!* would be pulled out for them to see. They would also visit a scene builders' shop on Eleventh Avenue to tour vast lofts echoing with hammers and saws as glamorous new sets came together, as well as—a first for Classroom/New York—a 14th Street studio where artists would show them how they made puppets and props; peripheral to theatre proper, perhaps, but friends of her son Jack's.

Fashion Merchandising visits vied with Theatre as the company's bread and butter. No enthusiast, Viv nonetheless felt pleased at having made contacts at the Bob Mackie, Geoffrey Beene and Angel Estrada showrooms, even at Calvin Klein's (if only the underwear division), not to mention F.I.T., Celanese House, the Color Board and Alpaca Board.

Classroom/New York groups got a lot for their money, Viv reflected as she gathered the pages of Meldover's program.

Meanwhile, Helen, pastmistress of the art of speaking in a voice inaudible three feet away, murmured on the telephone; Viv figured it an invitation to think she was talking about *her*, but thought it more likely Helen was merely dispatching the latest bulletins on Manhattan life to remotest Queens.

"Back in a few," Viv told her.

Helen raised an eyebrow as if granting permission reluctantly. "All right," she said.

Downstairs, Viv went into the copyshop off the lobby.

"*Hey*-a, Viv, what you got for us?" asked the counterman.

"Another program, Ali. Need this soon as possible, please. Twenty copies, stapled?"

266

"You got it."

She returned upstairs, used the grubby ladies room near the elevators and re-entered the suite. Jewell ripped an oblong of yellow paper off a pad and handed it to her.

"Your son just called," she said. "He'll be downstairs at noon."

"Oh, good. Thanks, Jewell."

Back at her desk she lit a cigarette. One thing she and Helen had firmly in common was that both smoked.

"Your phone rang," said Helen, interrupting her own conversation. Viv preferred that Jewell answer her phone, if need be, although Viv answered Helen's when the occasion arose.

"Yes, thanks."

Cocking her head against the telephone handset, Helen resumed looking into her mirror.

A few moments later Viv's boss bustled in.

"Morning, Viv, how's it going?"

She followed Phil into his office to report that everything seemed fine with the Easter groups, that Meldover was landing and its program at the copyshop. Still in his coat, he sat down and pulled out the company checkbook.

"Great, Viv, but can you please talk to 'em for me? Judith wants to cut out to the mountains early."

Viv gulped. "Yes, guess I can."

"Good. In that case, be on my way."

He handed her the check for Nolan Bucher, their theatre consultant, who would address Meldover at its arrival, and got up and left, radiating smiles.

Phil had founded Classroom/New York a decade earlier after knocking about for years in PR jobs. Dog-eat-dog business, that of tour operator, especially in the N.Y. student-group segment, long dominated by two established firms. But

Phil came up with a twist, incentivizing faculty leaders to bring groups to town by making their own airfare and hotel rooms free. It was simple: He priced the visits so students subsidized teachers.

That he happened to know the Bergen County family that owned the Westphalia Hotel was a stroke of luck. It was a respectable Times Square warren of 500 rooms built (inevitably) in 1929—15 stories of pale, if sooty, brick topped by another five of ogive-arched dormers poking out from oxidized green copper, one of those self-consciously dramatic rooflines New York builders once delighted in.

The Westphalia prospered in the decades when the neighborhood was a tourist lodestar; after Times Square became better avoided, the hotel suffered but survived. It took care in choosing its guests, willing to endure a low occupancy rate for the sake of tranquility, confident in the long-term value of the underlying real estate. The man who built it left it to his daughter, and her husband long managed it. Its low rates were the backbone of Classroom/New York's pricing.

Now two things were happening: After several lean years—nothing hits students' disposable income like a recession!—this year was proving unexpectedly fat; Viv guessed Phil would net $50,000 by June, and he was *out*. Soon as the end-of-semester groups had been and gone, he meant to retire to his house in the Catskills. Moreover, he was selling the business to her. They would split the profits for five years, and she would then be sole owner: Viv was going to be a businesswoman.

Not an easy decision. She feared for the company's future. She knew—*knew*—that most professors who requested materials advertised their proposed visit at a price higher than Classroom/New York charged them, meaning to pocket the difference. As college teachers, they felt entitled; why, she could not say, but she was familiar with the phenomenon. But often that higher price was *too* high, prevented the minimum twelve participants from signing up; they were outsmarting themselves.

The other thing that was happening was that the owners of the Westphalia chose that moment to sell.

Worse, the new owners were the Disco Duo. Famous for running the most notorious disco of the 1970s, a den of sex, drugs and celebrities, and freshly released from federal prison (for tax evasion), they were intent on building upon the unpretending bones of the Westphalia a hip new hostelry. Doing so would require a top-to-bottom renovation; the higher room rates needed to pay for it might well put Classroom/New York out of business.

So to take charge of the business now, under pressure as it was, and with Nat coming closer to retirement, had taken much thought.

Viv looked out her window. Stripes of rain obscured whatever was going on at Y&R, but she thought she could make out a cake and candles.

# 51.

NAT FELT AWE at the roster of those the Board of Editors had broken bread with over the years. They ranged from Lee Kuan Yew to Otto von Hapsburg, arms dealer Adnan Khashoggi to gambler Nick the Greek; not to mention successive CEOs of General Motors, General Electric and Exxon. It was said Churchill had once been served up and roasted but, if so, that was before his time.

But he smiled to remember the use Jack made of the lunch with the pretender to the throne of the Austro-Hungarian Empire: Visiting a friend in the Tyrol, only to find his friend's father an unreconstructed Nazi openly hostile to the American guest, Jack let drop that his father had met—oh, and *quite liked!*—Otto von Hapsburg. For all that Hapsburg was famously anti-Nazi, Jack's host's attitude towards him reversed as if by magic.

Datality CEO Chad McGann emerged promptly from the elevator, a well-preserved ex-college linebacker with a sweep of hair breaking into silver at the crests, shooting his cuffs with an expression of faint surprise as he was escorted through a lobby whose glass walls looked across to the upper reaches of the Exxon and Equitable Life buildings. The youngest of his complement of flacks preceding him, he was greeted warmly by *Ducats'* Managing Editor and its publisher, and conducted to a room where bartenders were already supplying editors with drinks. The publisher was there for the drinks portion of the proceedings only; OrbsCorp's famous church-state division meant he would vanish before the meal began.

Nat observed McGann. What went with the money madness of these captains of industry was the *grooming*. To him who showered and shaved every day, attended to hair and nails, dressed always in fresh and decent clothing, it was a wonder how the personal grooming of these guys could be of such a higher order altogether: Hair plumped and shining, never one out of place, fingernails luminous, skin tanned, beautifully tailored, they radiated color in the kind of glow Nat associated with rich women. Surely it restricted their effective spheres of action to limos and corporate suites? It was also true they looked overfed; flesh was encroaching on McGann's features.

Then everyone turned in astonishment as another colleague entered calling, "*Hello!* Hello, everybody, *hello!*"

It was Sidney Bunsen, pale and perspiring in a cream-colored suit, his mobile parchment features grimacing as if in pain.

The thing about *Ducats'* chief economist was that he had agoraphobia—suffered *agonies* of it. He felt fine within a certain circumscribed neighborhood, but couldn't stir beyond it without his heart racing and fluttering, his breath vanishing, joints going loose and limbs wobbly, darkness blotting out his vision. Within the area bounded to the west by Sixth Avenue, to the north by 86th Street, Lexington Avenue to the east and 45th Street—*sometimes* 44th Street—to the south, he was fine, but to cross any of those demarcations was to risk collapse. Even in Central Park, he flourished at the Wollman Rink, felt clammy and faint at the Bethesda Fountain. A golden prison, maybe, but a prison nonetheless.

The original Orbs Building, where Sidney had gone to work in 1936, stood within his borders, but the company's 1960 removal to the far side of Sixth Avenue had placed his office across the street from safety. The day the new building opened he gamely came in to hang pictures in his corner office, then lay down on the couch, trying to catch his breath while the company nurse checked his blood pressure. At lunchtime he repaired to The "21" Club, and went home.

The next day he came in just before lunch, and after lunch went home.

On the third day he came out of the elevator feeling so shaky and looking so like death that he was forthwith escorted to Lenox Hill Hospital, and home from there.

Home was a capacious duplex on Park Avenue at 74th Street, out of which — by a unique dispensation — he had worked ever since, several bedrooms converted to offices for his secretary and numbers-crunching assistants. He had not, until now, been back to the OrbsCorp Tower — not in 23 years. Generations of staffers had met Sidney only at home or at "21" or out on the town within his prison walls.

Today, the Managing Editor gasped, "It's *Sidney!*" McCann displayed grace in the unexpected situation, helping Sidney into a chair and modestly crouching down next to the old man.

The tableau was touching and historic. The afflicted economist had seen Datality's potential back in the 1930s, when no one else had, and from the start predicted greatness for it. Datality struggled not to succumb to the Depression, but it came close — mortgaging its properties and slashing workforce and salaries so as to fund research at its North River laboratory; it hung on by the fingernails.

Vindication had been its, of course, and Sidney's. The Second World War found uses for Datality's punchcard machines, and when, after the War, the company began making computers, it burgeoned, doing more ever since to change society than the auto companies or oil companies that hogged the top of the *Ducats 499*. Datality had broken into its top ten 20 years earlier, and though it wasn't at the top yet — oil companies don't budge easy — in 1983 it expected to take in revenues of more than $40 *billion*.

And Sidney Bunsen had predicted the whole astounding saga. His belief in the company remained firm, in fact was stronger now than ever. Datality's future was the article of faith by which he lived, and his pride in its success such that despite palpitations and shortness of breath he was come to the wrong side of Sixth Avenue to pay homage to McGann, grandson of the founder and for ten years past the behemoth's CEO.

Sidney sat crumpled in his chair, his little hand enfolded in McGann's large ones, McGann showing solicitude and respect for his elder. The scene would be spoken of for years to come; McGann's flacks vanished, *radiant,* to their separate dining room ("The kids' table," one said; "Same exact menu," the publisher's assistant replied).

"There, I feel better," Sidney declared, preparing to move to the lunch table. "Yes, I do indeed."

Nat looked on with particular interest. Before coming upstairs, he'd re-read the story he edited a few months back about Datality's leap into personal computers and the tiny startup it went into business with to accomplish it, a company called Qweet. Datality brilliantly brought to market the first practical PC, but couldn't be bothered to do in-house so mundane a task as writing code for an operating system to make it work. Datality manufactured enormous mainframes, each housed for life in glass-walled rooms cooled to temperatures that required acolytes to wear sweaters: Why would *it* do software on so small a scale? So it hired Qweet, a tiny outfit in Albuquerque, New Mexico, to write the code.

But, lo, Qweet's programmers, chatting over burritos at Pancho's, Nat's own Albuquerque favorite (downmarket but delicious, where one summoned more refried beans by raising the little Mexican flag on the table), came to realize that however labor-intensive writing code might be, the cost of *reproducing* it was the cost of a floppy disk. Moreover, Datality's PC had already been cloned by a dozen companies, and Qweet's operating system could power them all: Its profit potential was *unlimited*. In editing the story, Nat caught a whiff of its ambitions, how its principals—kids who couldn't be bothered to finish college—dared think that the growth of the personal computer could make Qweet *bigger* than Datality.

Datality's latest quarterly report—featuring a small but startling earnings miss—hinted at what Nat suspected might be the future: A drop in mainframe shipments was almost, but not quite, offset by a rise in PC sales. But mainframes cost $2 million and up; a PC, $2,000. In effect Datality was cannibalizing its chief product with one that cost a thousandth as much.

Nat wondered if Qweet weren't poised like Pac-Man to eat Datality's lunch.

## 52.

BY THE TIME VIV put on her coat to go downstairs and meet Jack, she had touched base with her group leaders and been assured all was well, and the rain at last was easing. Across the airshaft she saw Y&R's usual lunchtime desertion.

"Going to lunch?" Helen asked, putting a hand over her phone with a particularly skeptical look. "Have a good one!"

Jack was the problem child. Or weren't they all? Except for Tommy, maybe, Tommy who as a college freshman consulted actuarial tables and consequently entered the long-lived occupation of English professor, and was—what was the word?—*affable* enough to pull it off. Always in Tommy's shadow, Fred went to work for the Federal Government, but around the time of his divorce became a consultant, whatever that was. Jimmy was still fishing for salmon out of Kodiak, Alaska.

No, Jack was the problem child. To Viv's and Nat's surprise he once described himself as the angry son of an angry son of an angry son. (*Where did that come from?*) On Tommy's advice, they steered him, too, towards the academy, but he kept balking, though getting some good degrees along the way. He'd tutored, he'd taught and now was doing research for a scholar in his 24th year editing the letters of a Victorian Viv had never heard of; Volume One was due any year now! To help annotate them, Jack daily moved wraithlike through the New York Public Library, apparently content to live his life amongst footnotes.

They kissed in the lobby, and Jack asked, "Where to?"

"Chock full o'Nuts?" suggested Viv, who, after all, was buying.

"Or the Bistro?"

"All right."

Bistro-on-Mad, a second-story French restaurant in the next block, offered particularly good food at moderate prices. But onion soup, a glass of wine, quiche or an omelet ran to $12 or $15, whereas a nutted-cheese sandwich and coffee on a revolving stool at Chock cost $5. But Viv enjoyed the Bistro, too, so didn't begrudge him.

As they crossed 41st Street, Jack said, "Still laughing at what happened last time I walked up this block with Dad."

"What was that?"

"Down the street a guy's coming towards us throwing suspicious glances to the side, behind him, up at windows? Say to myself, 'OK, here comes a crazy, just be *aware* and you'll survive.' Comes up and goes, 'Hi, Nat.' Dad goes, 'Hi, Ned.' Introduces us: Ned Hendler, number three at the CIA. Dad always said he thought he was a CIA plant at *Ducats*."

The similarity in names had been a mutual annoyance for years. They got each other's mail and phone calls, until Reagan named William Casey to head the CIA and Casey's pal Hendler joined him there.

"My closest brush with James Bond," said Jack. "Very disappointing."

"Hah!" said Viv.

Upstairs, they had just touched glasses of white wine when

Jack said, "Got news about Ian. One of his roommates called. He's gone blind, the end seems near, but apparently he's cheerful as ever."

"Oh!" said Viv, and chattered about her Meldover group.

Ian she'd met two years earlier, Jack's date for a play Viv had extra tickets for — a frequent perk — and she'd gone crazy for him: cute, literate and polite, at thirty a publishing executive. At *Balm in Gilead* it amused her to see Ian and Jack discreetly lean far, far over to watch Vincent Spano at extreme stage right take off his pants.

She'd seen Ian in light of a possible partner for Jack; Jack who one evening, having reached his mid-twenties with no discernible interest in girls, declared that he'd gone to see the Broadway play *Bent*. Viv rushed from the room in tears, while Nat summoned compassion into his voice to ask, "And what did you think of *Bent*?"

But a week after she met him, Ian went to St. Vincent's ER unable to breathe. It turned out to be pneumocystis pneumonia — he had what would soon be called AIDS. Viv was terrified for Jack's sake. From the hospital Ian went home to Minnesota. Jack wrote and occasionally called, and Ian made one return visit to New York, by then sporting what he good-humoredly called his "Auschwitz look," skin stretched over knobs of bone. Meaning it to be a treat, having in mind a gaudy stretch Lincoln with TV and bar, Jack hired a limo to take him and his roommates to the airport. What showed up was a staid black Cadillac. "Like my aunt's funeral," Ian remarked.

Now Jack asked, "Can I come to your talk? Sit in on Nolan Bucher? Or would that make you nervous?"

"No, no, sure," Viv said.

"Reminds me," Jack said. "Always at the library there's been this old guy in a raincoat? Taking notes at the reference shelves, going through the catalog, never speaking a word to anybody—*me* in 40 years, I figured. There every day, except the other day I realized I hadn't seen him in a bit. And there's his obit in today's *Times*: Turns out he was the legman for *Ripley's Believe It Or Not*."

"Job open?"

"Don't even."

Viv declined his suggestion that they visit the Berg Collection, saying she had shopping to do at Altman's.

"Walk you down."

After quietly augmenting her tip, Jack escorted her through the merest drizzle down a stretch of Madison whose seen-better-days air Viv enjoyed.

They climbed Altman's shallow stone steps and passed into the store. Lofty, bright, paneled in wood and glittering with crystal, its grandeur extended all the way to Fifth Avenue; Jack could walk through and be halfway back to the library.

"Thanks, Jack."

"Thank *you*, Mother. Enjoyed lunch. See you at 2:30."

## 53.

HELPING SIDNEY BUNSEN to his feet—"I'll try to eat something," the old man quavered—McGann escorted him to a long table overlooking Sixth Avenue that shone with silver, crystal and china. The dining room and everything in it was a showcase of fine corporate design circa 1960. Chandeliers dazzled, three walls were glass and the fourth hung with tapestries woven to a drawing commissioned from Picasso. The joke someone was sure to crack at every meal was that Picasso doesn't exactly aid the digestion.

McGann placed Sidney to the right of his seat of honor at table's end. Through mute nods and ready accommodation, adjustments were made and another chair drawn up over the *marble verde,* an extra place setting found.

Sidney sank gratefully down, then blanched at the RCA and CBS buildings that loomed across the street. Woven metallic draperies were quickly drawn.

Slowly he revived, the editors took their places, and at his end the Managing Editor stood up to welcome their guest, their chief economist, too, and to encourage questions throughout the meal. "It's nothing more than a working lunch, after all," Hank concluded.

Service of soup and wine commenced, and reminiscences ensued. Speaking more frequently than McGann himself, Sidney in his cracked, precise voice recalled Datality's dubious stature of 50 years earlier, how its legendary founder got out there every day with a smile and fresh white shirt, while behind the scenes frantic paper games kept things afloat; how only the War and its need to keep track of millions of soldiers, sailors and prisoners, billions of bombs and bullets, finally stiffened the house of cards.

Sidney awarded himself some credit, but not more than was modest. "I saw how it would be," he said. "I had faith in this remarkable man and his company." Shrewdly deferential, McGann let him do his job for him, declaring that Sidney's — and *Ducats'* — support had been crucial to Datality's survival.

Finally Sidney grew interested in the entrée. The main course was sautéed shad roe — first of the season — with asparagus and new potatoes, accompanied by a superb Château Haut-Brion.

Questions were asked of McGann amicably, even joshingly, especially about prospects for another stock split, leading to a celebratory discussion of the stock price generally. No company ever made more people rich than Datality had. *Ducats* forbade its staff to trade for a year in stocks they reported on, but Datality's rise had been so sustained and long-running that everyone at the table held shares in the company. Throughout the postwar period it was the market's most spectacular gainer, again and again running up to a price of hundreds of dollars per share, then splitting five-for-one.

Nat spoke up. "Wonder if I might ask about earnings?"

"Fire away," McGann said tolerantly.

"Your earnings missed your projection by three per cent —"

"Two point eight," scoffed McGann.

"PC sales rose, but just a small weakening in mainframe

leases hit earnings. Isn't this a pattern that's poised to continue?"

Everybody was so startled a waiter dropped a plate with an audible, "Oh, *shit!*" Sidney gasped, McGann did a slow burn and around the table food was shoved into mouths in silent determination to get past this gaffe.

"Come again?" McGann asked with a toothy smile.

"Isn't the earnings miss a sign you might be making the wrong bet on PCs?"

"Think you've lost me, given that we founded the industry."

"I'll be more specific," said Nat. "To create your operating system, you hired a tiny New Mexico outfit—"

"Qweet's done a bang-up job for us, too."

"But isn't your PC undercutting your core product—mainframes—just when cheaper clones are gunning for your PC? And by producing software for them all, isn't Qweet better positioned to take advantage of PC growth than Datality itself?"

"Look, Qweet's making *millions*," McGann said. "From *us*. Over $10 million last year! Not bad for a bunch of drop-outs. This much is true: A PC's not as profitable as a mainframe. But sell a million PCs, you're talking real money."

Sidney pulled at his collar and tie.

Nat persisted. "But put enough PCs together, they can do anything mainframes can do, at a fraction of the cost. And with Moore's Law predicting ever cheaper computing power, how can you be confident revenues will ever actually rise? Not to mention profits? Especially with the clones underselling you? Making Datality one of many PC makers, while Qweet monopolizes the software for all of them?"

Several editors started talking sharply at the same time—no way to treat a guest!—but Sidney's keening cry of distress drowned them out. His face gone the color of his wine, he struck his chest and wheezed, terror in his eyes.

"Let's go to the next room," Hank called. "Sorry about dessert." Quietly, he asked the headwaiter to call EMS and to summon Turk, OrbsCorp's doctor.

His chair pulled back, Sidney was laid on the floor. McGann and Hank hovering over him as editors hurried out, he gurgled, moaned, convulsed and went still. Turk, in shirtsleeves, burst in with his bag and began CPR. From the next room people peered fearfully over. EMS stepped —*flew*— off the elevator, and soon, leaving the floor littered with wrappings and tubes, was wheeling Sidney away, oxygen mask clamped to a face carved from alabaster. McGann shook hands all around and left.

Leaning his forehead to a window, Nat saw EMS 50 floors below load the gurney into an ambulance, the sheet covering it instantly splotched dark by a cloudburst, while McGann's party climbed into limousines.

Soon Hannah was eating pecan pie at her desk.

"Leftovers from your lunch, I think," she told Nat. "*Delicious!*"

# 54.

SHOPPING BAG IN EITHER HAND—Easter bonnet from Altman's in one, in the other Meldover's schedules—Viv bumped along the airshaft to her desk.

Helen reacted dramatically.

"Sitting here with crossed legs, Viv! Cover my phone?"

"Sure."

Helen flew down the hallway. Viv unlocked Phil's desk drawer, took out Meldover's tickets and began putting them and the schedules into folders printed with Classroom/New York's skyline logo. It was past one thirty; she had not quite an hour to make her way to the hotel.

Helen's phone rang. Viv swiveled and reached for it.

"Trasker Accounting, how may I help you?"

"Got the stuff!"

"Excuse me?"

"On the corner!"

"Sorry, I think you have the wrong number."

"The *stuff!* I got it! *Now!*"

The caller hung up. Viv was finishing her packets when Helen returned.

"See you went to Altman's again. You know Bloomie's

only two stops away?" Though she no longer tried to insist, it pained Helen that Viv persisted in shopping at Altman's when Bloomingdale's was so easy to get to.

"I like Altman's. Someone called, no name, says he's on the corner with 'the stuff.' Told him he had a wrong number."

"Oh *shit!*" said Helen. She grabbed her purse and sprinted out of the suite, yelling, "And you let him hang up! *Shit! Shit! Shit!*"

Viv left a few minutes later. It wasn't a long walk to the hotel, and she disliked taking cabs, but given the chanciness of the skies, not to mention the fact she was carrying a couple thousand dollars' worth of tickets, she hailed a dirty yellow Dodge. A shower commenced the moment she shut the door.

During the ride she found herself thinking of an incident from Meldover's visit the previous year. The group went to see the Ridiculous Theatrical Company's *A Tale of Two Cities,* a farce it enjoyed right up until Everett Quinton's nude takeoff of David's *Death of Marat.* At that point the group got up and walked out.

"I would *never* take off my clothes!" wailed an aspiring Meldover actress at the emergency discussion Father Donellan convened, which he requested Phil and Viv attend. The jubilee of condemnation, he was satisfied, made his point about purity. Meanwhile, The Ridiculous banned the college forevermore.

Showers had resumed as a fabulously handsome doorman greeted Viv under the Westphalia's marquee. With the Disco Duo's takeover the hotel had undergone an overnight change of staff: The new doormen, bellmen and desk clerks were men in their 20s, each better looking than the last, though so far, unlike the disco, no one was going bare-chested.

Viv found Jack near the grand staircase in a lobby of faded splendor.

"We've got a minute," she told him. "Want to talk to Sherry, learn the latest."

As they climbed to the mezzanine, the Disco Duo happened to be coming down the stairs, the short one staring so intently at Jack that he stumbled and had to grab at the railing with both hands. His partner dryly advised, "Watch your step there, Steve."

Finding Sherry in her office, Viv asked about the outlook for rack rates.

"Well, Viv, they're going up," Sherry said. "Times Square's waking up from a long sleep."

"And we stuck by it through thick and thin, Sherry. Never took rooms at the Tesla or the Westsider or anywhere else — always stuck with the Westphalia."

"I know it, but can't *begin* to tell you what renovations will cost. This I *can* say, we're doing a floor at a time, be two, three years before the whole building's done, and for unrenovated rooms we won't be charging much more than we do now."

"But for renovated rooms?"

"So *beautiful*, Viv. Carlo Magnus himself is doing them. Setting up a model room soon, you'll have to take a look. See, he's making a virtue of the room size so we don't have to take walls down, which in the long run will help costs. But you can't pour millions into a property and not raise rates."

Viv picked up Jack outside the office.

"What'd she say?"

"Nothing I didn't know."

They descended to the lobby, where plump fingers plucked at Viv's arm.

"*Viv!*"

"Father Donellan!" she said. "Welcome to New York!"

Father Donellan, short, chunky, pink-faced, cast a nervous glance up at the boy standing beside him, a tall youth with prominent cheekbones and sun-streaked hair. Viv thought: *handsome!*

"Thanks, Viv, thank you. Want you to meet *Gerald*. Gerald, this is Mrs. Handler."

The good father, having generously eschewed the private room group leaders were entitled to, and specified his preferred roommate, was sharing with Gerald.

"Hi, Gerald," said Viv.

"Welcome," said Jack, with a smile.

Gerald nodded in acknowledgment before his head snapped after a passing bellman.

"My God, the *staff!*" said Father Donellan. "Such lookers! Like heaven will be, I imagine, except, of course, with clothes on. (Oh yes, heaven's *nude!*)"

"Shall we go downstairs, meet the group?" Viv suggested.

Usually Phil addressed groups in a mezzanine meeting room, but it wasn't available, forcing them to the basement site of the storied 1930s nightclub, The Golden Trough. Chairs were set up in what proved to be a cellar raised to glamour by virtue of walls spray-painted gold. (Sherry explained that Andy Warhol had recently thrown a party there, and the genius spray-painted *everything.*)

The group trailed in and took their seats. Father Donellan had brought 14 girls and three boys—sweet kids who, like kids everywhere, only wanted to know what to like and what to snub.

Nolan Bucher appeared uncertainly at the bottom of the steps. Viv waved him to the table up front and distributed folders. Father Donellan sat down next to Gerald and anxiously leaned into him.

Viv formally welcomed the group, and after discussing their schedule went on to outline some safety considerations.

"New York's a wonderful city, but it's bigger than what

you're used to, and it calls for behaving with good common sense. Be aware of your surroundings—that's the key to staying safe.

"For the ladies: Don't let go of your purse. Stay conscious of it always. When you eat, don't hang it from your chair, put it on your lap. On the street, hold on to it—don't let it hang behind your arm. Guys, my husband wants you to know that New Yorkers keep their wallets in their *front* pockets—too easy to have your back pocket picked. *Um.* He's had his picked twice."

Father Donellan whispered into Gerald's ear.

She continued in the same vein, giving specific instructions on how to use the subway and how to cross the street. The dose of realism delivered in her rather flat voice seemed to reassure the kids.

"And now, to talk about the plays you're going to see, here's the chief drama critic of the New York *Times*, Nolan Bucher."

The Butcher of Broadway was a pleasant-looking man of forty, balding and a little heavy. Remaining seated, and consulting a copy of their schedule, he discussed Broadway generally, especially its postwar history, the distinctions between Broadway and Off-Broadway and the shows Father Donellan had chosen.

"You're seeing some tasty ones. *Brighton Beach Memoirs* is a hot ticket," he said, "and Amanda Plummer in *Agnes of God* you won't forget any time soon."

When he finished taking questions, Viv slid him the envelope containing his honorarium, Phil's check for $75.

Father Donellan stood up. "You have your tickets," he told the group. "We'll meet at the theatre at 7:30. On your own till then. At six o'clock Gerald and I are eating at Hawaii Kai, one of the great showbiz hangouts, and anyone who wants can join us. Used to be Birdland, they tell me the dwarf doorman was Charlie Parker's good friend. OK, be safe! Have fun!"

He also reminded Viv that at 5:00 o'clock he was buying her a drink at the revolving bar atop the Marriott Marquis Hotel.

"Looking forward to it, Father."

Father Donellan hastened after Gerald, who had abruptly gotten up and walked out of the room.

Meanwhile, Bucher was praising Viv's performance to Jack: New Yorker, no doubt about it, but imparted her tips as a Midwesterner and thus was credible. "Very effective," he concluded.

He left with them. At the door, they went in three directions, Viv kissing her son on the lips.

It was 3:30, and rain was falling harder. An awkward hour and a half on her hands, Viv opened her umbrella and after a walk under theatre marquees went underground to take the 42nd Street Shuttle back to the office; she wasn't one to kill time somewhere smoking and drinking. After the drink with Father Donellan, she'd meet Nat for dinner—where, to be decided. And after dinner, they'd buy tickets to something at the half-price booth. Rain was pounding down too hard to think of doing that now, besides the fact that at this hour on Holy Thursday the twin lines would stretch to discouraging length whatever the weather.

# 55.

THAT AFTERNOON NAT felt more an outsider in the OrbsCorp Tower than in years. Through his open door, he sensed the corridors were fraught. No one, not all afternoon, stuck in a head to consult about a story's wording or direction, or about anything at all. Everyone shunned the killer.

Meanwhile, a thunderstorm moved over the island, a vigorous spring clash of dark clouds boiling eastwards. Rumbling penetrated even Nat's windows as struts and ladders of lightning dropped to the tops of buildings, dashing them with brilliance, and endless buckets of rain tipped onto Manhattan.

Before going back to Sidney Bunsen's story—his *last* story, he realized with a pang—Nat picked up one of the *Ducats Top Tier* sidebars. This one was about a Florida mogul too mean to occupy the ocean-view penthouse of a highrise he owned, living instead in the one with a view of the parking lot. Amusing, but *Lord!* the writing! The writer was one of *Ducats'* tech-savvy new breed of business journalist, stylish and charming on TV, but desperately reluctant to commit words to paper. Like pulling teeth, getting copy out of these kids, much less grammatical copy—harder yet *good* copy. This piece, a third draft, was still full of knots.

Finished, Nat in trying to fold it up found himself playing an accordion of springy computer paper. Tamed at last, into his tray it went, and he turned again to Sidney Bunsen's piece. Soon a youth stepped into his office (with trepidation, Nat sensed) and silently lifted the sidebar into his cart, on its way to an Atex operator. That operator, when finished keyboarding the changes, would place Nat's mark-up together with the resulting "clean" in the proofreaders' wire basket on the copy desk, there to remain until one of a team of proofreaders (the losing team) came and got it.

Nat decided to go to the kitchen. As he passed his secretary's desk, he picked up a pie-smeared saucer and fork; speaking low on the phone, Hannah nodded her thanks.

The very hallway seemed alien as colleagues, glimpsing him, darted out of sight. Nat was reminded of coming to New York to apply for a job at *Orbs* magazine after quitting the Grand Junction *Daily Item*. His first interviewer, before passing his clippings up the line, told him—not unkindly, just giving the rube a heads-up—"I *don't* think you're one of us." But Nat got the job, and thrived at it, too, deft as he found colleagues to be with elbows and knives. After more than a quarter-century with the company, he had some knife-fighting moves of his own.

The most exquisite put-down he ever got came early on when he found himself interviewing Eisenhower's Secretary of the Treasury, Robert B. Anderson, who at one time had overseen Texas' vast Wagonner Ranch. Nat's widowed grandmother sold the family spread on Wilbarger County's Beaver Creek to the Waggoners in the 1890s, and for some reason Nat so informed the Secretary. Fingers pinching at a pinstriped sleeve as though to pluck a flea, Anderson said, "Oh, a *nester*."

Sitting down again with a fresh mug of coffee — wondering why he preferred the taste from cardboard cups — Nat looked outdoors. From his study on Riverside Drive he loved watching the rain, but here in the office it seemed a gritty, gray-on-gray assault; a reminder that New York — unlike, say, Paris — was made not for love but for money.

He regretted Sidney's collapse and death. Lord, yes; but how was it his fault? Asking questions overdue for Wall Street's cossetted favorite? Returning to Sidney's story, he calmed down as his pencil cut unnecessary words and found sharper ones, transposed phrases, freed the thrust of the argument to come alive — redeeming the soul of the piece, he hoped, helping it speak to readers. If he did his work well, Sidney's proclamation of renewed prosperity would stand as a memorial to the man and his insight. The first paragraphs were starting to read well.

Suddenly he jumped to his feet and rushed down the hallway. Flashing in his mind's eye was the image of a usage error he'd failed to correct in the sidebar, one of those misplaced modifiers that can wriggle past even expert eyes.

He blundered into the windowless Operations room. Atex terminals were mounted on instruments of torture, armatures which had an operator peering over a keyboard at a screen next to a seat intended, when the scheme was fully implemented, for a single proofreader to stare at the selfsame amber phosphors. Apparently as punishment; the setup resembled the old witch-dunking chairs. Certainly it represented a win for typesetters in their ancient war with proofreaders, and for the beancounters who couldn't believe it paid to employ two proofreaders instead of one.

Nat hoped some grownup would step in and point out there's nothing personal in correcting errors and that there's a reason why proofreaders work in pairs. Anyway, he heard the issue was going to the Newspaper Guild.

Operations told him the proofreaders already had his sidebar.

Nat turned down their side corridor. The team in the first cubicle had it, the woman chanting its prose in monotone, interleaving proofreaders' code—*slam, com, point, ital, rom, quirk*—and knocking on her desktop to indicate capitalized words. The efficient tradition of one reading the mark-up aloud while the other silently tracked along the clean, pencil in hand, dated to the birth of printing.

Falling silent, she looked up uneasily; an editor was never a happy sight there.

"My sidebar? One more thing, if I can have it back for a minute, please."

"Sure, Mr. Handler."

A flurry of paper—the accordion now torn into single pages—and Nat trotted back to his office with mark-up and clean. He hunted the clean for the error niggling at his brain and found it, lurking so invisibly the proofreaders, too, had let it lie. He corrected it, then found a page that looked out of place:

> ... redolent of summer and her own peculiar aroma, though it was still spring. But the sun pummeled him, weighed him down, forced him to the grass unable to move, instincts surging—happy.

*The hell?!*

Proofreaders often were writers themselves, and apparently one had accidentally given up a page of manuscript. Nat evened up the stack, placed that page perpendicular in the middle, and carried it back. He found the team sitting up straight, super-alert; the man, seeing his page, looked relieved.

"Thanks, found it," Nat murmured, asking himself as he returned to his office, *Am I smirking? Poor fellow's stuff's no good.*

One desk drawer Nat kept locked. In it resided a novel he'd been picking away at for years. He took it out sometimes when he ate a sandwich at his desk and the telephone let him alone. In those moods where he regarded himself as a failed drudge, the manuscript represented what he still hoped was the future, what he'd been aiming at since he was a kid. Fair to say it was giving him trouble to finish, though when finally perfected he looked forward to shopping it from the eminence of Editors Row.

He took it out now, on this afternoon when he was left in preternatural peace. Though neatly typed (by Viv), the manuscript bore an air of age. Deftly plotted, though, he was sure of that. It was a Colorado newspaperman's first-person account of his wife's rape and murder, a crucifix left jammed between her legs; a worthy addition to the hardboiled genre, Nat hoped, especially with the twist that the narrator turns out to be the killer.

Today he had an addition to make, one he owed to his mind's freeflow during the walk to work, when things tended to come loose and fetch up in new ways. Somewhere around 59th Street *newspeeperman* had wafted into his unconscious. *Nice!*

But as he looked for an instance of *newspaperman* to replace, he saw something he'd never noticed before, an aggressive — worse, a *lifeless* — quality to his story, characters shoved around for ungenerous ends, nothing of *art* to it.

*Damn. Damnation!* Was he never to write a book?

Oh, he'd written a book, all right, about JFK's sex life; unpublished — *thank God!* — because of the assassination. The facts were out now, but Nat was happy not to have been the one to spill the beans.

But for a moment—just for an instant—he remembered the President's mistress whose beauty drove him so crazy. *Gee, Pam must be about 50 now.*

He cleared out the drawer, transferring the pages to his briefcase.

"Nat?"

His Managing Editor was leaning in at the door.

"Yes, Hank?"

"Can I come in?"

"Please."

Hank gently closed the door behind him.

"Nat, just to say—because sometimes silly things need saying—I hope you don't feel responsible for Sidney? You were just asking the questions he should have asked. Hell, he *used* to ask them, no one better, but then he got—cozy. Cozy, and old, and rich. Made a fortune in Datality stock."

"Lucky man."

"'Up to a point, Lord Copper.' Anyway, Nat, not your fault."

"Thanks, Hank. Appreciate it."

Hank left the door open. Feeling better, Nat dialed Viv's office number. The receptionist telling him she thought Viv was gone for the day, he went back to Sidney's story.

# 56.

JEWELL HAD LOOKED CONCERNED on Viv's return from the Westphalia.

"Oh, Viv, a *Leilani* just called? Says it's urgent?" She handed her a message slip.

"Thanks, Jewell."

Leilani's friend since 1959, Viv always thought her and her husband an odd couple: Leilani the Hawaiian beauty queen — prize of her husband's stint in the Honolulu bureau — and Hardy Owens a journalist with a roving eye. His *Orbs* magazine column, *The Pinnacle,* recounted the ordeals of Presidents Kennedy, Johnson and Nixon. The bestseller it birthed — *The Loneliest Pinnacle* — included photographs pairing him with his subjects: Kennedy grinning infectiously, next to a broadly smiling Hardy Owens; Johnson, weathered and put-upon in half-tones, Owens beside him equally grave and gray; Nixon warily appraising a crowd, Owens at his shoulder looking even more suspicious. Nowadays he ran a high-powered PR firm, Owens/Assoc.

The friendship prospered for two decades. Leilani and her husband visited Katonah for poolside weekends, and Viv and Nat sometimes stayed at East 81st Street. But soon after Viv and Nat moved to Manhattan, there came a break—absurd, unfortunate, but final.

Owens one day had called Nat to ask if he'd be interested in ghost-writing Jake King's memoirs. The money would be good, he assured him. King starred in a hit TV show, *Homicide Hawaii!*—Hawaii being the connection—and between scenes had already dictated some pages. Nat agreed to look them over.

He duly spent a weekend arranging and rewriting, and sent the package back to Owens saying that, no, he didn't want the job, because he couldn't see a book there: King was dull to the bone.

A month later, reading the Sunday papers, Viv reached for the *Daily News* supplement *Parade* and found Jake King grinning from its cover. Inside, *Jake King's Hawaii!* consisted of the fragments Nat edited. Not that he wanted credit, but a *Parade* cover story meant someone had gotten paid for *his* work.

Nat called Owens, who insisted he be his lunch guest at the University Club.

Over pan-seared salmon Nat brought up the *Parade* piece and said he felt owed something; what was published, preliminary though it was, *he* had put together. Amused, Owens smiled and dabbed at his lips. He had gained weight since Washington, was cultivating a resemblance to the Bourbon kings of France.

Harrumphing twice, he said, "That mishmash of yours, Nat? Don't you know *anything* about magazine writing? Amazed it sold. Should have said something before. Too late now."

Nat stood up, chair clattering, and stalked out.

"Pathetic," Owens launched after him. "Nat Handler, you're *pathetic!*" Such was his volume that marble floors and paneled walls echoed: *"Pathetic!"*

But Viv and Leilani kept up with each other after their husbands' quarrel. Leilani was the *chicest* creature Viv knew, exotic and svelte. They regularly met for lunch in Leilani's East Side purlieus, and alternated paying the bill. If Viv beat her to La Côte Basque or Lutèce—terrific splurges—she would order white wine, and there would come Leilani, flying á la Veruschka out of a livery town car, dispensing money to a panhandler as she crossed the sidewalk, to arrive at Viv's table with a blossoming smile and the scent of gardenia.

Their friendship was based on their finding themselves fish out of water in Washington a quarter century earlier; based on the luaus they threw in the Handlers' back yard for *Orbs* wives wearing muumuus, on their Georgetown hula-dance lessons.

The friendship never failed, but Viv was aware it wasn't particularly intimate; questions weren't asked, confidences not exchanged. Leilani had no children; her life was devoted to entertaining on her husband's behalf, until suddenly she took up painting, with a teacher and a loft studio in a grimy warehouse district newly dubbed *SoHo*. Though no longer invited to the apartment overlooking Central Park, Viv attended openings of Leilani's energetic abstract works that were said to find success in the rich market for sofa-size.

Viv carried the message slip to her desk. Helen was gone, but a graphic artist down the line of offices was standing in another's doorway, so she went into Phil's office, closed the door and used his phone.

"Leilani? Viv."

"*Viv.* . . ." She was crying.

"Leilani, what *is* it?"

"Viv, can I stay with you, please? For a few days?"

"Yes, of course."

"Right now, please?"

"Of course," Viv repeated. "Meet you at my building in half an hour?"

"Thanks."

*OK,* Viv thought, *an hour snatched out of my busiest day; but that's life.* She might simply have called the doorman, but Leilani's tone worried her. Five minutes later she was on Grand Central's platform, at Times Square in ten, in 30 minutes was rushing home from 79th Street as lightning bleached Broadway and thunder tried to shatter brick and stone.

Leilani was sitting hunched on a lobby bench, head wrapped in an Hermès scarf, Jackie-O-sized sunglasses shielding her eyes, a Louis Vuitton bag at her feet.

"Leilani," said Viv.

Leilani raised her bruised face, a black eye blossoming larger than her glasses. In a small voice she said, "Hello, Viv."

"Let's get you upstairs," Viv said briskly, and led her past Rueben to the elevator. When the doors closed, she said, "*Oh, Leilani.*"

"It was Wallace. Don't know what we're going to do with him."

Viv remembered the original Wallace, a friendly German Shepherd sweeping Georgetown coffee tables clear with his tail. That Wallace was long gone, of course, but he'd been succeeded by others of the same name, marvelous creatures who, it amused Viv to see, played along with the notion Leilani was in charge even as she listed 90 degrees tugging at the leash.

"My fault, I was teasing him."

"He's a good dog, I'm sure," Viv offered, unlocking the door and taking her into the study, which doubled as guest room. Tossing cushions, she handily pulled the couch into a bed. "Make yourself at home, Leilani. Bed's made, towels in the bathroom, extra key in the desk drawer. Help yourself to anything you find. I'm a bit pressed for time — meeting a client for drinks, then Nat and I are going out to dinner and a show. You're welcome to come along?"

"Thanks, a night in's what I need."

"We'll be home by 11:00 or 11:30." Mindful, then, of the spectacle her refrigerator provided — her perpetual diet required it be bare, save perhaps for carrots or a bowl of almonds — she said, "Menus are in the first drawer if you want to order in. The Chinese is especially good."

Though the gutters were running, the thunderstorm seemed to have spent its force when Viv hurried back to the IRT. At 72nd she crossed to the express just pulling in. It had a seat, even, and the rush downtown gave her a chance to catch her breath, to sit looking at nothing amidst vibration and incandescent flares and columns rushing past.

New York was a town of so many moving parts, she was amazed it ran as well as it did.

Recalling the thunderstorm's warmth, she closed her eyes for a moment. Tomorrow, April began; May would bring her 40th wedding anniversary and loveliness to Manhattan. She loved May's long, lingering evenings, how New York's dread lifted when the apple and cherry and pear trees burst into bloom.

She was at the Marriott Marquis faster than a cab could have taken her; a few minutes late, even so.

For two years she'd watched its construction. First a dozen buildings, including five theatres, were reduced to a field of rubble; she couldn't afterwards recall what they looked like. Then a tremendous excavation began, digging a hole that required steep earthen ramps for dump trucks to haul away the dirt. Far below ground level a crane was assembled, a stork-like thing that commenced pulling upwards beneath it a concrete cylinder—pulled it 500 feet into the air before girders began to clothe it with floors.

Now the hotel was open; this was only Viv's second visit. Its sky-high rates were part of the upwards pressure on the Westphalia's.

She strode into the lobby, a room 45 stories tall with glass elevators shooting up and down, and sped to the bar at the top, The View. There, with deliberation, unconsciously fearful of being split like a wishbone, she stepped across the seam of the rail on which it revolved (in fact at a most stately pace) and went over to Father Donellan, hunched against a window.

"Oh God, Viv, it's *Gerald*," the priest said, raising his tear-streaked face as she folded in across from him. "He's *gone*. I was in the shower, called for a towel—*no answer!* I'm *frantic!*" He heaved with sobs. "Should we report it to the police? I think we should. Probably we should. His parents would want me to—the *loveliest* people. Shouldn't be *here*, I should be at the *police* station," he wailed. "Viv, what should I *do?*"

"Don't you imagine he's just taking a walk? First time in New York?"

"Oh God, if anything *happens*, his parents will *kill* me!"

"Father, you need a drink."

The waitress had to wait for the priest, smacking his lips, to settle on the inevitable.

"A *Manhattan*, I think? Yes, please, a Manhattan. Seems appropriate, no?" he added brightly. "What a fantastic view. Know I'm going to Windows on the World this trip? Made reservations *months* ago!"

Windows was the fashionable restaurant atop the north tower of the World Trade Center. The reach of its view, practically to the Poconos, at her sole visit reminded Viv of the Denver restaurant of her youth, The Promontory, and of meeting there the boy who seemed the love of her life. *If I'd married J.T., I'd have been a young widow,* she'd thought. But in leaving she made the mistake of leaning into a window to take in the height, been sickened by the sensation of falling and hadn't been back.

The drink helped restore Father Donellan's calm. "You'd have laughed, Viv: Some of the girls ventured out, just to reconnoiter? Weren't ten steps down the sidewalk before they heard a gunshot and hit the deck. Backfire. So embarrassed, they got up laughing like crazy, hit the deck again." He sipped. "It's nice here – like a gyroscope, is that it? The motion goes with the liquor, that's what I mean."

The room revolved relentlessly, but there was a gyp aspect: However tall the hotel, it was shorter than the building next door, so for part of their circuit they were merely peering into offices. To Viv, backing into a widening view of Times Square, lights beginning to sparkle against gray, it felt like being in the groove at the end of a record, going round and round, *stuck.*

And had just time to think how soon the age of compact discs would make her simile obsolete when the priest perked up. Viv saw Gerald walking expressionlessly towards them. His hair was mussed, and there was something kissed-up to his mouth and cheeks.

"Oh, *Gerald!* Just saying your folks would *kill* me."

"Went for a walk, Father. *Sorry,* Father."

"All that matters is you're *here.*"

A squall hit the windows with a *thump* that sucked at the panes. Across Broadway Viv saw colors running off buildings and signs.

Father Donellan and Gerald were making her nervous, particularly as they whispered about the chances of the boy's getting a drink despite being underage. "We'll give it a try," Father Donellan murmured. "Priests usually get their way."

Viv signaled the waitress, decisively paid the tab, wished

them a pleasant stay, got up and crossed the seam. Worried about lurching, she didn't, though it was more of a challenge after a glass of white wine.

From the lobby she called Nat.

"All done, honey. How about you?"

"Done *in* — but ready to go. Where shall we meet?"

"Sam's?" Viv suggested, naming a theatre hangout unspoiled by tourists, and only steps down 45th Street from the Marriott Marquis.

"Sam's it is. Be there in ten, ten or fifteen."

"Love you."

"Love you."

Then Viv called home, and was pleased that at the sixth or seventh ring Leilani gingerly answered.

"Hello?"

"Leilani, it's me! How are you getting on?"

"Fine, Viv. It's so nice here."

"Good. Hope I told you, Nat and I are going out. Welcome to join us, if you feel up to it."

"I'd rather stay in, I think."

"All right, then. See you elevenish, twelvish."

Despite the rain, the sidewalks were filled with people going home. Umbrella battles were taking place. The ubiquitous little folding umbrella was lately giving way to enormous golf umbrellas that parted crowds like icebreakers, most often wielded by men whose lifted chins and pushed-out lips proclaimed joy at finally having a big one.

Viv waited under the hotel's marquee for a lull, then dashed down the street and into Sam's.

"Evening, Mrs. Handler, by yourself?"

"No, my husband's coming."

Viv loved Sam's. Nothing fancy, more casual than Joe Allen's, less touristy than Sardi's. Two storefronts wide, it had brick walls hung with theatrical posters and offered good, unpretentious food, though food was not exactly the point.

Sam's was most fun after a show when, stepping in for a drink or dessert, she and Nat found themselves part of the stir greeting Lois Smith's entrance, or Barbara Barrie's, or the teenaged Mathew Broderick's. Edward Albee was a late-afternoon regular at the bar, which Viv made the mistake of telling a client who happened to be writing a thesis about him. The client waylaid him, Albee turned loftily away and a new thesis topic had to be found.

Tonight, seated on a banquette against the wall, she ordered wine and — why not? — nachos, and worked out of, but did not check, her raincoat. Their departure had to be speedy if they were to win their theatrical Russian roulette of scoping out TKTS just before curtain. Fortunately, Sam's always got everyone to the show on time.

Sipping wine, happily buried in the restaurant's buzz, she realized with a thrill that one of the men at the next table — the one eating with the vitality of a corpse — was Tom Hulce, who in two hours would be chewing the scenery in *Amadeus*.

# 57.

NAT ENTERED SAM'S, found Viv's table, bent to kiss her — her breath sweet with the house white — lay his imposing coat beside her and, brushing back his hair, sat down.

"Seems to have stopped raining," he said.

"Finally."

"Lordy, could I use a drink." A waiter materialized and Nat said, "Gin martini, please, very dry? A double?"

"So how was your day?"

"Oh, straight from hell. Yours?"

"Oh *no*, what happened?"

"Editors' lunch with Datality's CEO, and of all people Sidney Bunsen happened to attend, I asked some questions — and Sidney up and died. Heart attack, right there at the table. Which right now makes me a pariah."

"Oh, Nat!"

"Got me thinking about retirement."

"Oh, *Nat!*"

"To the point of running some numbers. And we'll be all right, Viv — we'll be *fine*. Anyway, not right away, and when I *do*, we can hang on in New York long as you like."

"Sit on the benches along Broadway?"

"If that's what you want."

He didn't mention his discouraging discovery about the novel; his laden briefcase was leaning against his shin. His drink came, with another wine for Viv. They ordered—scallops for her, New York strip steak for him—and lifted their glasses.

"And how was your day?"

"Well, no one *died*. Had a nice lunch with Jack, and he came to meet Meldover—spoke to them myself. Crisis or two, solved themselves. Asked about the hotel renovations, which I'm still worried will price us out. Oh, and we have a houseguest."

Viv noticed Tom Hulce's head slightly inclining towards them as she spoke.

"Who's that?"

"Leilani's staying a few days. She's black and blue. Says she was teasing Wallace, and he attacked."

Nat buttered a roll and took a bite. "Do you believe her?"

"That the dog gave her a black eye?"

He breathed out heavily. "Hardy's a dreadful man. Did she want to join us?"

"No. Feel like a terrible hostess, Campbell's Soup is about all there is. Suggested she order in."

Dinner soothed them, the room's flow of conversation, rituals of breaking and buttering bread, the sounds incidental to eating and drinking, leaning back to facilitate the delivery and removal of dishes, the stage wait for the entrées. Their handsome waiter was an out-of-work actor.

Nat drank rapidly, and his two martinis, plus wine with his steak, had their effect—a function, thought Viv, of eating nothing since his prematurely ended lunch. Savoring her scallops, she tried to point out the celebrity sitting beside them, but Nat registered perplexity at the workings of her brows.

He was too busy thinking — but not speaking — of a certain disastrous Caribbean visit several years earlier which seemed to have some bearing on the kind of day he'd had. Every February *Ducats'* editors converged on one or another beauty spot to thrash things out for the coming year; that time it had been a resort on the French side of Saint Martin. Nat and Viv — she lying poolside with other wives — half-expected, or more than half-expected, that Nat would emerge from it as Assistant Managing Editor, taking the first step of the hoped-for two-step to Managing Editor that would crown his career.

First on the agenda was the publisher's proposal to reduce the magazine's size and increase the frequency of its publication. *Ducats* debuted — inauspiciously — shortly after the 1929 Crash as a monthly beautifully printed in color on oversized rag paper, 11 inches by 14, and bearing an outrageous cover price of $1.

Now, the publisher proposed that the country's premier business magazine — battered by "a low, dishonest decade" (Nat thought Auden's epigraph for the 1930s apt for the '70s, too) — be cut down to ordinary magazine dimensions and issued fortnightly. With most of his colleagues, Nat reluctantly came round in support, willing to discard nostalgia in exchange for a livelier presence in the marketplace.

But when he tried to communicate a crucial caveat, something went terribly wrong. All he meant was to emphasize that because reading is sensory, sensual — "not just the eye feeding abstractions to the brain, it's the paper's weight and *feel*, the *sheen* of the ink, the *look* of the words, the *font*, the font's *history*, because we're physical creatures and *everything's* tactile. Apologies to the Atex people, of course" — it was crucial that the new format retain the high production values *Ducats* was known for, the ample white space, elegant layout, crisp typography and distinctive graphics.

How could what he said be disputed? Much less taken as an attack on the idea of the makeover?

But the Atex crack gave one particular colleague—the button-pusher promoted in Nat's stead, as it happened—an opening, and he called Nat a *Luddite*. So frustrated was Nat at the apparent impossibility of getting his meaning across, what with the other's refusal to take the point, that finally he'd snapped back profanely, *cursed*. In embarrassment everybody drew up their knees and pursed their lips, looked outdoors at the turquoise waters and swaying palms. Thus Nat's career would end at its present plateau. *Never saw that coming*, he admitted. *Guess the better man won.*

Still thinking of Leilani, thus of Washington, Viv found her thoughts turning to Nat's long-ago obsession with a woman whose claim to fame was sleeping with President Kennedy. Dangerous interval! The shrew's cheap appeal had Nat slavering after her when only harm could result, harm to their marriage *and* his career. He'd been obsessed with possessing the siren, if only finally between the covers of a book; Viv felt pretty sure about that. Then not even a book. *Thank you, Lee Harvey Oswald!*

She'd always looked forward to greater intimacy with Nat after the kids left home. And she loved New York City. But Nat was consumed with work even in the evening, impatient for the squeaks and buzzes of the modem to bring more of it. And now she'd signed up for at least another five years herself, and no one had put a gun to her head, either.

*My life's been nothing but postponements*, she thought, her mouth full of buttery scallops. *I'm like the kids on a road trip asking, "Are we there yet?" But maybe you never want the answer to that question.*

Nat reached his fork to probe her plate, maundering about

how he used not to like sharing but got over that, and other inhibitions, with the move to Manhattan. He failed to notice she wasn't inviting him to steal scallops as she talked more freely—now that Tom Hulce and his companion had left—about the passage of time.

"Just keeps speeding up," she said. "So mysterious. Used to think, *Well:* the future—things will be all right *then*, kids grown up and gone. *Now. . . .*" She was a little drunk herself.

"Aren't we the most wantingest creatures?" Nat remarked.

"Not complaining, believe me."

"What they never tell you as a kid," he said, "when you're trying to grow up, get educated, do your best, is you're going to lose in life as much as you can possibly gain—*more*, all the way through, and everybody you ever met *knew* it the whole time."

"Not sure I'd go that far," Viv murmured.

She had cheesecake—why not?—but began adverting to her watch.

"Right." Nat autographed the air and their check came. Against his protests she paid it and they left, suddenly part of the theatre district's curtain-time flurry. The low, illuminated cloud cover lent something like glamour to the scene.

Against the tide of pedestrians, they walked over to Duffy Square. Flaps of canvas printed sideways "TKTS" hung from a tubular structure meant to disguise a trailer with ticket windows at one end. It took nerve to approach it so late, but the line moved at a lightning pace.

Not that Viv minded waiting. She liked watching the scene and overhearing tourists worry whether *Cats* would be available. Last time, she found herself behind a man who repelled a dispenser of discount coupons to the nude *Oh! Calcutta!* with, "Mister, I'm here with a church group, and I would *never* go see *Oh! Calcutta!*" When he got to the window he said quietly, "One please for *The Best Little Whorehouse in Texas.*"

"What do you think?" asked Nat.

"*Man and Superman?*" Viv suggested. Shaw's play was in previews at Circle-on-the-Square, a splendid theatre-in-the-round five minutes' walk up Broadway.

"Long one," Nat cautioned.

"That's OK."

"Fine."

And while he went up to the window, only having to wait on a tourist asking about *Cats*, Viv watched cars and cabs and people, everyone urgent and excited, shook her head pleasantly at the last touts working the line, glanced upwards at the glittering Coca-Cola and Sony signs. By day she scoffed at the billboards bolted to the dreary old façades, but by *night – !* The zipper of white bulbs at the base of the old Times Tower skittered with news of a disarmament proposal.

Nat flashed her the tickets, and they set off up Broadway at their going-to-work pace. The throngs thinned short of their goal, 50th Street halfway to Eighth Avenue.

By two minutes to eight they were seated and skimming the *Playbill*, anticipating the treat in store. The theatre was less than half filled, typical for previews, before the Butcher of Broadway had weighed in to tell New Yorkers what to think. Viv surveyed the minimal set. Associating Shaw with opulent Edwardian interiors, she regretted having to forgo them, though looking forward to seeing so many of her favorite actors; old friends, they seemed.

As the lights went down, Nat—replete, warm, a little high—fumbled for her hand.

Richard Woods as Roebuck Ramsden opened the cozy scene—cozy until his ward Ann Whitefield pounced on her prey, Jack Tanner, and they began fighting the liveliest battle of the sexes ever written. Viv and Nat laughed and laughed at declaration and riposte, flight and pursuit. Under assault, red-faced, his spittle flying in supercharged arcs at Ann Sachs, George Grizzard recalled Jack Tanner's adolescence:

> The only man who behaved sensibly was my tailor: He took my measure anew every time he saw me, whilst all the rest went on with their old measurements and expected them to fit me.

They roared! The woman on the hunt, the man desperate to escape, yet knowing escape to be unsatisfactory, too; roared in recognition of the nature of woman and man; roared at the ritual conflict playing out, sharply observed and so true.

Reminded by Shaw, Nat was thinking—but so was Viv—how at age 18 each had signed up for their own all-or-nothing, doing so blindly, but with no idea it was blindly. The bond then forged had never been perfect or free of tension, for years seemed a stalemate or succession of truces; but lately, even tonight as they laughed at the telling blows each sex struck on stage, it was coming to feel like peace.

At intermission they sipped wine and talked about Easter.

"Bought my bonnet," Viv said. "I'll bring it home tomorrow."

"Good."

Act III moved the scene to Spain's Sierra Nevada, where Philip Bosco as the brigand Mendoza kidnaps Jack Tanner. "I am a brigand"—he introduces himself—"I live by robbing the rich." Replies Tanner, "I am a gentleman: I live by robbing the poor." A dream continues the earlier debates, now between devil and Don Giovanni and Doña Ana and her statue-father, the Commendatore.

It was rich, perfect, *funny*, the funnier as they recognized how once it had been between them, the struggles and hurts, everything a fight (but never a *fight*), which they, too, could now contemplate as though all had taken place in dreams.

As the dream dispersed, and before Act IV dawned, Nat whispered, "Wonderful, but—"

"I'm *dead*," mouthed Viv, and they crept out.

It was already past 10:30.

## 58.

IN THE LOBBY they helped each other into their coats and walked out the 51st Street side.

"Hate to leave early," Nat said.

"I'm beat, though."

"Marvelous stuff."

"*Mmm.*"

He offered a cab ride home. At Eighth Avenue they took up a position on the uptown corner. Yellow night clouds were rushing along. Still wet, the pavements wavered with fluid blues, reds, yellows. Couples on the intersection's downtown side nabbed the first cabs, but one — windshield bleeding red — took the last of a light and veered to the curb beside them.

Amazingly, it was a bulbous Checker in imperial yellow, one of the last of the breed; it seemed a divine gesture. Ascending to the vast interior, they huddled in the seat's middle, feet not halfway to the folded jumpseats. Their hands found each other's.

"Fifty-Five Riverside Drive, please," Nat said. "That's at 78th."

They looked out their respective sides as, carried in state, they overtook people striding along.

"Shall we bring something home for Leilani?" Nat asked, the Checker rounding Columbus Circle and taking Broadway's tangent.

"She's all right."

"Maybe she'll have a nightcap with us."

"April starts in a few minutes," said Viv. "Next month, our 40th."

"*Gawd,* has it been that long?" Nat said, squeezing her fingers.

At Lincoln Center hands splayed into the street for cabs; the great houses were letting out, and sidewalks and intersections teemed.

"Holiday weekend," Nat remarked again.

"For some," Viv replied.

The taxi went through the expansive intersection at 72nd Street—the Central Savings Bank clock high overhead said *11:02*, then *11:03*—turned at 78th, passed West End and went down their block, headlights finding hints of cobblestones beneath the asphalt.

Viv got out while Nat satisfied the driver.

Henry the doorman greeted them, but was interrupted by an addled old lady in tiara and feather boa going out to hit the dance floor, as she did every night. The building's most famous resident, Disco Sally was in her 80s, her grinning husband, in a sparkly shirt behind her, almost 60 years her junior.

"Henry, we need the toilet plunged," Disco Sally said. "*Again.*"

"Yes, ma'am, I'll see to it. Good night, Mrs. Handler. Good night, Mr. Handler."

"Night, Henry," said Viv and Nat as they walked to the elevator hand in hand.

# Envoi

# *Virginia*

THE LAST PHOTOGRAPHS of Nat and Viv together were taken at their 70th wedding anniversary party, Viv in her wheelchair resplendent in Navajo and Zuñi Indian jewelry, Nat stooped next to her smiling broadly. Arrayed behind them were their sons, grandchildren and great-grandchildren. Viv always said if she'd known how much fun the grandchildren were going to be, she'd have had them first.

Their friends, most of them aged neighbors from their retirement community, watched the photo session approvingly before resuming what Nat called the "organ recital" of aches and pains at the buffet and open bar. The party was a great success.

Theirs was a long, useful and rather opulent retirement in the Southern town they moved to from New York. Viv volunteered for years at the renowned local research library, and undertook her own researches into her family tree, a quest that took her and Nat to courthouses and libraries across the country. Her father's blood proving to run a deep shade of blue, she happily delved into eleven generations descended from Jamestown settlers. After writing up the results, she had the Daughters of the American Revolution vet them by applying for membership. Accepted, she attended two meetings and resigned. She had what she wanted, and didn't much care for "those biddies."

Nat meanwhile wrote three novels that drew on his upbringing. To his deep satisfaction, they were published by university presses, praised by reviewers and enjoyed by readers. He never wrote his memoirs, scoffing at the notion that he'd ever done anything important, but later, reflecting how irrecoverable the past is without its witness statements, wished he had.

After Viv's death—her gentle fade-out—Nat stopped writing, even as new memories began failing to stick. But old ones stayed. On the eve of his 95th birthday, he told one of his sons his earliest recollection, dating to his family's 1928 move from Mesa, Arizona to Zuñi, New Mexico: sitting on his mother's lap in the mess of the original Route 66's construction, watching as enormous horses pulled their Model T out of a mudhole.

www.ingramcontent.com/pod-product-compliance
Lightning Source LLC
Chambersburg PA
CBHW051609100726
47898CB00001B/293